THE YELLOW EARTH

The Yellow Earth

A Film by Chen Kaige

With a Complete Translation of the Filmscript

Bonnie S. McDougall

The Chinese University Press

ISBN 962–201–499–2

THE CHINESE UNIVERSITY PRESS
The Chinese University of Hong Kong
SHATIN, N.T., HONG KONG

Printed in Hong Kong by Nam Fung Printing Co., Ltd.

Contents

Preface

The film *The Yellow Earth* is assured of a permanent place in the history of twentieth-century world cinema. Several factors have contributed to its remarkable success, not the least being the attempts of the official film world in China to suppress it or denigrate its achievements. Yet its supporters both inside and outside China have called it the best film made in China since the 1960s (or even since the 1940s), and one of the major films in the history of the Chinese-language cinema. This is not perhaps a very ambitious claim; the film's welcome, however, in the international art film circuit, is clear indication that Chinese cinema can be judged by world standards. *The Yellow Earth*, for international audiences, is not an arcane product of interest only to sinologists or sinophiles but a moving poetic essay on human dignity.

To sinologists, the film has an additional significance: it is one of the first and most outstanding cinematic contributions to the brief renaissance in literature and the arts which began in China during the Cultural Revolution (1966–1976). It was not until after the death of Mao Zedong and the fall from power of his supporters in 1976 that this renaissance came above ground and flourished, but its inspiration and its earliest products date from the early 1970s. For obvious reasons, the cinema was one of the last areas where the new wave surfaced. The following study of *The Yellow Earth* is primarily an examination of the film in the context of the new movement in the arts generally.

The first chapter discusses the multiple meanings of the film, drawing on reviews and critiques in the Chinese and foreign press and unpublished sources from 1984 to the beginning of 1987. Where not otherwise credited, the views expressed are my own, though it is not always easy to separate my own opinions from the insights I have heard and read from others over several years. Chapter Two describes the history of how the film was made, and compares the film-makers' intentions with the final product. Chapters Three, Four, Six and Eight describe the treatment given to the film in China; Chapters Five, Seven and Eight describe its reception abroad. I have not analysed the more technical side of the film's achievements, or set the film in the context of the contemporary Chinese cinema except in passing; nor have I given much weight to the criticism meted out by professional film theorists, critics and other cultural bureaucrats in China.

I first met Chen Kaige 陳凱歌 in 1982, as a friend of the poet Bei Dao 北島 (Zhao Zhenkai 趙振開) whose works I was then translating, and agreed to make a translation of the filmscript of *The Yellow Earth* in autumn 1984 (before I had seen the film). By the spring of 1985 I had completed a rough draft of the translation of the "literary" script (*wenxue juben* 文學劇本), but unhappy with its verbosity and also its distance from the actual film, I began to translate instead the "tabulated" or working script (*taiben* 臺本). The *taiben* was not only a better guide to the film but also seemed to me superior as literature in its more concise formulations of the plot, characterization and descriptions of the setting. I therefore began the translation of the filmscript from a mimeographed copy of the *taiben* lent to me by the director with his own corrections, and completed it in the summer of 1986; for the present book, it has been further revised to correspond to the published version which appeared in 1987. For their corrections of the script and of the translation, I am most grateful to Chen Maiping 陳邁平 and Chen Kaige; I am also grateful to Liu Baisha 劉白沙 and Liang

Yongsheng 梁永生 for their assistance. I am particularly grateful to Wong Kin-wai 王建慧 for her unusually meticulous copy-editing and to Anders Hansson for his equally conscientious proofreading.

In the meantime, the film had become famous beyond anyone's expectations. T. L. Tsim 詹德隆, director of The Chinese University Press, expressed interest in a book of the film as early as the summer of 1985, and Chen Kaige gave a cautious blessing to the project. The present book grew into its present form largely between September 1986 and June 1987. Though the film's history continues, it seems reasonable to halt the narrative at the end of 1986.

Very many people helped in the collection of material for the account that follows. Stephen C. Soong 宋淇, Tony Rayns, Anders Hansson, Jean Wakefield, Geremie Barmé and Garrie van Pinxteren supplied press cuttings from Hong Kong, Britain, the United States, Australia and the Netherlands. John Minford and T. L. Tsim, from beginning to end of the project, offered assistance and encouragement with writing and publication. The Institute of Contemporary Art in London kindly supplied me with a video-tape of the film for my research and with stills for illustrations used in this book. To the students and staff of the institutes of East Asian studies in Aarhus, Leiden and Oslo, my thanks to their lively reception of preliminary and incomplete versions of the manuscript in the spring of 1987, with special thanks to Anne Wedell-Wedellsborg, Jørgen Delman, Stig Thøgersen, Lloyd Haft, Tony Saich and Mark Elvin. David Holm read through several chapters and made very useful suggestions. Paul Clark is specially to be thanked for his eight-page list of corrections, suggestions and comments, and for supplying the Japanese references. Thanks are also due to the following for helpful suggestions and advice generally: Elisabeth Eide, Royall Tyler, Lars Ragvald, Göran Sommardal, Lü Daxiang 呂大祥. I acknowledge with thanks illustrative material povided by the Guangxi Film Studio and Southern Film Company Limited.

In addition to the above, I want to mention especially the invaluable support I received from friends in China and abroad. Primary among them are Chen Maiping and Danny Yung (Rong Nianzeng 容念曾), both friends and collaborators of Chen Kaige. Zhang Yimou 張藝謀 and Gu Changwei 顧長衞 patiently initiated me into some of the mysteries of cinematography in China. From Chen Kaige's family—his late mother, father, sister and former wife—I received endless hospitality and help in my endless enquiries. From Chen Kaige himself, I received five years' generous efforts to assist me in my work.

BMcD
October 1989, Olso

Abbreviations Used in Notes

BJRB	*Beijing ribao* 北京日報 (Peking daily)
BJWB	*Beijing wanbao* 北京晚報 (Peking evening news)
BR	*Beijing Review*
BYDY	*Bayi dianying* 八一電影 (August First films)
CD	*China Daily*
CL	*Chinese Literature*
CQ	*China Quarterly*
CR	*China Reconstructs*
DDDY	*Dangdai dianying* 當代電影 (Contemporary cinema)
DYCZ	*Dianying chuangzuo* 電影創作 (Film creation)
DYXK	*Dianying xuankan* 電影選刊 (Film selections)
DYXZ	*Dianying xinzuo* 電影新作 (New films)
DYYS	*Dianying yishu* 電影藝術 (Cinema arts)
DYYS CKZL	*Dianying yishu cankao ziliao* 電影藝術參考資料 (Research materials on cinema arts)
DZDY	*Dazhong dianying* 大衆電影 (Popular cinema)
FEER	*Far Eastern Economic Review*
GMRB	*Guangming ribao* 光明日報 (Enlightenment daily)
HQ	*Hongqi* 紅旗 (Red flag)
HS HTD	*Huashuo Huang tudi* 話説《黃土地》 (Speaking of *The Yellow Earth*)
HTD	*Huang tudi* 黃土地 (The yellow earth)
JSND	*Jiushi niandai* 九十年代 (The nineties)

PR	*Peking Review*
QNWX	*Qingnian wenxue* 青年文學 (Youth literature)
RMRB	*Renmin ribao* 人民日報 (People's daily)
SoF	*Seeds of Fire* 火種
TYE	*The Yellow Earth*
WHB	*Wenhui bao* 文匯報
WYB	*Wenyi bao* 文藝報 (Literature and the arts)
WYYJ	*Wenyi yanjiu* 文藝研究 (Studies in literature and the arts)
XGC	*Xin guancha* 新觀察 (New observer)
XHNB	*Xinhua News Bulletin*
ZGQN	*Zhongguo qingnian* 中國青年 (China's youth)
ZM	*Zhengming* 爭鳴 (Contention)

Transliteration

Except in place names for which there is an established Post Office spelling, I have adopted the *pinyin* system now in use in China.

Chen Kaige as a soldier in 1974.

Chen Kaige and Zhang Yimou shooting *The Grand Parade*, 1985.

Gu Qing bids Hanhan return.

Gu Qing and Hanhan enjoying their midday meal in the field.

Cuiqiao at the village wedding.

Gu Qing transcribing the towmen's song.

Cuiqiao and Hanhan at the bank of the Yellow River.

Cuiqiao's father with her now-abandoned straw stool.

Cuiqiao on her wedding night.

The waist-drum dance, Yenan.

Chen Kaige with a Japanese film group at the Peking Film Studio, 1987.

Bonnie S. McDougall with a member of the film crew of *The King of Children* in Yunnan.

Chen Kaige in Tokyo, 1986.

Bonnie S. McDougall with Chen Kaige and members of the film crew of *The King of Children* in Peking.

Chen Kaige on location in Xishuangbanna.

1. The Plot

The story of *Huang tudi* 黃土地 (The Yellow Earth) is on the face of it extremely simple, yet its implications are subtle and multiple, and summaries of the plot in the Chinese press range from merely misleading to indisputably wrong.

The film begins in the spring of 1939. The Eighth Route Army soldier Gu Qing 顧青 is travelling through Shaanbei 陝北, the northern part of the province of Shaanxi 陝西 in China's northwest. His mission is to collect folk songs for adaptation in the army's propaganda work. He follows a bridal procession to a poor village, where he transcribes the local wedding songs. Putting up for a few nights in the cave home of one of the poorest peasants, he meets the fourteen-year old girl Cuiqiao 翠巧, her father, who is in his forties, and her young brother, Hanhan 憨憨, about twelve. He tells them about the social reforms in Yenan 延安, headquarters of the Eighth Route Army and the Chinese Communist Party, emphasizing education for women and freedom of choice in marriage. The next day, he joins the family in their work in the fields and teaches Hanhan an Eighth Route Army song. The same day, a matchmaker arrives to arrange for Cuiqiao's wedding a few months away. Gu Qing returns to the cave and announces that he will leave the next day. Cuiqiao begs to be allowed to follow him, but he replies that since he is an army cadre he must seek permission. He promises to return, but Cuiqiao knows it will be too late to save her. Back in Yenan, Gu Qing witnesses the vigour and revolutionary spirit shown by normally taciturn peasants.

Cuiqiao, however, is married off to a much older man, and on their wedding day shrinks from his embrace. She resolves to flee to Yenan, but in crossing the Yellow River is engulfed in the waves. Gu Qing returns to the village in summer, when the men in the village are taking part in a rain prayer ceremony. Hanhan sees him in the distance, and tries to make his way through the dense throng to reach him. The opening sequence in the film was a long-distance shot of the yellow, barren soil of the vast mountains and gullies; the final shot is a close-up of the yellow, barren soil.

Accounts of the plot in the English-language press in China reduce the film to a commonplace formula: a Party cadre comes to a backward village to· release the revolutionary potential of the people, and the younger generation in particular make him welcome and stretch out their hands towards the new life. The tremendous controversy raised by the film and the efforts to restrict its release, however, show that there is more to the film than these summaries would indicate. Nevertheless, nowhere in the hundreds of articles written about *The Yellow Earth* is there a concise statement of the objections raised to the film: they are too sensitive to mention openly, either in the articles that praise the film or those that condemn it. In the account which follows, therefore, I refer to "codes" in which both objections and commendations are phrased.[1]

The most noticeable feature of the plot is negative: the absence of class struggle in the village, in contrast with earlier treatments of the same theme such as *Li Youcai banhua* 李有才板話 (Rhymes of Li Youcai), *Wang Gui yu Li Xiangxiang* 王貴與李香香 (Wang Gui and Li Xiangxiang) and *Bai mao nü* 白毛女 (The White haired girl) from the 1940s, or the novels of Zhao Shuli 趙樹理 and Zhou Libo 周立波 in the 1950s. In this film, the enemies of the villagers are the poverty of the soil and the unreliability of the rainfall, with not a landlord, Nationalist general or invading Japanese in sight. The Party had abandoned its former emphasis on class struggle in

1978, so that its absence from this film was not a departure from current policy; nevertheless, *The Yellow Earth* still created a sensation among old Party cadres. To understand the strength of their reaction, it is necessary to consider why the film was seen as a statement on some of the most central issues in modern Chinese history.

In this regard, the title, location and period of the film are each of great significance. The colour yellow has always had a special reference to self-identification by Chinese people (descended from the Yellow Emperor, cradled by the Yellow River), but Chinese self-descriptions traditionally tended to focus on black hair. In the nineteenth century, "yellow-skinned" was a derogatory term used by foreigners, but by the middle of this century, the terms "yellow skinned" or "yellow race" were used by the Chinese as a neutral self-description. The colour yellow regained its former association of glory in the 1980s. In 1981, for instance, a Taiwan campus song celebrating the "yellow skin" of the "descendants of the dragon" by Hau Tak-kin 侯德健 (Hou Dejian) became immensely popular among young people in Taiwan, Hong Kong and China,[2] and the film-makers used the terms *Yan Huang zisun* 炎黃子孫 or *Yan Huang houyi* 炎黃後裔 (descendants of Yan and Huang [yellow]) in talking about the film.[3] The words "yellow earth" in the title, adopted by the director during shooting, therefore suggest the Chinese people as well as the Chinese earth.

The location of the film is also extremely important. The area of north and central Shaanxi is commonly regarded by Chinese as the cradle of Chinese civilization,[4] where the earliest and most fundamental features of Chinese culture first appeared and developed around the deep bend in the Yellow River; the Yellow River is also often called the cradle of the Chinese race.[5] The title and the location together therefore suggest that the film refers to the Chinese people over the whole country and over the whole of Chinese history.[6] In a collective statement published immediately after the film was first released, Chen Kaige, Zhang Yimou and He Qun 何羣 confirm this by referring several times to the Chinese as the descendants of the Yellow Emperor, to the Yellow River as the cradle of Chinese civilization, to the yellow earth as the subject of their film, and to "the yellow earth" as the preferred title of their film.[7]

The significance of the historical period is linked with the significance of the location. It was during the late 1930s and early 1940s that the Chinese Communist Party became a mass organization with direct or indirect power over vast areas of the country, and the policies worked out at that time were also the basis of those pursued after 1949. To set a film in the present might limit its significance merely to the present; to set it in this period can imply that the most fundamental Party policies are being brought under consideration.[8] The site of the action is an area not far from Yenan, which, as the first location of extended Party government, became the symbol of Communist Party rule over the whole of China. The combination of that period and that locality, in other words, implies that the condition of the peasants shown in the film was to characterize the whole Chinese peasantry, and by extension the whole Chinese race. To stress the local peasants' "backwardness and ignorance," as critics claimed the film did, was to suggest the failure of the Chinese Communist Party to transform this condition even up to the present time.

The theme of folksong collection and the actual use of folk songs in the film also goes beyond the immediate setting. The Yenan plan to collect folksong to use as propaganda has its roots deep in Chinese history. The most admired section of the most ancient anthology of Chinese poetry is generally supposed to be a collection of folk songs made by government officials in order to inform the ruler of current opinion, one of the earliest instances of state involvement in literature and the arts. Known as *caifeng* 采 風 , the custom was continued into the Han dynasty as one of the means by which the state justified its rule over its people. When the Chinese Communist Party began in the late 1930s to collect folksong, it was following in the same tradition.[9] The theme of Yenan-style *caifeng* in *The Yellow Earth* inevitably drew attention to the relationship between the Yenan Party leadership and the peasants of the Shaanbei countryside, though critics generally avoided making the connection.[10] Chen Kaige himself, in collecting and rewriting the folk songs in *The Yellow Earth*, is catching a private echo of the tradition.[11]

Finally, the structure of the film itself suggests that more is being conveyed than just the tragic story of a single peasant girl. The narrative part of the film is in the realistic mode, and here every attempt was made to achieve an impression of ordinariness and naturalness.[12] Set against this ordinariness are three long sequences—the wedding procession (up until Gu Qing enters the courtyard) and its repetition at the time of Cuiqiao's marriage; the waist-drum dance at Yenan; and the rain prayer ceremony together with Hanhan's attempt to reach Gu Qing. These three sequences are highly stylized, in contrast to the rest of the film (motion against stillness, light against shadow, and exaggeration against understatement), implying meaning beyond the simple narrative.[13] The long descriptive sequences on the yellow earth and the Yellow River, and especially the arrangement of the characters in the picture-frame in these sequences so as to give unusual weight to the environment, again indicate underlying meanings in the relationships thus suggested. These non-realistic devices are only partly successful in that not all viewers perceive them or understand their significance. Nevertheless, they are evidence that the film-makers were consciously working within the customary framework in modern Chinese theory and criticism that treats works of art as complete models of political constructs.

Looking back on their work, the film-makers took every opportunity to affirm that they intended the film as a statement on the

Chinese people, Chinese history and the present situation in China. In an interview made shortly after its completion, Chen Kaige stressed this aim again and again. While fully aware of the current emphasis in China on urban life and material prosperity, he claimed that he wanted his first film to portray the simple, rough life of Chinese peasants, whom he described as "the strength of our people"[14] and "the majority of our population, the basis of our whole people and our country;"[15] in Cuiqiao he saw "the hope of our whole people."[16] "We are poor people in a poor country, compared to the developed countries, but like the people of Shaanbei, for thousands of years we Chinese people have pursued enlightenment and prosperity... We must positively accept new ideas, but at the same time we should respect our traditions, and gain strength from history... We must know ourselves clearly. This is the immediate significance of our film."[17] "The aim of the film is to explore our national character."[18] In his statement to the film crew before setting off on location, Zhang Yimou similarly claimed that the cinematography was designed "to express the unquenchable spirit of the Chinese people," and repeated the same idea in an interview after the film was completed.[19] The film-makers, their supporters and their critics in China all agreed on the film's implicit frame of reference: Gu Qing stood for Communist Party policy, Cuiqiao and her family for the older and younger generation of Chinese peasants and also for the Chinese people as a whole, and the yellow earth and Yellow River for China, the Chinese people, and the history of Chinese civilization.

Apart from the three highlighted sequences, which will be discussed more fully below, there are many other elements in the visual and narrative presentation which add depth to the meaning of the film. First and most controversial was the depiction of the poverty of the land and its people, most strikingly in the close-ups of the barren earth throughout the film. Many of the symbols of poverty convey additional meanings. For example, the wooden fish at the wedding feast, provided "just for the show," can also be seen as a kind of passive refusal to accept fate, or even as art or ritual substituting for material wealth. Outside the cave home, the "couplets" on the door are not the customary auspicious sayings written in Chinese characters but black circles stamped by the bottom rim of a rice bowl; although the peasants in this area are illiterate, they still decorate their lives. Peasant art is ritualistic: the three members of the family do not sing for entertainment, only on public or private occasions for grief or joy. The two most striking instances of the peasants' creativity are the parallel sequences of the waist-drum dance at Yenan and the rain prayer ceremony; the violent movements and noise in these two sequences shows the energy and passion of the normally silent and outwardly passive peasants, and the difference in tone between the two sequences shows the two aspects of the Chinese character. To some critics, the rain prayer sequence especially was part of the film's "glorification" of rural backwardness; to others, both sequences show peasants creating their own culture in the midst of poverty, thus asserting their own human worth.

Many elements in the film refer to the continued existence of feudal attitudes in the countryside, especially in regard to women. The value of a girl is shown in the disposition of Cuiqiao's bride price (half goes for her mother's funeral, the other for her brother's betrothal), and the custom of marrying children to adults is the immediate cause of the film's tragedy. Cruel as they are, the upholders of these customs are not insensitive: Cuiqiao's father is not happy about his daughters' fate, but simply asks, "What's love when there's no food?" If he beats Cuiqiao, it is not for personal gain but to ensure the continuance of the family as a productive unit in the only society he knows. It is not an evil power that enforces these feudal customs, only the tyranny of the earth and the seasons. The peasants' fatalism is coloured with a kind of pride which is the foundation for their own self-respect and dignity.

Although fatalism must be regarded as a fault in contemporary China, it is also compulsory to respect peasants for their capacity for suffering. The director chose an old man drawing water from the Yellow River as his primary image for rural hardship and determination to survive, and other images of or about the river water are central to the film's story. Cuiqiao does not complain that she carries water from the river a mile away, although the startled Gu Qing feels it is too precious to use for washing his feet, nor does she seem to notice that the water she carries is half mud. The struggle to survive is arduous but the peasants perform their tasks without complaint. On another level, however, just as Cuiqiao's own family determines her unhappy fate, the Yellow River water which sustains their life eventually destroys her. Here the multiple associations of the Yellow River give a deep sense of irony to the film.

Although the film does not condone superstition any more than it condones child marriage, some details show a deeper understanding of its role in peasant life than is usual in conventional Marxist ideology. Like art, it is a way in which the peasants make their hard lives more tolerable, and it also stands for a primitive environmentalism. When Cuiqiao's father makes an offering of a few grains of millet to the sky before eating, Gu Qing laughs, but the father rebukes him, asking if he has no respect for the earth. Primitive as their farming methods may be, the peasants none the less have an attachment to the land that goes beyond its exploitation. The scene foreshadows the rain prayer ceremony at the end of the film, and the sympathy created at this point carries over to that sequence. The attitude implied in the film towards superstition, as to tradition in general, is deeply ambivalent.[20]

Some details in the plot or presentation were contested as misleading or inappropriate. The veteran director Ling Zifeng 凌子風

claimed that if the village were in White (Nationalist) territory, then an Eighth Route soldier would not have been able to move around so easily; if it were a Red or "Liberated" area, there would have been more signs of communist influence.[21] Chen Huangmei 陳荒煤 , although a harsh critic of the film, felt obliged to point out that at that period the Nationalists and the Communists had adopted a policy of cooperation, and movement between the two areas was relatively free.[22] Ling Zifeng also claimed that the area in question was sparsely populated, so that the presence of so many villagers at the rain prayer was unrealistic.[23] Another hostile critic, Wang Shushun 王樹舜 , also noted the apparent inconsistency in the deserted landscape around Cuiqiao's home and the sudden appearance, when the plot demanded it, of hundreds of people to take part in the drum dance sequence.[24] (Here he confused the drum dance with the rain prayer sequence, since the drum dance took place in Yenan, several hundred miles away.) The critics were correct; the director admitted that he employed many more people than was necessary or probable in the vast but sparsely settled north China plain, but did so in order to increase the impact of the sequences and underline their significance.[25] Wang Shushun also mistakenly believed that folksong collection started only after the forum on literature and the arts in 1942.[26]

Some critics, wanting Cuiqiao to be more heroic, ask why she married in obedience to her father and ran away only after the wedding? Deng Baochen 鄧寶宸 implies that it was the husband's "big hand," but does not explain what he sees as the symbolism of the hand, the only visible part of the husband.[27] Chinese critics have generally avoided clarification of this episode. The hand, which is extremely dark in contrast to Cuiqiao's pale face, could be simply a symbol of cruelty, but her father had also beaten her without provoking her flight. The director explains that Cuiqiao obeys her father because she senses that his cruelty is due to ignorance and does not exclude sympathy for her plight; he adds

9

that this kind of tenderness is harder to resist than outright oppression.[28] Even the director, however, apparently does not quite dare make explicit the message of the "black hand". It is most likely that the "big hand" (as it is described in the script) stands for the rape implied in the consummation of the marriage, so that it was sexual violence which finally impelled the girl to seek a new life. This is implied in Chen Maiping's explanation that the husband whose face is not shown stands for all male peasants, including both the father and the peasants who join the army and carry out the revolution.[29] Wang Zhongming 王忠明 makes a similar point with less precision but more enthusiasm, claiming that the hand "universalizes" Cuiqiao's bridegroom: it is not an individual man who causes her to shrink back, but any husband at all under these circumstances.[30]

Deng Baochen also raises and answers some other questions on the plausibility of Cuiqiao's story. Why didn't she wait for daylight to cross the river in safety? Because her absence would be discovered at daybreak and her husband's family would set off in pursuit. Why did Gu Qing refuse to take her with him when she asked? Because it was not a Liberated area and it would have created a bad impression for Gu Qing to carry off even a reluctantly betrothed woman (in a Liberated area a woman could not be betrothed against her will).[31] Gu Qing's replies to Cuiqiao, that there are regulations, and that he must consult the leadership, evoke bitter laughter from Chinese audiences, and perhaps the film-makers could not resist playing to the audience at this point. Within the context of Gu Qing's characterization, we could alternatively read his rejection of her as symptomatic of his lack of responsibility. It remains a weakness in the storyline that many viewers realized; people leaving the film were heard to sigh, "If only he'd taken her with him it would have been all right!"[32]

The manner of Cuiqiao's death was apparently too sensitive to attract much open discussion. In the original story she commits suicide when she fails to escape from the bonds of feudal marriage after her hopes have been raised by the visiting Eighth Route soldier. By showing her as trying to flee to Eighth Route headquarters, the film-makers seem to be casting the story into a more orthodox mould. But as she meets death on her way across the river, a new kind of ambiguity is introduced. Her death may be seen as destruction by the same forces that nurture life: since the Yellow River is a symbol of the Chinese people, it is also the Chinese people that destroy her, not through cruelty but through tender ignorance. (There may or may not be an additional reference here to the Communist Party, which describes itself as the people's saviour.) Alternatively, her death from drowning as she attempts to escape a feudal marriage and reach communist headquarters may imply that the peasants' true problems are not class oppression but Chinese tradition and the Party's failure to develop adequate policies in regard to village life. Cuiqiao's death with the words "The Communist Party [will save us all]" on her lips can be read as a sign of her heroic determination and faith, but it can also be seen as the futility of unrealistic expectations.

One of the film's supporters, Shao Mujun 邵牧君, claims that a "scientific analysis" of the film leads to the inescapable conclusion that Cuiqiao was deliberately attempting suicide, and moreover that her decision was first formed at the time of her farewell to Gu Qing on the hillside. According to this interpretation, the song her father sings on Gu Qing's last night in the cave home foreshadows her suicide; the next day, realizing that Gu Qing can't save her from her fate, she sings as he disappears from sight, "I'm afraid that from now on, I'll never see you again" and "Folk songs can't save me, poor Cuiqiao." Shao Mujun also believes that her parting words to her brother show her determination to end her life, although to save distress to her father and brother she pretends she is fleeing to the Eighth Route Army.[33] (These effects may have been caused by the combination of the original storyline and the

11

film-makers' belief that Cuiqiao's death is necessary for the implied meanings of the film.)

Some critics thought that the death of Cuiqiao three-quarters of the way through the film made the structure unbalanced.[34] Other critics regard the protagonist either as Gu Qing, or as the yellow earth, or even as the four characters and the environment together considered as a whole, so this opinion was not given much weight. Another critic argued that her death was a sign of the futility of individual resistance without a class movement (Hanhan, in contrast, runs towards Communist Party leadership and therefore will be saved).[35] One young critic read two meanings into Cuiqiao's death: one, that this image of positive progress is swallowed up by the symbol of the Chinese race—the Yellow River; or two, that she merges into one body with the Chinese people.[36] Most critics were prepared to agree with the director that her tragedy was inevitable in that period of history,[37] and also that from an artistic point of view it adds a deeper level of meaning to the film.[38] It is her death which provokes the father's tears during the rain prayer ceremony and Hanhan's attempt to break through the crowd, so that her tragic fate makes the structure of the plot more dense.[39] At different times the director claimed different factors as responsible for her death. Discussing the acting, he notes that it is ordinary life that kills Cuiqiao, but elsewhere that it is her father's ignorance and fatalism that lead to her death. More commonly he says it is the Yellow River to which she sings her songs, or the Yellow River from which she draws water, that engulfs her. In the drowning sequence, the shots of the Yellow River are cut from turbulence to quieter waters to the shore and to a rock on the shore, showing the eventual gentleness of the river: this adds a further layer of ambiguity to the symbolism of the Yellow River.[40]

The characterization is as ambiguous and controversial as the plot. Gu Qing is shown as well-meaning but singularly lacking in sensitivity: he fails to notice the girl's plight, and, by awakening her desires without fulfilling her needs, is ultimately responsible for her half-suicidal death. Despite his peasant background and willingness to lend a hand in the fields, he is also blind to peasant sensitivities in several instances: writing down the song at the wedding feast, trying to make conversation at the first encounter with the father and laughing at Hanhan's song. In these scenes he almost seems to parody a type of patronizing literary bureaucrat bringing enlightenment to the masses.[41] (In the Chinese-language press he is mostly described more accurately as a "worker in literature and the arts" or suchlike rather than as a common soldier.[42]) As he begins to learn more about the family, however, he puts aside his notebook: he fails to take down Hanhan's half-comic, half-despairing song, the father's lament for child brides and Cuiqiao's farewell. He parts from Cuiqiao with an awkward consciousness of inadequacy; in the final sequence he disappears altogether, and only the barren earth remains.

Several critics see the relative ordinariness or "coldness" of Gu Qing as a shortcoming in the role or in the performance.[43] Western viewers tend to welcome it as deliberate departure from the conventional figure of an heroic communist;[44] they, however, are not obliged to consider Gu Qing as anything but a simple soldier-cadre from the Eighth Route Army. The whole tradition of post-1949 cinema and the arts, however, compels the native critic to treat Gu Qing as a symbol of Communist Party policy. Given the film-makers' awareness of this tradition and their own aims in making this film, Gu Qing's failure to rescue Cuiqiao or to reach her brother are not matters of film realism but of political allegory, and the stylized presentation of the relevant sequences can be seen as the film-makers' signal of this change in mode. Several critics therefore offered different justifications of Gu Qing's "coldness". One claimed that all the characters, Gu Qing included, are deliberately blurred so that they come across as types rather than as individuals: Gu Qing is a "type" of army cultural cadre.[45] A more far-reaching (or far-fetched) reading interprets Gu Qing's ordinariness as allowing him to be on the same level as the other characters, not somehow suspended in mid-air as conventional Party "saviour" heroes are usually depicted, and suggests that while his powers as an individual to save the family are limited, as a symbol of Truth he transforms their lives.[46] A less ambitious reading has Gu Qing acting as an "observer" on behalf of the audience, or even as the film-makers' mouthpiece.[47]

There was also controversy about the characterization of the father and Hanhan as typical peasants. Again, the film-makers knew themselves to be working within the convention that all major characters in a film are "typical", i.e. representing a certain social class or stratum. The common charge was that the father and Hanhan were presented as backward and stupid. In a possible attempt to defend the film, Deng Baochen describes the father as not being indifferent to change as he listens to Gu Qing.[48] Other, even friendly, critics might not agree, and the director himself notes that though the father was moved by Gu Qing's account of women's emancipation in Yenan, his generation—at that time and at that place—were not able to change their fundamental beliefs.[49] (In this context, it might be noted that friendly critics sometimes made fundamental errors about the film plot. Li Tuo, for instance, apparently believed that Hanhan was a grandson.[50]) One critic points out that when the father sings for Gu Qing on his second night in the cave home, it is not to help the Eight Route Army or to please Chairman Mao but so that his guest will not be in trouble for failing to accomplish his task.[51] According to the same critic, the father is shown in the film as concealing deep emotions behind his impassive exterior: at home his eyes are dim and his movements slow, but in the fields he is active and capable, talking coarsely but affectionately to his ox; his hospitality to strangers might stop short of lively conversation, but he offers the last drop of hot water in the home to his uninvited guest; he expresses his sympathy for his daughters' fate in the song he sings for Gu Qing; he displays grief and hope in the tear-streaked face he raises to the heavens as the jar of holy water sinks into the pond.[52]

Hanhan's silence has been variously interpreted by critics. One veteran objected to Hanhan's "doltishness" on the grounds that children are by nature lively and appealing.[53] His name, meaning "foolish" or "naive", is probably to be regarded as his childhood nickname rather than his formal name, and Cuiqiao apparently feels that even by village standards he is "silly", but Gu Qing knows better. As pointed out by a Hong Kong critic, the dumb protagonist in the 1960s film *Serfs* finally speaks when he is saved at the end of the film by the PLA; in *The Yellow Earth*, on the other hand, Hanhan breaks his silence when he is joined by Gu Qing in tending the sheep but relapses into silence again throughout the remainder of his visit, and when finally he tries to reach Gu Qing at the end of the film, his cries are inaudible through the invocations to the Dragon King.[54] Two Western sinologists found the most striking message of the film in Hanhan's character and "the deceptive silence with which he preserves his individuality."[55] Most Chinese critics saw Hanhan's silence, like his father's, as a realistic portrayal of peasant reticence especially in the face of strangers, and a break with the convention that makes peasants articulate spokesmen against class oppression. Hanhan's silence is created by his circumstances: herding sheep from sunrise to sunset, he never hears a human voice all day, only the bleating of his sheep. At home, he is awed into silence not so much by the stranger as by his own father: when his father goes out, Hanhan cautiously moves over to Gu Qing's side. Like his father, he conceals strong emotions behind his passive exterior, but finds it hard to express them. One critic finds him particularly moving as a visual image;[56] many viewers praise his sudden burst into song.[57]

There was no controversy about his sister. All Chinese critics who discussed her role described it with approval as embodying the traditional virtues of Chinese women: gentle, hardworking, uncomplaining, brave and determined.

Many critics complained that the three set pieces, while superbly filmed, are not well integrated into the plot. The film's supporters point out that they not only form the basic structure of the film but also convey the film's deeper meanings. For instance, the first wedding procession is filmed in a highly stylized manner up to the point where Gu Qing enters the courtyard: this sequence is then repeated when it is Cuiqiao's turn to be married. The first bride is unconnected with Cuiqiao, but her fate is nonetheless the same: the repetition of the procession implies that the custom of child marriages is part of a never-changing cycle of peasant life, an ancient and unchanging tradition without happiness or joy, just the ritual of established custom. Therefore when it comes to Cuiqiao's marriage, instead of showing her unhappiness as an individual, the film conveys the idea of an inescapable fate for all like her. Shao Mujun points out that in the first wedding courtyard Cuiqiao is shown five times against the characters "Three submissions, four virtues" (referring to a woman's successive submission to her father, husband and son), these characters foreshadowing her own destiny.[58]

The stylized mode of the drum dance similarly signals a deeper layer of meaning in the sequence. Originally the director avoided placing it in a specific location or even indicating that it took place around Yenan, afterwards claiming that the vigour of the dance and the clear blue sky behind the dancers were to have signified a Liberated area;[59] studio pressure obliged him to identify it with the label Yenan. One critic claimed that this is the only sequence where a clear blue sky is shown.[60] In fact, there is also blue sky behind Gu Qing as he makes his way over the hill towards Hanhan in the rain prayer sequence; in the rest of that sequence either the sun is shown in a kind of hazy glare or else the sky is overcast as in the foreshadowing scene where the father makes his offering of millet grain to the earth. The exaggeration in the excessive numbers of dancers and the uniform neatness of their costume primarily conveys the strength and vigour of which the normally passive peasants are capable. Its position in the film is also significant: it links the scene of Cuiqiao's wedding with the scene of her flight, and represents the change in her thinking which took place between the two events. A Western viewer saw the drum dance as also representing Cuiqiao's fantasy of Yenan.[61] A hostile Chinese critic claimed that coming directly after the wedding night scene, the drum dance sequence is tainted with its sorrow and is not the wholehearted joyousness that, according to her, the director must have intended.[62] Another interpretation sees deliberate irony in the celebrations in Yenan coinciding with Cuiqiao's deepest anguish, her would-be saviour Gu Qing watching the fun unaware of his protégé's tragic fate.

To many senior Chinese viewers, the most offensive element in the film was the rain prayer sequence. Whereas the same critics accepted the "exaggeration" (meaning, roughly, stylization) of the drum dance sequence because of its "positive" nature, they regarded the similar "exaggeration" of the rain prayer sequence as negative or even voyeuristic. Some critics doubted its actual connection with Chinese reality: Ai Mingzhi 艾明之, for instance, felt it was like an excerpt from a cowboy film about North American Indians, and Han Shangyi refused to believe that Chinese peasants ever wore wreathes around their heads.[63] In fact, although the numbers and uniformity of the participants are exaggerated, the details of the ritual are based on local information, and documentary sources attest to its ancient origin and present existence. Whether authentic or not, this portrayal of peasant superstition was seen by orthodox critics either as a contemptuous exposé of rural backwardness and ignorance or else, even more offensively, their glorification. To the film's supporters, the film neither shows

17

contempt for the peasants nor tries to glorify them, but is an exploration by the film-makers of new ways of understanding themselves and the world; the final sequence is essential in that it suggests the relationship between man and society, society and nature, nature and society.[64]

Many critics singled out the drum dance and rain prayer sequences as the major contrast in the film. The simplest interpretation of the contrast is that the former shows the strength and progressive nature of the Liberated area while the latter symbolises the backwardness and ignorance of the Nationalist area.[65] Yu Yanfu 于彦夫 credited the director with the more subtle perception that on the same earth, two such very different life conditions could co-exist.[66] Some critics thought that even the latter sequence showed a spirit of resistance with a potentiality for revolution.[67] It is not clear whether or not statements such as the latter can be taken at face value: they may represent an attempt by the speakers to defend the director from criticism on political grounds, just as some of the director's own claims seem sometimes to do.

One of the film's supporters pointed out the significance in the order in which the two sequences appear; conventionally, the Yenan sequence would have come last, promising hope and change for the future. By placing the rain prayer at the end, followed only by shots of the barren yellow earth, the film-makers open up the possibility of several interpretations.[68] The most obvious message is that peasant vigour as represented by Yenan is still a limited phenomenon, poised against the enormous weight of traditional fatalism. Another reading, commonly adopted by the film's supporters, is that the latent energy shown by the peasants in the rain prayer is in itself a sign of hope: it only awaits proper organization to be transformed into a positive force for change; the film shows respect for their unrealized aspirations and admiration for the beauty of the rituals that they create in their desperation. A third interpretation is hinted at in the juxtaposition of similar wording in the peasants' rain prayer and Gu Qing's song as sung by the disembodied voice of the dead Cuiqiao: the peasants invoke an outside force (the Dragon King/the Communist Party) to appear as their saviour. In this reading, peasant superstition will not be overcome by the Yenan spirit but merely transferred, with the active encouragement of the Party, to the Yenan leadership.[69]

The final sequence of Hanhan going towards Gu Qing is also highly ambiguous. Most critics interpret it as Hanhan "swimming against the tide"; Ai Mingzhi even criticizes it for being too direct and unsubtle, an instance of the director forcing his ideas on the plot.[70] Others see the significance of the sequence in its last moments: Hanhan fails to reach Gu Qing, Gu Qing fails to reach Hanhan. The slow motion repeats of this sequence are seen by some as not mere stylization (as most Western audiences would inevitably judge[71]), but as a symbol of the Party's repeated failures to solve the problems of the yellow earth.

Notes

1. The most important document in the debate on *TYE* is "Diwujie jinjijiang pingweihui bufen pingwei guanyu yingpian *HTD* de fayan zhailu" 第五屆金雞獎評委會部分評委關於影片《黃土地》的發言摘錄 (Extracts from speeches about the film *TYE* by panelists of the fifth Golden Rooster Award adjudication panel), first circulated in *DYYS CKZL*, 1985.5 (5 April 1985): 2–48; together with reprints of articles on the film and interviews with the filmmakers, it was reprinted in Chen Kaiyan, ed., *Huashuo HTD* 話說《黃土地》 (Talking about *TYE*) (Peking: Zhongguo dianying chubanshe 中國電影出版社, 1986): 1–36. The filmmakers' point of view is best represented in their statements from the spring of 1984 before setting off on location: see Chen Kaige, "*HTD* daoyan chanshu" 《黃土地》導演闡述 (Statement on the directing of *TYE*), 6 April 1984, reprinted in *Beijing dianying xueyuan xuebao* 北京電影學院學報, 1985.1 (June 1985): 110–115; Zhang Yimou, "*HTD*

sheying chanshu" 《黃土地》攝影闡述 (Statement on the cinematography of *TYE*), 31 March 1984, reprinted, ibid.: 116–19; and He Qun, "*HTD* meishu sheji de shexiang" 《黃土地》美術設計的設想 (Ideas on the art design of *TYE*), 7 April 1984, reprinted, ibid.: 120–22 and in *HS HTD*: 298–300. The first two statements were amplified and compared with the final product in two interviews conducted by Xiao Luo for *DYYS CKZL*, No. 15, 1984, "Huaizhe shenzhi de chizi zhi ai—Chen Kaige tan *HTD* daoyan tihui" 懷著深摯的赤子之愛——陳凱歌談《黃土地》導演體會 (Nourishing a sincere love for the innocent—Chen Kaige discusses his experiences in directing *TYE*), reprinted in *HS HTD*: 264–84; and "Wo pai *HTD*—Zhang Yimou tan *HTD* sheying tihui" 我拍《黃土地》——張藝謀談《黃土地》攝影體會 (Shooting *TYE*—Zhang Yimou discusses his experiences in the cinematography of *TYE*), reprinted in *HS HTD*: 285–97.

2. For the English translation see Hau Tak-kin, "The Descendants of the Dragon", *CL*, September 1983: 98–99. For a connection between the song and the film see Ah Fan 阿帆 (Hong Kong), *HS HTD*: 313–14.

3. See Chen Kaige et al., "Shaanbei caifeng shouji" 陝北采風手記 (Jottings on collecting folksong in north Shaanbei), *DZDY*, September 1984: 14–15; repeated in Chen Kaige, "Qianli zou Shaanbei" 千里走陝北 (Going a thousand li through north Shaanbei), *DYYS*, April 1985: 29–31, esp. 29.

4. See for instance this enunciation as a cliché by Chen Maiping, *HS HTD*: 200; also Xia Yan 夏衍 , Luo Yijun 羅藝軍 and Hu Bingliu 胡炳榴 , *HS HTD*: 5, 10, 33; [Li] Jinsheng 晉生 , *HS HTD*: 174; Zhou Chuanji 周傳基 , *HS HTD*: 213; Dong Zhi 董志 (Hong Kong), *HS HTD*: 304; Hao Dazheng 郝大錚 , *GMRB*, 27 June 1985: 3.

5. Similarly Li Chao 李超 as a cliché, *HS HTD*: 114; Wang Dehou 王得後 , *HS HTD*: 134; Ah Fan, *Da gong bao* 大公報 , 27 April 1985.

6. This association between the title and the location with "the cradle of the Chinese culture" was made by Sun Naixiu 孫乃修 , *GMRB*, 4 July 1985: 3.

7. Chen Kaige, "Shaanbei caifeng shouji": 14–15. See also Yu Qian 余倩 , *HS HTD*: 126.

8. This was indirectly admitted by the makers of *TYE* and other new wave films set in the late 1930s, at a seminar on the new films in February 1985; see Benkan jizhe 本刊記者 (Our own reporter), "Zui

nianqing yidai de dianying tansuo" 最年青一代的電影探索 (Film explorations by the youngest generation), *DYYS*, April 1984: 26–28.

9. See David Holm, *Art and Ideology in Revolutionary China* (Cambridge University Press, forthcoming), Chapter Four. For a post-1949 example of the conscious use of the *caifeng* tradition in film, see Wai-fong Loh 陸惠風, "From Romantic Love to Class Struggle: Reflections on the Film *Liu Sanjie*," in Bonnie S. McDougall, ed., *Popular Chinese Literature and Performing Arts in the People's Republic of China 1949–1979* (Berkeley: University of California Press, 1984): 165–76, especially p. 173.

10. See for example He Zhongxin 何鍾辛, *HS HTD*: 1; Ye Xiaonan 葉小楠, *HS HTD*: 231.

11. See Chen Kaige, "Shaanbei caifeng shouji":14–15.

12. Chen Kaige, "*HTD* daoyan chanshu": 111–12, 113, 114–15 and *HS: HTD*: 272, 274.

13. Chen Kaige, *HS HTD*: 277.

14. Chen Kaige, *HS HTD*: 267.

15. Chen Kaige, *HS HTD*: 266.

16. Chen Kaige, *HS HTD*: 268.

17. Chen Kaige, *HS HTD*: 268; see also 275–76.

18. Chen Kaige, *HS HTD*: 277.

19. Zhang Yimou, "*HTD* sheying chanshu": 116 and *HS HTD*: 285; see also *HS HTD*: 287, 288, 293, 295.

20. Chen Kaige, *HS HTD*: 270.

21. Ling Zifeng, *HS HTD*: 17.

22. Chen Huangmei, *HS HTD*: 23.

23. Ling Zifeng, *HS HTD*: 17.

24. Wang Shushun, "Chuangxin chuyi—dui *HTD* deng jibu yingpian de qianzhe" 創新芻議——對《黃土地》等幾部影片的淺析 (Some tentative opinions on innovation—a preliminary analysis of films such as *TYE*), *DDDY*, February 1985: 52–55, esp. 54.

25. Chen Kaige, *HS HTD*: 279–80.

26. Wang Shushan, "Chuangxin chuyi": 54.

27. Deng Baochen, *HS HTD*: 14.

28. Chen Kaige, *HS HTD*: 271; see also 278.

29. Chen Maiping, *HS HTD*: 199.

30. Wang Zhongming, *HS HTD*: 119.

31. Deng Baochen, *HS HTD*: 14.

32. Reported by Wang Shi 王石 , *HS HTD*: 189.
33. Shao Mujun, *HS HTD*: 261.
34. Quoted by Chen Maiping, *HS HTD*: 199; Li Chao, *HS HTD*: 112; [Li] Jinsheng, *HS HTD*: 171.
35. Han Xiaolei 韓小磊 , *HS HTD*: 84.
36. Ye Yancai 葉言材 , *HS HTD*: 93.
37. Chen Kaige, "*HTD* daoyan chanshu": 111.
38. Chen Kaige, *HS HTD*: 271–72.
39. Chen Kaige, *HS HTD*: 272.
40. Chen Kaige, *HS HTD*: 271–72; cf. Ye Xiaonan, *HS HTD*: 232–33.
41. Wang Dehou comes close to implying this; see *HS HTD*: 136, 138.
42. For instance Zhang Chengshan 張成珊 , *HS HTD*: 103; Wang Zhongming, *HS HTD*: 118–19; [Li] Jinsheng, *HS HTD*: 167; Wang Shi, *HS HTD*: 181; Ye Xiaonan, *HS HTD*: 230.
43. Zheng Dongtian 鄭洞天 , *HS HTD*: 45–46; Li Tuo 李陀 , *HS HTD*: 54; Deng Baochen, *HS HTD*: 15–16; Ye Yancai, *HS HTD*: 92–93; Li Chao, *HS HTD*: 115; Ye Xiaonan, *HS HTD*: 230; anonymous critics, *DYYS*, April 1985: 27; Ma Rui 馬銳 , *DYYS*, September 1986: 17.
44. For example, Tony Rayns, *Monthly Film Bulletin*, October 1986: 295–98; Ian Bell, *The Scotsman*, 19 August 1985; Derek Malcom, *The Guardian*, 7 August 1986; Adrian Turner, *The Observer*, 10 August 1986.
45. Wang Zhongming, *HS HTD*: 118–19.
46. Hao Dazheng, *HS HTD*: 148–49.
47. Tong Daoming 童道明 , *HS HTD*: 192.
48. Deng Baochen, *HS HTD*: 14.
49. Chen Kaige, *HS HTD*: 269–70.
50. Li Tuo, *HS HTD*: 53.
51. Wang Shi, *HS HTD*: 182.
52. Wang Shi, *HS HTD*: 183–84.
53. Han Shangyi 韓尚義 , *HS HTD*: 19; see also anonymous critics reported in *DYYS*, April 1985: 27.
54. Shi Qi 石琪 , "*HTD*, shang, xia" 《黃土地》上、下 (*TYE*, I and II), *Mingbao wanbao*, 25–26 April 1985.
55. Geremie Barmé and John Minford, (eds.), *Seeds of Fire: Chinese Voices of Conscience*, (New York: Noonday Press, 1989): 253. See also the Hong Kong critic, Dai Tian 戴天 , *Xin bao* 信報 , 16 May 1985.
56. Wang Shi, *HS HTD*: 184.
57. See Wang Dehou, *HS HTD*: 134.

58. Shao Mujun, *HS HTD*: 258.
59. Chen Kaige, *HS HTD*: 279.
60. Zheng Dongtian, *HS HTD*: 42, 45.
61. Paul Clark, *Chinese Cinema: Culture and Politics since 1949* (Cambridge: Cambridge University Press, 1987): 181; first expressed in "Viewer's Guide" (see below): 43.
62. Tan Min 譚敏 , *HS HTD*: 83.
63. Ai Mingzhi, *HS HTD*: 10; Han Shangyi, *HS HTD*: 19.
64. Chen Maiping, *HS HTD*: 200.
65. Han Shangyi, *HS HTD*: 20.
66. Yu Yanfu, *HS HTD*: 3.
67. He Zhongxin, *HS HTD*: 2; Deng Baochen, *HS HTD*: 13.
68. Shao Mujun, GMRB, 25 July 1985: 3.
69. See *Zhengming*, July 1985: 51.
70. Ai Mingzhi, *HS HTD*: 10; also some of the film's supporters, e.g. Hao Dazheng, *HS HTD*: 146 and Chen Xihe 陳犀禾 , *HS HTD*: 253.
71. See for instance Annan, quoted below Chapter Eight: 123.

2. The Process
(November 1983 to August 1984)

The creation of a new cinema in China after the end of the Cultural Revolution was due chiefly to the efforts of a new wave of film-makers, now known as the "fifth generation" to have appeared in the Chinese film world since its beginnings in the 1920s. The new wave consisted of the first batch of students to graduate from the Peking Film Academy since its reopening for full degree studies in 1978. (The academy, founded in 1956, is still the only tertiary institution for the training of professional film personnel in China. A film school was established in Shanghai before the Cultural Revolution but existed only for two years; there were no specialist film schools in China before 1949.) The academy consists of five departments: directing, acting, cinematography, design, and sound recording, and courses take four years. Competition for places is fierce: particularly in the summer of 1978 when the first nationwide entrance examinations since 1965 were held. Since candidates were tested on merit as well as on political reliability, the number of hopeful applicants was almost more than the school could handle. About ten thousand applications were made for the 150-odd positions available.

The class of '78, as it is known, included many talented young film-makers whose maturity and independence, developed during the Cultural Revolution, set them apart from previous generations in the film world. Their immediate prospects on graduation, however, did not seem promising. Some were assigned to the half-dozen full-size feature film studios, but since the major studios were already overstaffed, they could expect years as "assistants". Others were posted to the handful of small provincial studios that were founded or enlarged in the late 1970s and early 1980s for the purpose of implementing the general policy of decentralization. On graduation in 1982, the director Zhang Junzhao 張軍釗 , the cinematographer Zhang Yimou (plus one other graduate from the same department) and the art designer He Qun were thus assigned to the new Guangxi Film Studio 廣西電影製片廠 in Nanning 南寧 . Restructured as a feature film studio in 1978 from earlier film units in Nanning, it was run by a bureaucrat with no staff and no knowledge of film. What might have looked like a bleak prospect was actually a great opportunity. It was here that these three young graduates produced in 1983 the controversial *One and Eight* (一個和八個)[1] from what had started out as a student exercise. Work on *One and Eight* began in June and the film was completed by October. In September, Zhang Yimou proposed to the studio that the new graduate director Chen Kaige be invited to Guangxi to collaborate with him on another film. The studio, still happily unaware of the storm that *One and Eight* would produce, was pleased with the film and agreed to Zhang Yimou's proposal. Although Zhang Yimou and Chen Kaige had not been close friends at the academy, they knew each other well and respected each others' work. Chen Kaige had been assigned as an assistant director at the Peking Film Studio 北京電影製片廠 , the second oldest studio in the country and one of the most famous. At this studio, however, he faced the prospect of an indefinite and depressing future as another director's "gofer". What Guangxi had to offer him was a chance to make his first independent film, at the extraordinarily early age, for China, of 32.

Chen Kaige arrived in Nanning in November 1983 and immediately began looking at scripts. Zhang Ziliang 張子良 , a Xi'an Film Studio 西安電影製片廠 scriptwriter, had found an essay about an incident in north Shaanxi during the early years of resistance to

Japan, and had worked it into a filmscript. Xi'an Film Studio was not interested, but Zhang Yimou, who was from Xi'an himself, thought it showed promise and passed it on to Chen Kaige. After some discussion, Chen Kaige and Zhang Yimou obtained the initial approval of the studio for the project. In January 1984 a team of five set out from Xi'an for north Shaanxi to look at the area and rewrite the film script: Chen Kaige, Zhang Yimou, He Qun, Zhang Ziliang and Zhao Jiping 趙季平 , the composer.

Before taking on this assignment, Chen Kaige already had strong ideas of his own about what he wanted to convey in film. Talking two years later about his state of mind in 1984, he said that he had come to believe, from his own experiences and from his readings in Chinese history, that suffering was the normal course of history; he thought the common practice in literature at this time, to complain about private unhappiness and the injustices in an individual's life, was futile.[2] Just after finishing the film, he spoke of wanting to express a sense of the greater maturity and confidence that some at least of this generation had achieved through their suffering, and of wanting to convey his generation's capacity for both happiness and sorrow, their ideas on past history and their hopes for the future.[3] In film terms he wanted to explore not the conventional beauty of riverine landscapes (known in Chinese aesthetics as "soft beauty") but its opposite, the "hard beauty" rarely seen on the Chinese screen. Although he had never been to the north-west, it appeared in his imagination as a vast and bleak landscape that would add great strength to a film.[4] It was also the kind of harsh environment that was more appropriate to the knowledge he had gained about his own country and its people, knowledge he would never have obtained as a young urban intellectual in the ordinary course of events.[5] In the story of Cuiqiao, he also wanted to convey more than one person's tragic destiny, but was not sure how to do this. The purpose of the January trip was to search for ways of expressing these still unformulated convictions; it was only after a month in north Shaanxi that his ideas clarified and took shape. According to Zhang Yimou, at this stage they were not even wholly committed to making the film: they would decide after scouting around.[6]

Both the director and the cinematographer later stressed the importance of this visit on all aspects of the film: colour, light, picture composition, tempo, music, dialogue, gesture and structure.[7] In answer to repeated questions about the influence of foreign films on *The Yellow Earth*, both tended to reply that the major influences were both traditional aesthetics and the nature of Chinese society itself. First as students at the film academy and later as film professionals, both had been able to see relatively large numbers of foreign films, and both wanted to challenge the thirty or more year old conventions of the Chinese cinema. It would have been easy for them to have adopted flashy new techniques and create a thoroughly fashionable modern film. Instead they chose the much more difficult approach of bending new techniques to express new ideas in the context of a traditional society depicted in its own aesthetic. Basic to this process was the belief that technique was never its own end but a means of informing a realistic presentation with artistic and philosophical vision. Below we shall examine the way in which the film-makers' aims and intentions were given shape, successfully or otherwise. At the risk of repetition, all statements of intention will be dated in relation to the time the film was made, and, where relevant, examined for the possible influence of internal or external factors.

The team set up headquarters in Yenan and spent the next few weeks travelling extensively round the countryside. The contrast between the reminders of revolutionary history in Yenan and the poverty of the land around them made a deep impression that was eventually conveyed in many non-verbal messages in the film.[8] In later criticism, many people claimed that the film-makers were too young to understand this period in Chinese history, but several

Yenan veterans admitted privately that they had a very firm grasp of the time and place.[9] A re-examination in the early 1980s by older Party intellectuals of the role of the wartime bases laid particular emphasis on the fact that the countryside around the revolutionary base areas had remained poor up to the present day.[10] The urban "Educated Youth" (EYs) who had returned to the cities from the base areas or other parts of the countryside felt qualified to contribute to this debate. The EYs who formed the film crew, with their headquarters in Yenan, were constantly reminded both of the revolution which was to have transformed the countryside and of the land's poverty. The problem was an inescapable part of their daily life.[11]

If their witness to the poverty of the area informed the philosophy of the film, the knowledge they gained of the local arts and their place in the lives of the local people was equally important in forming the aesthetic basis of their work. They gained their first insight into the art of the local people at Ansai 安塞 county, where they came across an exhibition of peasant paintings and papercuts. In the crude simplicity of these local products, they found a natural sincerity lacking in the works of professional painters, and He Qun, the art director, was even moved to tears. A recent group of French visitors had called one of the papercut artists "the Matisse of the East"; back in Peking, Chen Kaige repeated the story (turning Matisse into Picasso),[12] and later spoke about the influence of the peasant paintings and papercuts on the pictorial composition of the film.[13] Even more stirring was the team's first encounter with the waist-drum dancers of Ansai. While filming in Yunnan 雲南 the previous year, Chen Kaige had seen some local Jingpo 景頗 dances and wondered why this kind of artistic vigour had disappeared from the Han race; at that time, though waist-drum dances were common in the Shaanbei countryside, few people in urban areas knew about them, and the kind of Han dances that found their way on stage as folk dances had been modified to the point of complete insipidity. The primitive colour and life of the reality was so different that Chen Kaige was still in a state of high excitement on his return to Peking at the end of the month, repeating with relish the story that the French visitors, seeing a performance by only three drum dancers, were startled by their strength and power.[14] The papercuts and drum dances that the film team saw in Ansai reminded them that China's brilliant ancient civilization had been created by these people, and also that these people were still capable of an artistic energy that put their own generation to shame: "without enough to eat (until the recent past), they wanted to describe happiness in their art, while we well-fed educated people wanted to describe misery."[15] The team also spent a lot of time sitting in people's homes chatting; the peasants did not speak much, but what they did say was full of meaning to the team and found its way into the revised script.[16]

Finally, in Jia Xian 佳縣 , they reached the banks of the Yellow River. "At dawn one morning, we saw an old man filling two buckets of water on the bank of the Yellow River, his back bent and stooped as he walked away—someone after all drew water from the Yellow River; the Yellow River waters after all would flow through the parched land. You could say it was on that morning that we realized what and how we should write."[17] The original script had featured neither the yellow earth nor the Yellow River; the image of the yellow earth had not yet emerged, but the Yellow River became the starting point for the script revision.[18] According to the director's statement to the film crew a few months later, after the working script had been completed, the Yellow River appeared to him as an image for the Chinese people.[19] It was also then his image of the artistic direction of the film.

The studio, however, was not happy with the first draft of the revised script that was submitted, and it was rewritten several times before a working version was agreed upon in February. The major rewriting was carried out by Chen Kaige, staying in a small hostel in an outer suburb of Peking in order to concentrate more intensively on the script revisions. It was at this time that some of the incidents and conversations recorded in the January visit were incorporated into the script, such as the unhappy marriage of an old peasant's elder daughter, and the same old man's sayings "Where's love when there's no food", "Wine and meat friends, millet and wheat spouses" and "Why sing when you're not happy or sad".[20] The outline for the rain prayer ceremony was also added at this time. According to the director, this sequence was based on the oral testimony of elderly peasants living in that area, who advised them on details of the wreathes and actions.

Another important addition were the songs. The folk songs in the film are also based on material collected by the film team in Ansai. Hearing that there were a lot of peasants in the area who knew many local songs, they invited people to sing for them. One man in his late thirties, He Yutang 賀玉堂 , first refused, saying that once he started singing he was unable to control himself and would not be able to stop for two to three hours. They heard him out, and it was true that he lost himself entirely in his singing: he would laugh or cry and seemed almost crazy. Asked who taught him the songs, he said that no-one had taught him, but that his grandfather often used to sing. He himself was very poor, only barely able to support his family of four or five children. Chen Kaige was very moved by this man's singing and decided to record his songs. They met another three times and became good friends. The character of the poor singer in the film is based on him.[21] To incorporate his songs into the film, the words in some cases had to be altered to fit in with the story line, and the overt sexual content common to the songs in that area had to be modified.

The basic ideas for the visual style of the film, also formulated in the script at this time, were the result of repeated discussions with the cinematographer and art director in January and February. The original script had described a landscape of flowers, flowing water and birdsong in the valleys, but according to the director after the film's completion, he decided together with the cinematographer and designer during the script revision that the primary visual element was to be the vast expanse of yellow earth. They paid a great deal of attention to the appearance of the landscape, believing that the environment was of primary importance in shaping the lives of the people who lived there: although the earth was barren, it still contained great warmth, and in this also the director saw a symbol of the Chinese people.[22]

"Warmth" and "hope" are two words stressed by the director and cinematographer in their post-film interviews, and many of their supporters quoted them directly or otherwise praised the film for conveying these messages. The question arises whether these statements are more defensive than wholly apposite. Other criticism, not necessarily hostile, points out that the overall effect of the cinematography is to create an effect of depression and monotony. Tan Min assumes this to be a shortcoming in the film-makers' technique; in other words she prefers to accept the intentions and query the results.[23] Most Western critics accepted the result and praised the film for it. Other Chinese critics simply condemned it.

Another problem in relying too heavily on the film-makers' own statements of intent is that these statements are not always consistent over time. Before shooting the film, the director described the Yellow River as the primary image in both the picture composition and the story structure; in the post-film statement it became secondary to the yellow earth.[24] It is not in fact quite clear when the yellow earth replaced the Yellow River as the primary image; when the later statements were made, the yellow earth had become the title of the film and may have been seen in retrospect as primary from the beginning.

At the pre-location stage, the director gave only two general instructions to the cinematographer and the designer: one, that except in the deliberately stylized sequences, the visual composition should aim at ordinariness; and two, that without ethnographic pretensions, the details of clothing and props should be correct. More concretely, he wanted Zhang Yimou to abandon the striking visual effects of *One and Eight* in favour of "the calmness of concealed strength". To this end, and also to create the right kind of historical atmosphere, he required a fixed camera wherever possible. For instance, in the cave scene at the beginning of the film, he allowed at the most only four camera positions for each sequence, with absolutely no change of focus: the "still life" thus created was to give the sense of a stultifying oppression. For the drum dance sequence, on the other hand, the reverse effect was needed so that full use could be made of a moving camera.[25]

In March, a team of ten people set out again for Shaanxi, and this time a specific location was decided upon in Ansai. The next step was to choose the actors, a task pursued by Chen Kaige and Zhang Yimou in Peking, Shanghai and Guangxi. By mid-April, the cast and the technical staff were all assembled: a crew of twenty-six people whose average age was only about twenty-three. As in all Chinese film-making, everything was very carefully planned in advance for greater economy on location. The statements made by the director, cinematographer and the designer to the crew at this stage show how much preparatory thinking had already gone into the film, and also their firm belief in the originality of their ideas and their own creative ability.[26]

On 16 April the film crew returned to Shaanxi, set up their headquarters in Yenan and began shooting the following day. They ran into many difficulties, but what they lacked in technical equipment and experience was made up for in enthusiasm and hard work.[27] (Danny Yung received from Chen Kaige an impression that the equipment used for shooting the film was less than adequate—for instance, they had no two-way radio to use in the long-shots—but avoided questioning him closely about this.[28]) The director recalls that the rain prayer sequence took three days to film, seven to eight people directing the invocations with only two or three megaphones between them.[29] The film is set in early spring, when the earth is at its hardest and driest, but was filmed during the summer; to achieve the right appearance, the film crew carefully removed every blade of green from the site.[30]

Shooting generally began about four in the morning and often went on until nine at night. Since most of the exterior shots were taken at dawn or dusk, sometimes only four or five scenes could be shot per day. There are no union rules on working hours in the Chinese film industry, either for adult or child actors, and with tiny production budgets there is considerable pressure to finish on schedule, especially out on location. Since there was little shooting taking place during the day, however, there was still time for revisions to the script. For example, in the February script, Hanhan at the end of the film manages to reach Gu Qing and hand over to him the shoe soles that Cuiqiao had embroidered for him; this sentimental, optimistic scene is deleted in the final version. The songs were also further revised. The final title for the film occurred to Chen Kaige on the way back to their hostel in Yenan after the day's work. "Shengu huisheng" 深谷回聲 (Echo in the valley), the title of the original essay by Ke Lan 柯藍 , had been changed to "Guyuan wusheng" 古原無聲 (Silence on the ancient plains) in the February script, but Chen Kaige was still looking for something simple yet powerful. That afternoon, the prevailing yellowness of the landscape suddenly struck him: the peoples' skin was yellow, the earth was yellow, and even the cattle were yellow. It took some time for the title to be accepted, since to some people it had a common, unattractive sound, just as the story itself seemed to be yet another version of an old Party cliché.[31] According to Zhang Yimou, it was only adopted during the screening of the first rushes.[32]

The cinematography received almost universal praise from critics and reviewers, even those opposed to the film's content, and the close working relationship that developed between director and cinematographer is an important reason for the success of the film. According to Chen Kaige in 1986, both men are very strong-willed and independent, but in this project they worked together very well, not giving and taking orders but holding continual discussions at every stage of their work.[33] It is clear that Zhang Yimou contributed to the overall directing of the film, though the suggestion made informally by some commentators that he should have been credited as co-director is probably exaggerated. The style of Zhang Yimou's first film, *One and Eight*, is very different from *The Yellow Earth*, whereas there are strong similarities between the latter and the second film on which they collaborated, *The Grand Parade* (大閱兵); this supports Chen Kaige's claim to have influenced the cinematography, and some observers credit him with having further developed Zhang Yimou's considerable talents.[34]

Zhang Yimou set out his plans for the cinematography under four headings: colour, light, composition and movement.[35] Throughout he was conscious of breaking the rules, sometimes trying out ideas already used in *One and Eight*, sometimes trying for entirely new effects. According to one of the teachers at the film academy, these experiments had started already before graduation. An anecdote describes the iconoclastic mood of the '78 students: watching Chinese films from the 1950s and 1960s as part of their training, they would shout out which camera angle the director would use next. As their teacher observed, their guesses were usually correct.[36]

Colour was one of the main areas of innovation. Together with the director and the art designer, Zhang Yimou worked out not only a basic colour scheme of yellow, red and black, but also a method of colour montage that challenged conventional ideas on colour among Chinese film-makers.[37] Both director and cinematographer felt satisfied that their creative use of colour was one of the most successful achievements of the film.[38]

The most important factor in regard to colour was the decision to use the yellow earth as the primary image in the film. When the team first arrived in the north-west, Zhang Yimou was struck by the intense contrast between the blazing blue sky and the harsh yellow earth. To shoot the film according to the true intensity of these colours would create an effect similar to American westerns, and this was in fact his original plan. After discussion with the director and designer, however, he revised his concept of the earth itself: "poor as it was, it nurtured our Chinese race, it has the warmth of a mother, it gives us strength and hope."[39] To convey the warmth in the yellowness became a major aim of the cinematography. The exterior shots are of mostly of the earth itself, with little or no sky showing, and shooting was mostly carried out at dawn, at dusk or on days when the sky was overcast in order to create a soft tone. One of his film academy teachers endorsed Zhang Yimou's claim, but some critics thought that the "muddy yellow" of the yellow earth and the Yellow River gave a feeling of bleakness and oppression.[40]

The next most important colour in the film was red. Zhang Yimou realized that the same colour can produce different emotions by the use of colour montage. In the first wedding procession, for instance, the colour red dominates the picture frame. Not knowing the story, the audience at this point is only conscious of the superficial meaning of the colour red signifying a joyous occasion. It is only in the courtyard, when the expression on Cuiqiao's and Gu Qing's faces gives the audience a sense that something is wrong, that the red takes on a deeper meaning;[41] as the director points out, the contrast between the bride's red accoutrements and the black clothing of the peasants suggests the tragedy of the feudal marriage system.[42] In the second wedding procession, the use of red is clearly ironic. In consultation with the art designer, Zhang Yimou decided that the overall colour in Cuiqiao's wedding chamber should be red except around the edge of the picture frame (to make the red all the more striking against the bare walls).[43] The scene then switches to the drum dance at Yenan, where the colour red takes on a new meaning altogether. Finally, as Cuiqiao runs away from her new home, the redness of her wedding clothes becomes the redness of the revolution.[44] The link between these sequences was not contrived during the editing but a joint decision by director, designer and cinematographer in the early planning stages in February.[45]

The combination of yellow, red and black, with white as a supplementary colour, was based on both local custom and local peasant art.[46] Black is the traditional colour of peasant clothing in north China, signifying the common people from the beginnings of Chinese history. (Li Tuo thought that the preference for black went back as far as Qin and Han.[47]) White is the colour of the turbans worn by peasant men in north China, and its use in the film is mainly as a contrast to the black clothing.

Another aspect in which Zhang Yimou challenged conventional studio thinking was in the use of light. Usual practice was to aim at a highly defined clarity; Zhang Yimou felt that although clarity could be at times appropriate, Chinese film-makers paid too little attention to the dramatic effects that could be achieved through the modulation of light. His own aim in both *One and Eight* and *The Yellow Earth* was to use lighting sparingly, regarding this as the hallmark of a good cinematographer.[48]

The main lighting effect that Zhang Yimou wanted for *The Yellow Earth* was to enhance the feeling of warmth mentioned above. In most of the exterior sequences, shooting was done at dawn, at dusk or on cloudy days so that the harsh sunlight was softened, in order to give the film a luminous, yellowish glow, and the only sequence where the full glare of the sun was utilized was in the rain prayer scenes.[49] Zhang Yimou notes that two sequences were shot in brilliant light: the drum dance and the rain prayer, respectively conveying the sense of new life and death/rebirth.[50]

For the interior shots, the director required that the cave (constructed by the film crew) must appear as dark as cave homes are in reality: warmth was to come from the fire and the steam from the stove, with the aid of the oil lamp, plus discreet scatter and soft lighting at the direction of the cinematographer. All of the cave home scenes are "warm": even in the first encounter, the atmosphere must not be cold, since Gu Qing is only a stranger and not a hostile element.[51] In this sequence, the camera concentrates on close-ups of the father's face, its swarthy colour and wrinkles: he sits there like a statue in semi-darkness, shot with the oil lamp behind. According to the cinematographer, this method was adopted not only to express "a subjective concept," the suffering of the Chinese people over thousands of years, but also corresponds to the Shaanbei reality: the peasants sit on the *kang* 炕 like trees, not moving or speaking unless directly addressed. The next day, however, the father is shown as a different man out in the field: in the brighter light one can see his face clearly, his eyes alert and penetrating.[52] The daytime interior shots were all taken from the inside looking out into the brightness outside, so that as the characters went in and out the audience would also experience the sensation of coming in from brightness to darkness or the reverse.[53] Many critics were especially impressed with the cave photography, in particular with the camera's reliance on the set's own sources of light, so that the flickering oil light picks up the lines of suffering on the father's face and the reflection of the fire lights up Cuiqiao's face, while Hanhan by the door is in almost complete darkness.[54] Shao Mujun was particularly impressed by the camera swings from the darkness of the cave to the vast stretch of landscape beyond.[55]

Both director and cinematographer frequently claimed that the composition of the picture frame, in regard to such things as the compression of the landscape into one surface, with virtually no perspective and with human figures appearing as marginal, is based on traditional Chinese painting (including peasant painting) rather than contemporary Western film.[56] Zhang Yimou told interviewers that under the influence of Chinese paintings, he avoided direct front-on shots, but shot from the side or above or below, to create a picture surface "as flat as water".[57] Speaking directly after the completion of the film, however, Zhang Yimou also stressed that the film should clearly present a contemporary and not old-fashioned view of the historical past, and that the use of colour, light, composition and movement should each have a contemporary feeling.[58] The many scenes showing a tiny human figure against a vast landscape are influenced not just by traditional aesthetics in poetry and painting but also are designed to express the film-makers' appreciation of the vast distances and sense of space in the north China plateau as distinct from the south. These shots also try to convey the close relationship between the people and the earth; in particular, these figures make their entrances and exits not directly from left or right of the picture frame but from the earth itself, behind the fold of a hill.[59]

In the placement of the horizon in the upper half of the picture frame or beyond the upper frame is a technique which Zhang Yimou learned from the Chang'an school of painting 長安畫派.[60] Again, the technique was adopted not for its own sake but to convey the main image of the film and to express the film-makers' "subjective concepts." For example, scene 28 (shot 275) reads as follows: "The evening sun is about to set behind the ridge. The sound of the father urging on the ox reverberates against the earth and sky, plaintive and lingering. The row of three small figures, ploughing, sowing and spreading dung, proceeds slowly across the ridge, just as our people have proceeded throughout their long and arduous history…" The composition of this scene was inspired by a line from Shi Tiesheng's 史鐵生 short story "Wo de yaoyuan de Qingpingwan" 我的遙遠的清平灣 (My faraway Qingpingwan).[61] After reading this short story, which had created something of a stir when it first appeared the previous year, the director was so impressed that he decided to incorporate it into the film.[62] The Chang'an style provided the appropriate compositional technique. The film-makers regarded this scene as very important and spent a great deal of time getting it right. Zhang Yimou's only regret was that due to practical limitations it was not possible to use the Chang'an style more consistently throughout the film.[63]

One particularly effective contrast in picture-frame composition is between the drum dance and rain prayer sequences. In the former, the earth still occupies most if not all of the picture frame, but in the latter the horizon falls very low so that the sky occupies the main picture area. This defiance of the "golden section" disturbed many critics.[64] Answering charges that this excessive display of sky is due to the film-makers' excessive "subjectivity", Zhang Yimou claims somewhat unconvincingly that their exaggeration in presentation is to show the peasants' strength, and that in this world, after all, the sky and the earth are larger than anything else: if the earth in the drum dance sequence conveys the idea of abundance, then the sky in the rain prayer conveys the idea of vastness. He also notes that the worshippers look up to heaven for the answer to their prayers, so that it is appropriate for the heavens to occupy the greater part of the picture frame.[65]

Many critics commented on the long, slow pace of the film and the predominance of static camera work. Asked if he was influenced in this regard by Western films such as Antonioni's *Red Desert*, the director replied that rather he was inspired by the nature of Chinese society: to produce an effect corresponding to the long slow process of Chinese history and the stillness and simplicity of peasant life, the camera rarely moves itself, but pans or tilts only to follow the motion of the actors. The pace is therefore created by the actors rather than by the camera.[66] Zhang Yimou notes that in the use of statis to create a feeling of history he was influenced by the Japanese film *Doro no Kawa* (Muddy river), but also that stasis corresponds to the appearance of Shaanbei and the manners of its people.[67] In most of the scenes where action takes place, it tends to be slow and repetitive, again in imitation of the movements of north China peasants. Zhang Yimou felt that repetition was particularly important to convey the impression of the repetitive or cyclical nature of people's daily life, and to that end not only were whole sequences of actions repeated, but wherever possible he tried to use the same camera position, the same camera distance and the same light aperture to shoot different scenes. The intention of this is to create an impression of the long road that the Chinese people have followed.[68] (The slight variations within repeated sequences, therefore, are able to convey a great deal of meaning: for example, the change in Cuiqiao's manner in the three sequences bearing the river water home.[69]) In the drum dance and rain prayer ceremony, on the other hand, the emphasis was on violent motion: here Zhang Yimou used a hand-held camera and wide-angle lens for greater flexibility. However, because of practical limitations, he was not entirely satisfied with the result.[70]

Zhang Yimou's final challenge to convention was in regard to the information conveyed in the picture frame. Conventional wisdom held that the more information per frame the better, but Zhang Yimou believed that amount should be determined by theme and content. As an example where his aim was create an effect of great simplicity and purity, he described at length the repeated sequences of Cuiqiao drawing water from the Yellow

River.[71] The conventional portrayal of the Yellow River encompasses the river's great expanse and length, and the powerful turbulence of its current: in these scenes, however, apart from the opening shot, all the audience sees is the water filling the bucket, with Cuiqiao's figure in the foreground. In Zhang Yimou's words, to show the full magnificence of the river would be very beautiful but would have no connection with the story or its significance. These scenes, instead, emphasise the close relationship between the river and the peasants: the river that nourishes life and also destroys it. Zhang Yimou used a long-distance focus to draw the river and the figure of Cuiqiao together on the same plane, and again used scatter light and the natural light of dusk to create an atmosphere of warmth and intimacy.

The four main actors in the film were all professionals, and directing them did not raise particular problems. The father, played by Tan Tuo 譚托, is a member of the Xi'an [Western] Opera Troupe 西安歌劇團; trained in the Italian style, he performs his own songs in the film.[72] This was his first appearance on screen, and was followed by a role in Chen Kaige's third film, *The King of Children* (孩子王). Liu Qiang 劉強 (Hanhan) and Xue Bai 薛白 (Cuiqiao) are both from Peking. Wang Xueqi 王學圻 (Gu Qing) is from the army and subsequently played in Chen Kaige's television film "Forced Takeoff"[73] and in *The Grand Parade*. Wherever possible, local peasants were recruited as paid extras. The director found them very cooperative and very serious in their work; they needed to be told what to do, but understood and did not try to go beyond his direction.[74]

Chen Kaige directed his actors to strive for an effect of ordinariness and simplicity.[75] Many Chinese critics founding the acting too understated, wanting, for instance, Gu Qing to show more emotion on leaving Cuiqiao, or Cuiqiao to show more emotion after the encounter with the matchmaker.[76] Where critics found evidence of "Westernization",[77] the director was usually able to give a local source as inspiration: Hanhan's arms-in-sleeve silence as he farewells Gu Qing, for instance, is based on accounts by EYs of the way in which they were farewelled by the local peasants when they returned to the cities after their rustication.[78] In general, the slow and sparing use of dialogue was seen as an accurate reflection of peasant life on the north China plain.[79] Only one critic objected, claiming that Chinese peasants are very talkative.[80] According to some critics (including two otherwise generally hostile towards the film), the scene of Cuiqiao's wedding night was an excellent example of restraint in acting and directing.[81] Many Western viewers, however, found it distastefully melodramatic, especially in the unnaturally dark colour of the outstretched hand and the clumsy dubbing of Cuiqiao's laboured breathing.

Several critics mentioned the father's resemblance to the subject of Luo Zhongli's 羅中立 1981 prizewinning oil-painting "The Father", usually as a commendation.[82] Zhang Yimou notes that it was not a case of copying but two artistic endeavours reaching a similar end by different roads.[83] According to the director, the characterization of the father and much of his dialogue was based on an old peasant he met on his first visit to the film site. Describing him as a peasant philosopher, he claims that there were many people of this sort in Shaanbei.[84] Many Chinese and Western critics commented favourably on the acting by the father and son. Some Western viewers felt that in contrast to her brother and father, Cuiqiao was too fair-skinned and too pretty. On the other hand, most of her chores outside the home are done at dawn and dusk, so it is not unnatural that she should be paler than the farmers; and pretty girls can be found in Shaanbei.[85] No Chinese critic found her too pretty for the part. The script calls for her to display the same blankness as her brother, but in the film, her sensitive face reflects her emotions very delicately. No Chinese viewer criticized the actress or director for this either. The criticism that her "singing" (her songs are dubbed by a professional singer) is too prettified was more common. Some critics complained about the family's tattered clothes and other evidence of poverty.[86] Their surroundings are in fact depicted with a truthfulness rarely shown in the Chinese cinema, although to Western filmgoers they are still somewhat romantically picturesque.

On 26 June the crew packed up and returned to Guangxi, where the final editing took place. At this stage it was still possible to reshoot some scenes. Asked in 1984 about the rhythm of the film, especially about the long, slow passages "in which there seems to be no meaning but which hold a great deal of meaning," the director replied that the editing was largely a matter of experimentation.[87] One critic thought that the editing was the weakest point in the film; others thought it was one of the strongest.[88] The result was certainly very different from the usual Chinese feature film. Zheng Dongtian described the film as moving between documentary, prose poetry and drama, startling viewers with its departure from the familiar conventions of the Chinese or Russian cinema.[89] Li Tuo documented the length of the extra-narrative sequences and praised the combination of narrative montage with a documentary style; Ma Rui and Meng Hongmei 孟紅梅 criticized it with the same statistics.[90] Peng Jiajin 彭加瑾 praised the creators of *The Yellow Earth* and *One and Eight* for both breaking with convention and choosing scripts based on an essay and poem respectively.[91] Many critics compared the film to a poem[92] (variously a "lyrical epic", a prose poem, a symbolist poem, a poem by Du Fu 杜甫, a poem by Chen Ziang 陳子昂 and so on),[93] and the director Huang Jianzhong also found "poetry" in the director's written descriptions of his visit to Shaanbei.[94] One critic commented on its mythic quality, and at least one also compared it to an oil painting;[95] there was general agreement that it left behind the stagy theatricality of most Chinese films.[96] Although in most cases the film-makers felt that they were able to combine their "subjective ideas" (code for unorthodox opinions) with actual reality, it is clear that they were not always successful in this.[97]

The mixture of styles created confusion among some viewers, though at some points Chinese critics seemed to be deliberately obtuse. One film expert, for instance, claimed that it was "unrealistic" for the song at the beginning of the film to come in disembodied form, the singers or their whereabouts not being shown within the picture frame.[98] Another failed to understand the relevance of the wedding procession sequence, except in as it served to introduce the two main characters.[99] Some foreign critics saw the film's descriptive passages merely as pastoral romanticism or self-conscious "exoticism."[100] Even when only imperfectly understood, however, the non-realistic elements nevertheless made a very powerful impact on a wide range of audiences.[101]

The soundtrack recording was made in Xi'an 西安 where the musicians were based, and the songs were also rerecorded at the Xi'an Film Studio. Chen Kaige had originally believed that the music and the sound effects in the film would be as revolutionary and as artistically successful as his other ambitious plans for the structure and cinematography. He was particularly attentive to the placement of the songs in the structure of the film. For instance, Cuiqiao's songs as she draws water are sung to herself, and her tone is soft and sad. On the night of Gu Qing's arrival, she sings at the spinning wheel, the creaking wood "sounding thousands of years old". At first she sings softly, but after a pause raises her voice as if hoping that the visitor will hear, telling him that she could brave any hardship as long as she could escape marriage. The next day at the river bank, "the public official" (Gu Qing) is drawn into the words of her song, but she still feels unable to speak to him directly about her problem. It is only when she realizes that Gu Qing will leave without saving her that she opens her throat and heart, letting her song echo through the hills and valleys: her first three verses reassure him of her confidence in his

promise; as he gets further away she expresses her hopeless longing for his return; as she turns to go home she lets her despair take
over.[102] Most Chinese and Western critics agreed that the songs
were skilfully woven into the script.[103]

On the other hand, the use of a professional singer for Cuiqiao's
songs and the romantic orchestral accompaniment received some
criticism,[104] and after the first showings of the film, the director
conceded that the results had fallen short of the conception.[105] He
blamed this mainly on his own lack of skill, but also on an attempt
to bow to the box office. The team had realized that on the whole
they were going above the heads of the mass audience, and so in
order to appeal in at least one way to this audience they decided to
have Cuiqiao's songs performed in a "Westernized" (i.e. polished)
style accompanied by Western-style orchestration. Chen Kaige
describes the fault here as due to the mixture of two styles, but
Western audiences tended to describe the artifice of Cuiqiao's
singing and the sentimentality of the orchestration more simply as
a lapse in taste.

From Xi'an Chen Kaige moved back to Nanning to supervise
the final mixing. In one of his rare references to Western directors,
Chen Kaige mentioned that he was influenced by Korda's use of
music in the film *Nana*, in particular to the use of abrupt pauses in
the soundtrack. Some critics praised the effective use of silence in
the film,[106] but others criticized the clumsy postsynchronization
dubbing, the indistinct dialogue and the obtrusive sound effects
(such as the "wind through the valley", which sounds more like
an airplane).[107] Chen Kaige later acknowledged that he does not
understand fully the technology of sound mixing.[108]

The film was completed on 8 August 1984.

Since then, Chen Kaige has given innumerable interviews
about *The Yellow Earth*, though the best statement of his aims and
approaches is still the talk he gave to the members of the film crew
before setting out for location in April 1984. Thinking about the

production process two years later, Chen Kaige felt that on the whole, despite the practical difficulties they encountered during writing, shooting, editing and recording, everything went smoothly.[109]

Other members of the film team generally shared the director's satisfaction with the film and their own part in it. The only discordant note came from the art director, He Qun, who had already worked on *One and Eight* and who was also to be the art director of Chen Kaige's second film (but not his third). According to the scriptwriter, Zhang Ziliang, He Qun believed that he was not given sufficient recognition for his contribution. Zhang himself believed that He Qun's work in *One and Eight* and *The Yellow Earth* was the beginning of serious art design in the modern Chinese cinema.[110]

Before charting the reception of *The Yellow Earth* in China, it may be useful to add a few words about the actual and intended audience for Chinese films and the social status of film-makers.[111] By the 1980s, the potential domestic market for films was huge, and virtually every small locality possessed at least a film projection unit. Not all films reached far into the countryside: the number of copies made and the geographic distribution of a film was decided at the centre. From the early 1950s to the late 1970s, the actual audiences in the countryside were passive: choice was very limited and attendance was almost compulsory. To some extent this was also true in urban areas, where even in the early 1980s block purchase of tickets by work units was still common practice and viewers were not necessarily informed of the title of the film they were about to see.

In addition to this passive audience was an active urban audience composed of students, office workers (cadres) in Party and government units, and intellectuals: except at the height of the Cultural Revolution, this audience was generally able to attend cinemas spontaneously, exercise a choice over what they saw, and comment on the available fare by letters to the press, the annual vote on the most popular films of the year, and word-of-mouth recommendations. To some extent, therefore, this audience was able to influence the film industry. The most important audience to film-makers, however, was the numerically small critical audience, composed of upper-level Party cadres, intellectuals and the film-makers' own colleagues. To some extent this critical audience was homogenous in regard to educational background and prejudices, since film-makers (especially directors and scriptwriters) were members of the élite literary intelligentsia, and upper-level Party cadres also had previous or present close personal connections with the intellectual élite.

Whatever lip-service may have been paid to "the masses", film-makers generally ignored the passive audience, made some concessions to the active audience in order to gain popularity, and concentrated their main attention on pleasing the critical audience at the centre, where the fate of the film and of its makers was primarily determined. While adopting broadly conventional attitudes to these three audiences, however, the new film-makers such as Chen Kaige hoped to reach especially their own generation of young intellectuals and cadres. The debates on *The Yellow Earth* reported below were conducted mostly within the critical audience, but young intellectuals who were normally confined to the role of active viewers were also drawn in.

Notes

1. For Chinese film titles and dates see Glossary.
2. The history of the film's process and the account of the director's motivation up to this point is based on an interview by the author in July 1986. See also the statements made by Chen Kaige, Zhang Yimou and He Qun in April 1984, the joint article by all three in

DZDY September 1984, and the interviews with Chen Kaige and Zhang Yimou in late 1984 reprinted in *HS HTD* (full citations above Chapter One, note 1:19–20).

3. Chen Kaige, *HS HTD*: 264–65.
4. Chen Kaige, *HS HTD*: 275
5. Chen Kaige, *HS HTD*: 265
6. Zhang Yimou, "Jiu pai zhe kuai tu!—*HTD* sheying tihui" (Shoot this piece of land!—my experiences photographing *TYE*), *DYYS*, May 1985: 54–55.
7. See variously below in this chapter. Hao Dazheng remarks that the style, structure and language of the film are all "in the dialect of Shaanbei peasant life"; *HS HTD*: 151.
8. Chen Kaige, *HS HTD*: 265–66.
9. See for example Huang Jianzhong 黃健中 , *HS HTD*: 238.
10. I am grateful to Tony Saitch for drawing these debates to my attention.
11. Chen Kaige, *HS HTD*: 265–66.
12. Chen Kaige, *HS HTD*: 266.
13. See below Chapter Eight: 120–21.
14. Chen Kaige, *HS HTD*: 280.
15. Chen Kaige, *HS HTD*: 266–67.
16. Chen Kaige, *HS HTD*: 267, 69.
17. Chen Kaige, *HS HTD*: 267; see also "*HTD* daoyan chanshu": 111.
18. Chen Kaige, *HS HTD*: 276.
19. Chen Kaige, *HS HTD*: 267 and "*HTD* daoyan chanshu": 110.
20. Chen Kaige, *HS HTD*: 269.
21. Chen Kaige, *HS HTD*: 266, elaborated in conversation with the author.
22. Chen Kaige, *HS HTD*: 275.
23. Tan Min, *HS HTD*: 82–83.
24. Chen Kaige, *HS HTD*: 276.
25. Chen Kaige, *HS HTD*: 276; for his former teacher's impression, see Zheng Dongtian, *HS HTD*: 44.
26. See for instance the statements made by Chen Kaige, Zhang Yimou and He Qun in March and April 1984, before setting out on location (Chapter One, note 1:19–20).
27. Chen Kaige has always admired physical dedication in any line of work. See for example his admiration for the Japanese director

Imamura Shohei in his search for realistic effects for the film *Narayama bushiko* (Ballad of Narayama), reported by Wang Shi, *HS HTD*: 184.

28. Interview with Chen Kaige, Peking, August 1986.
29. Chen Kaige, *HS HTD*: 280.
30. *Ming bao wanbao*, 26 April 1985: 4.
31. *BR*, 10 February 1986: 30 and *DZDY*, August 1984: 12.
32. Zhang Yimou, *HS HTD*: 288.
33. Interview with Chen Kaige by two French students, July 1986, from notes taken by the author. See also Chen Kaige, "Qinguo ren—ji Zhang Yimou" 秦國人——記張藝謀 (A Xi'an man: recalling Zhang Yimou), *DDDY*, July 1985: 101–107.
34. For example Danny Yung. Geremie Barmé, on the other hand, who regards Zhang Yimou's cinematography as the major achievement of the film, sees the latter as having found his own path. See Bai Jieming 白杰明 [Geremie Barmé], *HS HTD*: 306–7.
35. Zhang Yimou, "*HTD* sheying chanshu": 117.
36. Zhou Chuanji, *HS HTD*: 211.
37. Zhang Yimou, "Statement": 117, 119.
38. Zhang Yimou, *HS HTD*: 288–90.
39. Zhang Yimou, *HS HTD*: 288.
40. See for instance Shen Songsheng 沈嵩生, *HS HTD*: 29 as compared with Tan Min, *HS HTD*: 82–83 and Xi Bai 犀白 (Hong Kong), *HS HTD*: 310.
41. Zhang Yimou, *HS HTD*: 289–90.
42. Zhang Yimou, *HS HTD*: 277.
43. Zhang Yimou, *HS HTD*: 290.
44. He Qun, *HS HTD*: 298.
45. Zhang Yimou, *HS HTD*: 290.
46. Zhang Yimou, *HS HTD*: 288–89; see also Zheng Dongtian, *HS HTD*: 45.
47. Li Tuo, *HS HTD*: 55.
48. Zhang Yimou, "*HTD* sheying chanshu": 117–18 and *HS HTD*: 294–96.
49. See Shen Songsheng, *HS HTD*: 29; Gui Ying 桂英, *Gong jiao bao* 公教報 (Hong Kong), 24 May 1985.
50. Zhang Yimou, "*HTD* sheying chanshu": 119.
51. Zhang Yimou, *HS HTD*: 294–95.

52. Zhang Yimou, *HS HTD*: 295; see also Chen Kaige, *HS HTD*: 268–70.

53. Zhang Yimou, *HS HTD*: 285–96.

54. Zheng Dongtian, *HS HTD*: 42–43; Shen Songsheng, *HS HTD*: 31. For a dissenting opinion, see Wang Dehou, *HS HTD*: 138–39.

55. Shao Mujun, *HS HTD*: 258–59.

56. See for instance Chen Kaige's remarks in Hong Kong in April 1985, recorded by John Minford, *FEER*, 8 August 1985: 32, and interview with Tony Rayns, *Time Out*, 833.

57. Zhang Yimou's remarks in Hong Kong in April 1985, recorded by Gui Ying, *Gong jiao bao*, 24 May 1985.

58. Zhang Yimou, *HS HTD*: 292. Zhang Yimou's comments on picture-frame composition are given in his *"HTD sheying chanshu"*: 118 and in *HS HTD*: 291–94. See also Ge De 葛德 , *"HTD huamian zaoxing de xieyi jichu"*《黃土地》畫面造型的寫意基礎 (The "non-realistic" basis for the picture composition in *TYE*), *DZDY*, January 1986: 9–8.

59. Zhang Yimou, *HS HTD*: 292.

60. Zhang Yimou, *HS HTD*: 292–93.

61. *Qingnian wenxue* 青年文學 , January 1983; English translation, "My Faraway Qingpingwan", *CL*, Spring 1984: 61–76.

62. Zhang Yimou, *HS HTD*: 293; see also Zhang Yimou, "Jiu pai zhe kuai tu!": 54–55. Zheng Dongtian, Ni Zhen 倪震 and Li Chao, who would have read Zhang Yimou's interview, also mention Shi Tiesheng's story in connection with the film; see *HS HTD*: 41, 67, 111.

63. Zhang Yimou, *HS HTD*: 293; cf. Ye Xiaonan, *HS HTD*: 232.

64. See Zhou Chuanji's analysis of their unease, *HS HTD*: 214.

65. *HS HTD*: 293–94; see also Ni Zhen, *HS HTD*: 74–75.

66. Interview by two French students, July 1986, from notes taken by the author.

67. *HS HTD*: 286. Zhang Yimou's comments on movement and repetition in the film are in *"HTD sheying chanshu"*: 118, 118–19 and in *HS HTD*: 286–88. On the debate around the use of movement see Shao Mujun, *HS HTD*: 259–60. *Doro no Kawa* (1981), was the first film by the director Oguri Kohei, who chose the muddy river as a symbol of a child's development, pure at the source but becoming muddy as it descends to the sea.

68. *"HTD sheying chanshu"*: 118–19 and *HS HTD*: 286–87.

69. See Zhang Chengshan, *HS HTD*: 104.

70. Zhang Yimou, *HS HTD*: 287–88. Generally this sequence was very highly praised; one dissenting voice was Hu Bingliu, *HS HTD*: 34.
71. Zhang Yimou, *HS HTD*: 295–96.
72. I am indebted to Paul Clark for the information on Tan Tuo's voice training.
73. See Chapter Nine, p. 142.
74. Interview with Chen Kaige by two French students, July 1986, from notes taken by the author.
75. Chen Kaige, "*HTD* daoyan chanshu": 114 and *HS HTD*: 272, 274.
76. E.g. Ye Yancai, *HS HTD*: 92; anonymous critics reported in *DYYS*, April 1985: 27.
77. E.g. Yu Yanfu, *HS HTD*: 4 and Yu Min 于敏 , *HS HTD*: 25. See also below, Chapter Three: 58.
78. Chen Kaige, *HS HTD*: 270–71, 272–73.
79. Many critics backed up Chen Kaige's claims on this point, e.g. Hao Dazheng, *HS HTD*: 151–52.
80. Ye Yancai, *HS HTD*: 93.
81. Wang Zhongming, *HS HTD*: 118; [Li] Jinsheng, *HS HTD*: 174; Tong Daoming, *HS HTD*: 195; Ye Yancai, *HS HTD*: 94; Wang Shushun, *DDDY*, February 1985: 54 (the latter two are otherwise generally hostile).
82. See for instance Xie Tian 谢添 , *HS HTD*: 3; Hao Dazheng, *HS HTD*: 152; Ding Daoxi 丁道希 , *HS HTD*: 156; Chen Maiping, *HS HTD*: 199; Chen Xihe, *HS HTD*: 255; *DYYS*, March 1985: 8. Ni Zhen speaks more generally of the Sichuan school of oil painting, *HS HTD*: 67.
83. *HS HTD*: 295.
84. *HS HTD*: 268–270. Hao Dazheng supports the director's claim, noting that slow speech by no means implies deficient judgment, only the mannerism of peasants from an area with little social intercourse; see *HS HTD*: 147.
85. See Chen Kaige on her model, *HS HTD*: 273–74.
86. One critic claimed for instance that even the poorest peasants in that area had padded door curtains to keep out drafts; see Ye Yancai, *HS HTD*: 91. Wang Shi describes the depiction of poverty in such details as clothing as unusually truthful, *HS HTD*: 184.
87. Interview with Danny Yung, Peking, August 1986.
88. Liang Xin 梁信 , *HS HTD*: 9 versus Hao Dazheng, *HS HTD*: 53–54,

Kong Du 孔都 , *HS HTD*: 97, and Zhou Chuanji, *HS HTD*: 217 and *DDYS*, March 1985: 3.

89. Zheng Dongtian, *HS HTD*: 43.

90. Li Tuo, *HS HTD*: 51, 57; Ma Rui, *DYYS*, September 1986: 17; Meng Hongmei, *HS HTD*: 223.

91. Peng Jiajin, *HS HTD*: 128; see also Zhang Boqing 章柏青 , *HS HTD*: 241.

92. Most notably Zhao Yuan 趙園 , *HS HTD*: 59–66 and Ma Debo 馬德波 , *WYB*, February 1985: 60–61. Kong Du says it departs from film narrative and achieves the effect of poetry, *HS HTD*: 96; Peng Jiajin, [Li] Jinsheng and Wang Shi say much the same, *HS HTD*: 128–32; 167, 170–73; 187.

93. Wang Dehou, *HS HTD*: 135; Tan Min, *HS HTD*: 83; Shao Mujun, *HS HTD*: 259; Li Xingye 李興葉 , *DYYS*, March 1985: 8–10; [Li] Jinsheng, *HS HTD*: 167. Du Fu and Chen Ziang are famous poets from the Tang dynasty.

94. Huang Jianzhong, *HS HTD*: 238–39.

95. Tong Daoming, *HS HTD*: 191; Wang Dehou, *HS HTD*: 135

96. For instance Zhang Chengshan, *HS HTD*: 103; Law Kar 羅卡 [Luo Ka] (Hong Kong), *HS HTD*: 116–17; [Li] Jinsheng, *HS HTD*: 166; and the anonymous film director quoted in *DYYS*, April 1985: 27.

97. See Zhang Yimou, *HS HTD*: 283, 296 for the film-makers' own admission of failure to reach some of their goals.

98. Quoted by Chen Maiping, *HS HTD*: 198.

99. Wang Shushun, *DDDY*, February 1985: 54.

100. See for instance the anonymous reviews in *The Economist*, 20 April 1985 and 16 November 1985.

101. See also the range of reactions from Western critics described in Chapters Seven and Eight.

102. The interpretation given here is my own. For a slightly different reading of the songs see Zheng Dongtian, *HS HTD*: 40.

103. For example [Li] Jinsheng, *HS HTD*: 173–74. Zhao Yuan and Hao Dazheng praised the integration of the songs, except for Cuiqiao's, into the script; *HS HTD*: 63, 153. Hu Bingliu was critical of the use of the songs and of the sound generally, *HS HTD*: 34.

104. For example from Li Xingye, quoted in *DYYD*, March 1985: 5, Zheng Dongtian, *HS HTD*: 46 and Deng Baochen, *HS HTD*: 15 (songs only). One Hong Kong critic liked the orchestration; see *HS HTD*: 311.

105. Chen Kaige, *HS HTD*: 282–83.
106. For example Zhao Yuan, *HS HTD*: 63; Wang Dehou, *HS HTD*: 139; Hao Dazheng, *HS HTD*: 153.
107. For example Wang Dehou, *HS HTD*: 139. Deng Baochen, on the other hand, thought that apart from Cuiqiao's songs, the music and sound effects were well done; see *HS HTD*: 15. Zhou Chuanji praises especially the father's voice effects but notes some problems in postsynchronization, *HS HTD*: 215–17, 219.
108. Interview with Chen Kaige, July 1987.
109. Interview with Chen Kaige, July 1986.
110. Interview with Zhang Ziliang, July 1987. Zhang Ziliang himself is a native of Shaanbei. During the Cultural Revolution he spent three years in a village near Gansu 甘肃 , then four years in the army in Hami 哈密 . Afterwards he was posted to the Xi'an Film Studio as a film process worker, and now works in the script department.
111. This topic is lamentably underresearched. For some introductory remarks, see McDougall,"Writers and performers, their works, and their audiences in the first three decades," in McDougall, ed., *Popular Chinese Literature and Performing Arts in the People's Republic of China 1949–79* (University of California Press, Berkeley, 1984), pp. 269–304, and Clark, *Chinese Cinema, passim*. The following remarks are based mainly on personal observation of film-makers and film audiences in the late 1950s and in the 1980s.

3. The Release
(August 1984 to February 1985)

The first screening of *The Yellow Earth* took place on 19 August in Peking. The senior critics and prominent literary figures (including the poet Ai Qing 艾青) who saw it in similar private screenings over the following weeks were almost unanimous in not liking it. The Film Bureau was even more decided in its dislike for the film and initially barred its public distribution. The opposition of these people did not come as a surprise, especially in view of the fate of the still unreleased *One and Eight*. On the other hand, the enthusiastic response of friends and colleagues gave the film crew considerable encouragement, and they began to believe that their work over the past few months had all been worthwhile. Changes were then made in the film which Chen Kaige later described as minor improvements stemming from the crew's more relaxed and objective mood.

Timing was an important factor in the release of *The Yellow Earth*. The less fortunate *One and Eight* was completed in October 1983 when the movement against "spiritual pollution" was well underway, and even its heavily revised version was not publicly released for almost two years. (It was subsequently shown on television in summer 1986 but not permitted release outside China until 1988; its appearance at the Hong Kong International Film Festival in 1987 did not count as an "outside" release.) By the time *The Yellow Earth* was completed, however, the movement had been discredited, and though its chief instigators were still in office, the political climate had changed. In spite of the film's controversial nature, therefore, it was passed for release within a month.

The Yellow Earth was first shown in public in Shanghai in September 1984. It was given no advance publicity, and as far as the director knows, no billboards were ever posted for the film in China until 1986. Although total box-office figures for particular films are in some cases widely publicized, Chen Kaige was never given box-office returns for *The Yellow Earth*. At this point, however, there was no need to supply figures. The film had a brief run at two or three cinemas, but audience attendance was low, and the film was withdrawn from circulation. The poor audience response embarrassed the film's supporters, who frequently felt obliged to make defensive remarks about audience levels. One critic pointed out, however, that *The Yellow Earth* appeared at a time of crisis in the Chinese cinema, when audiences for all kinds of films were shrinking, and that the similarly poor box-office of the prize-winning *Border Town* (邊城), another 1984 release but wholly conventional, was not held against it in any public statement.[1]

The first mention in the Chinese press of *The Yellow Earth* was a short note under the heading of "Studio News" in *Dazhong dianying* 大衆電影 (Popular cinema) in August 1984, together with coloured stills from the film on the inside front cover.[2] The next month's issue, coinciding with the film's release, ran a short article by Chen Kaige, Zhang Yimou and He Qun about their first visit to Shaanbei to gather material for the film.[3] In October, the film was one of several shown as part of a mass exercise in film criticism for young people sponsored by *Zhongguo qingnian* 中國青年 (China's youth), *Popular Cinema* and other organizations; one of the young reviewers wrote a very enthusiastic, almost gushing review of *The Yellow Earth* for this event, which was recommended the following year by the sponsoring committee for publication.[4] *The Yellow Earth* was not included in the special mass release of the year's new films when the 35th anniversary of the People's Republic was celebrated in October that year, but it made the second batch of anniversary releases in November.[5] In December it was listed in *Popular Cinema* among the month's new films, described as having attracted controversy during its trial run.[6]

Towards the end of 1984, when the controversial nature of the film was firmly established, Chen Kaige and Zhang Yimou were interviewed for the "internal" [restricted circulation] film magazine, *Dianying yishu cankao ziliao* 電影藝術參考資料 (Research materials on cinema arts).[7] Their statements of intent in these interviews were quoted by hostile and friendly critics alike as statements of fact about the film. Very occasionally a critic might express doubt about the sincerity of these statements, as for instance when Yu Min noted sarcastically that if the film-makers loved the peasants as they claimed, why did they not make films that the peasants loved?[8] In general, however, and in keeping with the importance given to orthodoxy in art and politics, intentions were regarded by critics as of equal importance with results; also, given the low level of art criticism in China, many critics fail to perceive any distinction between intentions and results. (An honorable exception to this is Yu Qian 余倩 .[9]) Further, both the film's supporters and the film-makers themselves tended to make claims about their intentions that seem primarily defensive in nature. For example, Chen Kaige replied in the following manner to the interviewer's question about the film's supposed voyeurism and glorificiation of peasant backwardness:

> Praying for rain is one of the most ancient rituals of our people, and one which survives even today. In the *Book of Songs* there are descriptions of peasants praying for rain during celebrations for good harvests. *People often begin praying for rain just as it is about to start raining.* [italics supplied] Thus it is not simply an expression of superstitious ignorance, since it also embodies a certain element of enjoyment. Our aim in filming this scene was not at all voyeuristic or calculated to

show up the ignorance of the peasants, but rather to express the formidable energy and force of the peasants. Although that energy is still blind and undirected, as long as it exists it has great potential *if properly tapped and directed*. [italics supplied][10]

Similarly, Zhang Yimou described Gu Qing coming over the hill in the final sequence as showing that only the Communist Party can awaken the peasants to be their own masters.[11] Not surprisingly, the film-makers defined their intentions or beliefs differently at different times and to different audiences; in a statement made two years later to foreign interviewers, for instance, the director was noticeably less cautious, even arrogant, in his definition of his aims in the film.[12]

At the annual meeting to survey the year's films organized by *Dianying yishu* 電影藝術 (Cinema arts) at the end of 1984, *The Yellow Earth* and the other new wave films on the whole were well received.[13] In the published report of the proceedings, very little direct criticism of the new films was made, but it is apparent from some of the responses that attacks had been made especially on *The Yellow Earth*. Chen Kaige, who spoke at the meeting, was obliged to defend himself and his fellow-graduates from charges of seeking foreign, Western and formalistic effects.[14] Backing him up, a researcher from the Film-makers' Association, Peng Jiajin, claimed that the film's chief value was not in its innovations but in its continuation of the national tradition of poetic art, and its continuation of Lu Xun's 魯迅 treatment of peasants. He also pointed out with some irony that the appearance of these "experimental films" by fifth generation directors, which could not be expected to sell cinema tickets, had coincided exactly with the current crisis in cinema attendences.[15] Box-office returns, however, were not a major topic at this meeting.

The first newspaper mention of the film was in a favourable review in the English-language *China Daily* in December 1984 by a friend of the director:

The film's success is largely owed to the director's faithful portrayal of the people and the revolution, but what is more, to his understanding and grasp of cinema aesthetics. He tried for something original, beautiful, national and powerful, something that had not been attempted. And he got it. The acting is impressive, especially that of the peasant man and the boy. They act convincingly and accurately so that they convey the inner worlds of the characters. [16]

The Yellow Earth continued to be shown privately in the new year, for instance at the fourth national congress of the Chinese Writers' Association. Over eight hundred writers attended the conference, which opened in Peking on 8 January 1985, and the film received a great deal of comment. Despite the film's limited distribution, the influential *Wenyi bao* 文藝報 (Literature and the arts) ran a review of it in February 1985, mentioning only in the last line the controversy that had already arisen.[17] In this context the review is surprisingly enthusiastic, even looking forward to mass audience reaction; it is also fuzzy on detail, reporting, for instance, that the cave home lies on the river bank.

An important event for the new wave cinema was the Seminar on Films by Young Directors and Cinematographers held in Peking in the first week of February under the joint sponsorship of the Film Publishing House and *Cinema Arts*;[18] the active organizers included Chen Kaiyan 陳凱燕 and Gu Xiaoyang 顧曉陽 . Four films were shown: *The Yellow Earth, One and Eight, On the Hunting Ground* (獵場扎撒) and *Bloodshed in Black Valley* (滴血黑谷). About fifty people were invited to speak, including the filmmakers themselves, several of their teachers from the film academy, older film directors, and also scholars, writers and artists outside the film world. Many of the latter group belonged to the same generation as the film-makers: the first to speak, for instance, was the painter Ma Desheng 馬德生 , followed by the writer and drama teacher Chen Maiping. The support they gave the new films was so enthusiastic that some of the senior people involved became embarrassed and tried to cut short the discussion.

One of the major points in Chen Maiping's speech was the open-ended nature of the film's images in contrast to the rigidly limited meanings of conventional Chinese films.[19] In this and other respects he set the film in the context of the new movement in Chinese poetry, fiction, painting and music, quoting Bei Dao's famous lines, "A million scintillating suns/appear in the shattered mirror."[20] In particular he praised the film's breakthrough from representationalism to "subjective expressionism", meaning by the latter not the early twentieth-century art movement but the film-makers' desire to express personal, unorthodox views.[21] Another speaker, Kong Du, similarly claimed that the film abandoned the language of film realism to enter "the aesthetic realm of expression."[22] The Lu Xun scholar Wang Dehou also defended the film's artistic innovations, quoting Lu Xun on the notion that divergent opinions were a common phenomenon in art.[23]

The first public debate over the film came in March 1985 with the publication in *Dianying xinzuo* 電影新作 (New films) of two articles, one pro and one contra, and four articles in *Dangdai dianying* 當代電影 (Contemporary cinema), three pro and one contra. Both bimonthlies, these magazines were among several established in the 1980s as part of a general expansion in the Chinese cinema. In *New Films*, Han Xiaolei, one of Chen Kaige's '78 classmates, not surprisingly supported *The Yellow Earth*; Ye Yancai, a self-proclaimed newcomer to the film world, saw himself as braving the tide by pointing out numerous inaccuracies and shortcomings.[24] Ye Yancai's main contention was that the film emphasises form at the expense of content: he gives as example the much-praised drum dance sequence which he describes as "stiff, forced, and unrelated to the picture."[25] Li Chao tried to refute Ye Yancai's charges, but his article did not reach print for another year.[26]

Of more public signficance was the debate in *Contemporary*

Cinema, regarded as one of the most authoritative and liberal-minded of the new film publications. The first three articles evidently address themselves to current criticism of the film and have a distinctly defensive note. Zheng Dongtian, head of the directing department of the Peking Film Academy, set the tone of the discussion by describing *The Yellow Earth* as a film which embodied the thoughts and feelings of a whole generation, and which in the barest thread of a plot encapsuled the fate of generations of Chinese people.[27] In response to critics who claimed the film presented a picture of backwardness and ignorance, he denied that there was any trace of condescension or ridicule in the film-makers' attitude, only compassion and indignation in the face of a continuing tragedy in the Chinese countryside: he saw the film as a profound attempt to come to grips with fundamental problems in Chinese history.

Zheng Dongtian analyses the sequence of the matchmaker's visit to show the portrayal of Cuiqiao as a symbol of the peasants' attempt to create a new life. Her mind just awakened with new hope, Cuiqiao is overcome with despair at the sight of the matchmaker. The camera focuses on the changing emotions on her face, as off-screen her father's slow, monotonous voice tells her of her fate: it is the disembodied voice of History, an impersonal cruelty imposed by the poverty of the land. Cuiqiao can only submit to her fate; she is faced not with deliberate viciousness but an ignorance which is both calm and tender. The change in her consciousness is shown in her songs: her first song expresses helpless submission; the song with which she farewells Gu Qing expresses her hope for change; the song she sings as she rows towards a new life expresses her faith in change. Cuiqiao drowns "in the current of history", but the roar of the waves "sounds louder and louder." (The contradictory nature of this interpretation of the symbolism seems to have escaped the author).

Zheng Dongtian next examines the philosophical implications

61

of the film's presentation of man and nature, taking as his example the sequence where the father is shown ploughing the family plot. In this scene, where man, animal, earth and sky are blended into one whole, we feel the relationship between man and earth, and as the father advances again and again towards the camera, we feel history stretching forward under his feet. As in the film as a whole, unusually realistic representation is combined with deep philosophical meaning. To take another example, the darkness in the cave home is not only more faithful to reality than previous film treatments had dared to present, but it also becomes an image of oppression and melancholy. Scenes of peasants tilling land, cave homes and the Yellow River are all very familiar in the Chinese cinema, but Zheng Dongtian found their presentation in this film particularly fresh, moving and thoughtful (for instance, the Yellow River as destructive as well as nurturing). He praised the film's attention to detail in acting, design and camera work, in each case technique being used to convey meaning. Despite a few shortcomings, which on the whole he believed were inevitable in the course of exploring new ground, he praised the film very highly and regretted its poor box-office reception.

The second article in this issue of *Contemporary Cinema* was by the well-known fiction writer Li Tuo, who characterized the film as "an intruder at the party".[28] A large part of the film's strangeness, he points out, was the attention given to elements in the composition of the film that are part neither of the characterization nor the plot. Primary among these are the images of the yellow earth and the Yellow River, which occupy about 700 feet of film, or almost a whole reel. The complex impression evoked by these two complementary elements goes beyond simple explanation; they are neither simple representations of geography nor just background scenery. A third important element is the depiction of local culture in the film, which in terms of screen time is even more important than the earth and river: altogether the three amount to about one-third of the whole film. Although this kind of quantification is not the major index in analysis of film structure, it does indicate the unusual degree to which the film underplays plot and character, thereby assuming a documentary and poetic colour. Furthermore, the film-makers manage not only to express in film terms the grandeur of the landscape and the aesthetic appeal of the local culture, but also to relate this specific area to Chinese culture as a whole and explore its influence on China's destiny.

Moving on to the characters in the film, Li Tuo points out that they seem initially unconscious of the hardship and tragedy in their lives, but instead of portraying their awakening in ways so familiar to Chinese audiences, we only have Cuiqiao running away from home and Hanhan offering her Gu Qing's sewing kit with its red star. At the same time as it celebrates the grandeur of the yellow earth, it also shows the poverty created by natural geography. Cuiqiao's twice-daily trek to the Yellow River for water and the farmers' pleas for rain shock us with nature's miserliness, but the father's affectionate words to the ox as it ploughs the soil is one of several examples showing the courage, optimism and determination of these people. Not only have they kept themselves alive for generation after generation in a stubborn, unceasing struggle for existence, but they are the creators of an ancient and brilliant culture. This culture now is, however, also a form of bondage. The portrayal of the father is a living example of this contradiction: he is both frank and suspicious, both generous and stubborn.

Li Tuo especially praised the film-makers for their spirit of experimentation. Rather than single out particular examples, he argued for the general necessity for experiment in what was still a relatively recent art form. Like Zheng Dongtian, he saw the box-office unpopularity of such films as a temporary phenomenon to be corrected by education and time, and denied that experimental films might interfere with the normal development of the Chinese cinema: of the several hundred films produced in the last few years, only a handful could be called experimental, and economic considerations prevent the production of a greater proportion. In short, there was no reason not to give the stranger a well-deserved welcome.

The theme of the third article, by Professor Zhao Yuan of the film academy, is the poetic nature of *The Yellow Earth*.[29] In many places his argument seems to be a defence of the unorthodox views in the film, so that "poetic" and other circumlocutions appear to be code words for the film's perceived attack on Party policies. For instance, denying criticisms that the ideological preoccupations of the film-makers produced forced effects, he claimed that the abstract concepts behind the film have become completely internalized, so that instead of making the film dry, they enrich and illuminate it. Again, where some people do not see the logic behind some of the "poetic lines" of the film, he claims it is because the logic is not "plot logic" but "theme logic". To some critics *The Yellow Earth* was part of the modernist trend in literature in the arts characterized by irrationality and obscurity. Zhao Yuan points out that the plot of the film is extremely simple and clear, but that its significance and emotional impact are largely due to three other elements in the film: the image of the yellow earth itself, the constant if unseen presence of the director (as the subjective intelligence providing the logic of the film), and the use of concrete detail to express abstract concepts. These three elements are characteristic of poetry, according to Zhao, especially modern poetry.

Zhao Yuan described the special quality of *The Yellow Earth* as its use of "blankness" or "empty space". Blankness is a special characteristic of poetry, and in fact a special characteristic of all traditional Chinese classical art forms; the Chinese cinema, however, has always lacked "blankness". Zhao Yuan saw the minimalist plot, dialogue, characterization and camera work in *The Yellow Earth* as allowing the "space" for philosophical reflection. "Space" is also important in the film sound track, for instance in the silences which precede the boy's and the father's songs. Zhao Yuan's final point is the "meta-realism" or "realism beyond realism" in the film. For example, Cuiqiao is the most "realistic" character in the film, but it is the father and the son who make the greatest impact: given the rich expressiveness of their faces, there is correspondingly less need for spoken dialogue. Colour, employed as part of the film language, and the visual imagery generally, also goes beyond mimetic realism. In his evidently strong desire to praise the film, Zhao Yuan concludes with rather confused statements about the "unity of exaggeration and mimesis" and the "literariness" in its "filmicness".

The final contribution was from Wang Shushun, who set *The Yellow Earth* in the context of other films from the "fifth generation" in 1983 and 1984.[30] His main criticism of *The Yellow Earth* and *One and Eight* was for not paying attention to their respective "representative environments", in other words, not presenting sensitive themes in keeping with orthodox Party treatment.[31] Acknowledging the originality of the new films in such areas as minimalist dialogue, plot, number of characters and number of shots, he also claimed that in *The Yellow Earth* the film-makers get carried away in their search for novelty. His main example is at the end of the rain prayer sequence where the villagers are shown rushing forward; since why and where they are rushing is not made clear, he concluded that its only purpose was to create a tide for Hanhan to go against, and accused the film-makers of glorifying superstition in their hunt for bizarre effects. He concludes with the warning that originality must not go beyond "national, traditional and realistic" aesthetic standards, and that art films for limited audiences are not to be encouraged.

With these articles, the terms of the public debate became clear:

apart from a few areas of generally agreed upon flaws and generally agreed upon merits, the participants lined up on opposite sides depending mainly on their support for or rejection of the "search", "deep reflection", "subjective expressionism" or "philosophical/poetic truth" of the film. "Search" was the most common and most neutral code word for the movement away from orthodoxy in the the arts since 1977. "Deep reflection", described either as a quality that the film-makers had invested in the film or as the response the film invokes in the audience, was also used by both sides as a code word for criticism of Party policy or practice within acceptable limits. "Subjectivism", on the other hand, was used to describe elements in the film that went beyond the normal limits, while overtly hostile criticism characterized the film in terms such as "unrepresentative", "unrealistic", "naturalistic", or even, in the worst case, "departing from the masses".

Notes

1. Shao Mujun, *HS HTD*: 256.
2. *DZDY*, August 1984:12 and inside front cover.
3. *DZDY*, September 1984:14–15.
4. Wang Zhongming, "Chu 'shou' bu fan—*HTD* ganyan" 出「手」不凡 ——《黃土地》感言 (A masterly first move—my response to *TYE*), *ZGQN*, May 1985: 47; reprinted in *HS HTD* (minus editorial comment): 118–20.
5. *DZDY*, October 1984: 5 and December 1984: 27.
6. *DZDY*, December 1984: 7.
7. Xiao Luo 小羅 (interviewer), "Huaizhe shenzhi de chizi zhi ai—Chen Kaige tan *HTD* daoyan tihui" (Nourishing a sincere love for the innocent—Chen Kaige discusses his experiences in directing *TYE*) and "Wo pai *HTD*—Zhang Yimou tan *HTD* sheying tihui" (Shooting *TYE*—Zhang Yimou discusses his experiences in the cinematography of *TYE*), *DYYS CKZL*, 15, 1984; reprinted in *HS HTD*: 264–84, 285–97.

8. Yu Min, *HS HTD*: 26. For the context, see below Chapter Four: 80–81.
9. See Yu Qian, *HS HTD*: 126.
10. Chen Kaige, *HS HTD*: 278–80; translation from *SoF*: 268, adapted by the author.
11. Zhang Yimou, *HS HTD*: 294.
12. Interview by two French film students, July 1986, quoted above Chapter Two: note 33.
13. Xiao Ou 小鷗 , "Duocai de xinxi, kegui de tansuo—zai jing bufen yishujia, pinglunjia tan 84 nian guochan gushipian" 多彩的信息，可貴的探索——在京部分藝術家、評論家談84年國產故事片 (Richly varied news, valuable exploration—artists and critics discuss domestic feature films of '84 in Peking), *DYYS*, March: 2–7.
14. "Duocai de xinxi": 7. According to Xiao Ou, the comments recorded in this article are based on his notes from the meeting and have not been checked with the speakers themselves.
15. Peng Jiajin, "Duocai de xinxi": 7.
16. Mian Mian, *CD*, 20 December 1984: 5.
17. Ma Debo, "*HTD*" (*TYE*), *WYB*, February 1985: 60–61.
18. See Benkan jizhe (Staff reporter), "Zui nianqing yidai de dianying tansuo—'Qingnian daoyan sheying yingpian yantaohui' jianji" 最年青一代的電影探索——「青年導演攝影影片研討會」簡記 (Film explorations by the youngest generation—a summary of the Seminar on Films by Young Directors and Cinematographers), *DYYS*, April 1985: 26–28.
19. Chen Maiping, "Zhe li shi xin shijie—*HTD* zhi wojian" 這裏是新世界——《黃土地》之我見 (Here is a new world—my views on *TYE*), *DYCZ*, July 1985; reprinted in *HS HTD*: 197–201, esp. 200.
20. *HS HTD*: 200–201. For the English translation of the poem from which these lines are taken, see "Notes from the City of the Sun" in Bei Dao, *The August Sleepwalker*, ed. and trans. by Bonnie S. McDougall (London: Anvil Press Poetry, 1988): 31.
21. Chen Maiping, *HS HTD*: 197.
22. Kong Du, "Tan *HTD* de gaikuoxing dianying xingxiang" 談《黃土地》的概括性電影形象 (A discussion of the generalized film images in *TYE*), *DYYS*, April 1985; reprinted in *HS HTD*: 95–98.
23. Wang Dehou, "Chenchen de *HTD*" 沉沉的《黃土地》 (The deep *TYE*), *DYYS*, June 1985: 33–35; reprinted in *HS HTD*: 134–39, esp. 134.
24. Han Xiaolei, "*HTD* de qingxu jiegou—jian yi gaipian de xian-dai minzu yishi" 《黃土地》的情緒結構——兼議該片的現代民族意識 (The

emotional structure of *TYE*—together with a discussion of modern national consciousness in this film), *DYXZ*, 2 (February 1985); reprinted in *HS HTD*: 84–90; Ye Yancai, "Huang tu xiamian shi qingquan" 黃土下面是清泉 (Below the yellow earth is a clear spring), *DYXZ*, 2 (March 1985); reprinted in *HS HTD*: 91–94.

25. Ye Yancai, *HS HTD*: 91, 92.

26. Li Chao, "Cong lanhuahua shi de gushi dao dui minzuxing de fansi—*HTD* shenmei jiazhi qiantan" 從藍花花式的故事到對民族性的反思——《黃土地》審美價值淺探 (From a child-bride type of story to a reflection on national character—a brief exploration of the aesthetic value of *TYE*), *HS HTD*: 107–15, esp. 107, 112.

27. Zheng Dongtian, "*HTD* suixiangqu" 《黃土地》隨想曲 (Thoughts on *TYE*), *DDDY*, 2 (March 1985): 42–47; reprinted in *HS HTD*: 37–47.

28. Li Tuo, "*HTD* gei women dailai le shenmo?" 《黃土地》給我們帶來了甚麼？ (What has *TYE* brought us), *DDDY*, 2 (March 1985): 36–41; reprinted in *HS HTD*: 48–58.

29. Zhao Yuan, "Guanyu zhege minzu de shi—tan yingpian *HTD*" 關於這個民族的詩——談影片《黃土地》 (About this national poem—on the film *TYE*), *DDDY*, 2 (March 1985): 48–51; reprinted in *HS HTD*: 59–66.

30. Wang Shushun, "Chuangxin chuyi", *DDDY*, 2 (March 1985): 52–55; not reprinted in *HS HTD*.

31. For instances of Wang Shushun's inaccurate charges against the film's authenticity see above Chapter One: 9.

4. The Golden Rooster (March 1985)

A major challenge to the authorities came with the national film awards in the spring. There are three annual prizes for film in China: the Golden Rooster awards 金雞獎 , given by the Film-makers' Association for best film, best director, best actor and so on; the Ministry of Culture awards, given to best films in different categories; and the Hundred Flowers awards 百花獎 , given to the most popular films of the year on the basis of a reader poll in *Popular Cinema*. That year, with two highly controversial films on its hands, the Guangxi studio decided not to enter any of its 1984 films for nomination for the Hundred Flowers awards.[1] On the other hand, the Golden Rooster awards, regarded as China's "academic" film awards since the panel includes teachers from the film academy as well as senior directors and critics, represented the only realistic chance *The Yellow Earth* had of winning a prize.

The adjudication panel for the Fifth Golden Rooster awards for 1984 was headed by two honorary chairmen—the elderly play-wright, scriptwriter, cultural bureaucrat and director Xia Yan, and the very powerful senior critic and advisor on film to the Ministry of Culture Chen Huangmei. Also on the panel were two other chairmen and twenty-one senior personnel from the studios and academies, including performers and directors. The panel met in Chungking 重慶 at the beginning of March 1985: *The Yellow Earth* was already so controversial that a special session was convened to consider its suitability. Most of the speakers referred ambiguously to the "film-maker(s)" or "author(s)" of the film;

some specified the director and the cinematographer as a two-man team jointly responsible for the film; a few singled out the work of the cinematographer. Where the cinematographer alone was mentioned, the praise was usually unqualified. Even the most enthusiastic of the film's supporters conceded that "of course" the film had defects, usually ascribed to the youth and inexperience of the film-makers, and often not specified. All speakers acknowledged that the film had merit, usually described as its "creativity" and its "search".

Within the apparent common ground was considerable disagreement as to the achievements of the film and its suitability as a prize winner. The chief concern was the theme or message of the film, usually described in terms of the film's portrayal of the "backwardness and ignorance" of the peasantry. The sensitivity of the question was generally referred to indirectly with a statement on the film's "rich historical associations". The clearest formulations were made by Xia Yan and Luo Yijun: since the area was the cradle of Chinese civilization and also an old liberated area, why were the people there shown as so poor and backward?[2]

The sharpest clash on this question was between Huang Zongying 黃宗英 , supported by Zhang Ruifang 張瑞芳 and Deng Baochen, and Xia Yan, supported by Ling Zifeng, Han Shangyi and Chen Huangmei. This was one of the very few occasions in the panel's deliberations when actual discussion between the speakers replaced set speeches, but the discussion roamed confusingly between disputes on fact and disputes on the correct attitude with which to deal with these facts. Xia Yan admitted that even now the place was poor and backward, but criticized the film as failing to express adequately the sense of hope that existed in the midst of backwardness and ignorance: especially since the area was so near to Yenan, where Party power had already existed for three years, "hope" should take more widespread and visible forms than "a spark in a girl's heart." Xia

Yan, who had himself spent the war years in the Nationalist interior, claimed that the influence of Yenan in those years had spread throughout the whole country, even throughout the world. In his opinion, the film-makers exaggerated the backwardness and ignorance of the peasants for artistic effect, and even saw "beauty" in this backwardness.[3]

Huang Zongying, a well-known writer, actress and film director, pointedly took up Xia Yan's challenge by asserting that Shaanbei, from where she had just returned, was even today actually more backward than portrayed in *The Yellow Earth*. Speaking with great vehemence, she claimed that "we, the offspring of the yellow earth", are still deep in feudalism and ignorance, but that the film overwhelmingly expressed an intense desire to throw off these influences that persist in us today. She praised the film for its courage, concluding by saying that she had never seen a film in which there was so much pain, anger and refusal to accept backwardness and ignorance, or so much feeling and hope.[4] The director Deng Baochen contrasted *The Yellow Earth* with Antonioni's documentary on China: the latter did show reality but did not perceive the hope behind the backwardness, whereas backwardness in *The Yellow Earth* is not portrayed objectively or indifferently. Deng also claimed that the film-makers did not take an indulgent stand towards this phenomenon but assumed a serious and historical perspective with the aim of awakening people to these realities.[5]

The director Ling Zifeng, whose films have been acclaimed by conventional spokesmen for their literary and artistic qualities, praised the artistry of *The Yellow Earth* but on the question of its message came down firmly on the side of Xia Yan. He criticized the film for failing to show any trace of change or development and thus not reflecting historical truth; this he blamed on the film-makers' search for "form" (code word for aesthetic values). The search for artistic effect must be on the basis of real life, and may not be "separated from real life" (code for departing from Party policy). Backwardness and ignorance are not the major charactististics of the Chinese peasantry, and the director and cinematographer are wrong in leaving this impression; leaving aside the question of spontaneous peasant protest, he claimed that "there must have been" an influence from Yenan.[6] Han Shangyi, an art director from the Shanghai Film Studio 上海電影製片廠, took the offensive by stating as his introduction that he fell asleep during the screening of films like *The Yellow Earth*. Some of his remarks were almost a parody of a Hollywood-producer mentality, such as his objection to "making the audience wait" in scenes where there was no movement or speech. Like Xia Yan, he gave the director credit for wanting to describe the "inner beauty" of the peasants, but stated that he does not succeed because "the subjective elements are too many, the objective elements too few" (code words for not following conventional Party wisdom). His close attention to these details somewhat undermines his claim to somnolence.[7]

Han Shangyi's aggressiveness provoked Huang Zongying into an even more emotional rejoinder. Professing distress at this response from a studio head, she stated that *The Yellow Earth* was made by "our children" who yet have more promise than the older generation such as herself.[8] Chen Huangmei tried to brush her defence aside by referring to her "motherly" sense of responsibility to the younger generation,[9] but Huang Zongying then spoke up for the third time, saying that her attitude was not that of a mother but of an artist, and herself went on the offensive by asking why the two most original films of 1984 had come from the small Guangxi studio and not from the major film studios such as Peking and Shanghai.[10]

Yu Min, a scriptwriter and editor at *Cinema Arts* and a more articulate opponent than his predecessors, pointed out that while the images of backwardness and ignorance in the film were extremely concrete and convincing, the images of hope and longing for a new life were mostly abstract and implied. He praised the film-makers for formulating the idea of hope amid backwardness but suggested that they were unsuccessful in portraying this hope effectively.[11] When Huang Zongying expressed her dismay at not being able to make a more effective defence of *The Yellow Earth*,[12] Shen Songsheng, as had some earlier speakers, then stated that he had found such scenes as the drum dance and the rain prayer both very powerful images of peasant strength. He agreed with Yu Min that not all of the positive images were readily comprehensible, but thought that nevertheless the atmosphere created in the film by "warm" photography was very positive. He also pointed out that the many static shots, which leave an impression of apparent changelessness, are balanced by shots which are full of very strong movement; the peasants' passivity and dumbness are only on the surface, and the film also shows their capacity for passion and change.[13] Lu Zhuguo 陸柱國 , an army scriptwriter, also thought that the peasants' potentiality for change was shown not in the plot or the dialogue but in the circumstances and atmosphere of the film.[14] Nevertheless, their arguments tend to support Yu Min's charge that the positive elements are abstract and implied rather than straightforward and dominant. Although Western critics felt this was a praiseworthy feature of the film, by many Chinese critics it was regarded as a deliberate attempt by the film-makers to let the negative elements predominate.

Although the discussion above all related to the question of Party policy in regard to the peasants, direct debate on the rights and wrongs of Party policy was avoided by all participants. The portrayal of the Party in the film, with the characterization of Gu Qing as its embodiment, was discussed only by Luo Yijun and even then rather indirectly. Luo described the older generation of film artists, including himself, as tending to treat both the masses of workers, peasants and soldiers *and* the leadership with too much respect, refusing to acknowledge the ignorance of the former and the fallibility of the latter; the new generation, being free from this historical burden, introduced a new breath of air into the film industry. The implication seems here to be that Gu Qing's failures to emancipate any of the villagers or even to collect much in the way of new songs may be read as a symbol for failure of Party policy, and by extension, an answer to the question why the land remained in such a backward state. Luo's own enigmatic comment is that while the creators of *The Yellow Earth* may not always be correct, the spirit of enquiry embodied in the film is extremely valuable.[15] Similarly, while Deng Baochen claims to see in Gu Qing an affirmation of the film-makers' confidence in the Party in contrast to the negativism of the "scar literature" of the late 1970s, nevertheless, by twice drawing attention to the originality of the film in its treatment of this period in Chinese history, Deng seems to be implying with approval that it tries at least to shed new light on Party policy.[16]

Interspersed with these critical remarks came repeated praise for the seriousness, dedication and hard work of the film-makers and for the originality of their approach. Many speakers described *The Yellow Earth* not simply as a good film but as extremely creative and original. Lu Zhuguo, like Huang Zongying and Zhu Xijuan 祝希娟, thought that the creativity shown in *The Yellow Earth* went beyond anything achieved by older directors;[17] Liang Xin saw the creators of *The Yellow Earth* as having opened up new territory in Chinese films.[18] Using slightly different terminology, Luo Yijun described them as carving out a new path in Chinese film aesthetics: whereas films like *Camel Xiangzi* (駱駝祥子) (directed by Ling Zifeng) and *Memories of Southern Peking* (城南舊事) (by Wu Yigong 吳貽弓) tried to create a "national" style by faithful detail of local custom or by a "poetic" atmsophere, *The Yellow Earth* and *One and Eight* tried to combine direct perception with profound ideas and feelings. He described the drum dance and rain prayer scenes as expressing in film terms traditional Chinese aesthetics, and saw *The Yellow Earth* as a starting point for a new Chinese cinematic aesthetics.[19] (These and the following comments were offered in set speeches and not as part of a discussion or in any particular logical sequence; they are rearranged here under topic.)

Many speakers, including Han Shangyi, Luo Yijun and He Zhongxin, noted the traditional aesthetics involved in the photography. Han Shangyi, pointedly excluding the director from credit, noted in particular the balance of space and mass.[20] Xie Tian and Yu Yanfu just as pointedly went out of their way to praise the close collaboration between director and cinematographer.[21] He Zhongxin, a director from the Xi'an Film Studio, noted the use of tiny figures placed against vast landscapes, as in traditional landscape painting.[22] Hu Bingliu, a director from Pearl River Film Studio in Canton, found a very strong "national form" in the film, in harmony with the content.[23] Zhu Xijuan (star of the original *Red Detachment of Women* [紅色娘子軍]) found it "very Chinese".[24] Some critics went out of their way to note the close connection between the style and the subject matter of the film. For instance, He Zhongxin praised the film as having the simplicity and earthiness of the folk songs that it includes. He noted the aesthetics in the sequences of drawing water from the Yellow River, showing the mud in the water: this he praised as beauty without artifice.[25]

Several speakers tried to characterize the film as romantic, realistic or naturalistic: in Chinese criticism, these terms are often used as code words for qualities such as aestheticism, orthodoxy and depiction of ugliness respectively. Some critics saw the film as "romantic", meaning that it employed "exaggeration" in sequences such as the rain prayer. Xie Tian, an actor and director from the Peking Film Studio, disagreed on the grounds that he felt the use of romanticism in this film justifiable as a means of expression.[26] (This is different to Huang Zongying's point that the rain prayer ceremony was true to life.) Some criticised the film as "subjective", meaning that it was too much an expression of the film-makers' personal (and therefore non-orthodox) point of view. Luo Yijun noted that many foreign films were too subjective, but by implication excused *The Yellow Earth* from this charge. On the other hand, he mentioned as a shortcoming that in places the film was "naturalistic", meaning that it showed some things (not specified) that may be true but were not beautiful.[27] Chen Huangmei similarly described the "ugliness" of the actor playing the wedding scene singer an example of undesirable "naturalism" as distinct from "realism".[28] Deng Baochen disagreed that the film was an example of naturalism, saying that the film creators "selected and refined" their material, and praised the way in which the film was both concrete and abstract in its artistic presentation. On the other hand, he found the rain prayer sequence too exaggerated and Hanhan's slow motion run as too prolonged.[29] Han Shangyi found the portrayal of the singer very moving,[30] but together with Ling Zifeng criticised the film for not being realistic in that the peasants looked too fat and healthy.[31] Hu Bingliu found nothing at all of naturalism in the film, which he saw not as an attempt at objective representation but as expression.[32]

Deng Baochen praised the multitude of meanings created by the images used in the film. For example, the yellow earth is shown as poor and monotonous, but also shown is the greatness and profundity of the earth as mother of the Chinese people.[33] Part of Han Shangyi's response, like that of many Hong Kong critics, was patriotic: the vast sweep of the camera made him feel the boundless vitality of the earth.[34] Huang Zongying praised the long shots of the hillsides, going up, going down, going up, going down … as symbolizing the slow and lonely route taken by the Chinese nation in history.[35] Giving credit to both director and cinematographer, Shen Songsheng from the Peking Film Academy spoke at length on the impressions created by the photographic imagery. He found that the unorthodox use of static shots for the landscape and to portray life gave the film a feeling of depth, oppression and melancholy. Life seems to have stopped, but the stillness is not absolute and eternal. On the outside, the people appear impassive, but the drum dance and the rain prayer, in different degrees, show the strength and vitality inside. The rhythm of the film is built on this alternation between stillness and movement. The vast scale of the landcape shots creates an impression of poverty and bleakness, but at the same time one feels the greatness and warmth of the land. The small figures shown against these vast landscapes symbolizes the relationship between man and earth: the great earth mother that has nurtured the Chinese race.[36] The repetition of scenes such as the wedding procession and drawing water from the Yellow River, like the refrain in a poem, represents the slowness of change in Chinese history.[37]

In China the director has not traditionally played an independent role in the film: he has been more of a technician than an "auteur". Chen Kaige rejected this tradition, and Ai Mingzhi, a scriptwriter from the Shanghai Film Studio, acknowledged the importance of the director's handling of the script in this film. While Ai Mingzhi praised the director for presenting his own views, he felt that there were several points where the director allowed his concept to override reality or aesthetic considerations, e.g. by placing the rain prayer sequence at the end of the film and in the depiction of Hanhan going against the tide in an almost literal sense.[38] Deng Baochen also made the same criticism in almost identical terms, though he personally was very moved by the sequence.[39]

Shen Songsheng spoke of the common attitudes by film-makers of the first graduating class. He pointed out that by that time, these young filmmakers had already created eight films, *One and Eight* and *The Yellow Earth* (the third and fourth), being the most controversial. One of the common points was that the directors went beyond the script to shape the film on the basis of their own understanding. Another was that they were not satisified with traditional methods of expression, and that they paid a great deal of attention to film technique. Finally, they all expressed very strong ideas of their own in their films; although their ideas were not always "correct", the film-makers did not turn their backs on the Party and their country. Shen was the only speaker to include the designer specifically as one of the "creators" of the film.[40]

There was less disagreement over the cinematography, everyone granting that it was outstanding. Ling Zifeng, Shen Songsheng and Zhao Huanzhang 趙煥章 were particularly impressed by the handling of the interior light in the cave home scenes.[41] However, Ling Zifeng found too much repetition in the long shots. In general he found that the cinematography went to excessive lengths in the search for originality so that it overpowered the content.[42] Yu Yanfu, like Ling Zifeng, claimed that though a lot of attention was given to the composition of the shots so that they looked stunning, the visual impressions had nothing to do with the thoughts or acts of the characters, which were therefore left unclear.[43]

Han Shangyi, on the other hand, specifically stated that as far as the cinematography was concerned, form and content were unified.[44] Shen Songsheng gave an example of this unity: the warm tones of the film, which aroused a sense of warmth among viewers, also created a sense that the land was not simply an environment but a blend of earth and man. Shen Songsheng thought that the film-makers constantly strove to create suitable form for the content, e.g. in the rain prayer sequence, but felt that they were not always successful, as for instance in the abrupt way the heads were lowered and raised.[45]

Unity (or the lack of it) between form and content is an overworked formula used sometimes very vaguely by critics to praise (or blame) a literary or artistic work. Hu Bingliu tried to be a little more concrete. For instance, he felt that the static shots with fixed camera were very effective in portraying thoughts and feelings, and that in fact there is kind of "concealed movement" in these shots. The use of empty space he found much better here than in *One and Eight*, describing the cinematography as part of the action of the story, a quality very rare in Chinese film-making. The complex blending of the elements in the story, the close relation between the earth and the people, is hard to express in words but is very ably expressed in cinematic language. His only criticism was that the inexperience of the director resulted in an inability to knit the sequences together smoothly into the film. On the other hand, he liked very much the rain prayer and the drawing water sequences, which he found both thought-provoking and full of poetry.[46] Zhao Huanzhang, a director from the Shanghai Film Studio, also praised the rain prayer, calling it much better than a similar sequence in a film of his own.[47] Xie Tian, who saw the film three times and found it very moving, thought the film full of poetic feeling. He praised its avoidance of the modern technique of speeding up images: this film slows down the images without becoming boring.[48]

In regard to acting, several critics found it too subtle. Yu Yanfu, a director from the Changchun Film Studio 長春電影製片廠 , criticized some scenes as over-stylized in the manner of Western cinema: for instance, in the final shots of Cuiqiao farewelling Gu Qing, when she tells him to take out his notebook and sings, he walks forward aloofly: the director does not show his inner conflict, and this to Yu weakened the impact of the scene.[49] The scene of Gu Qing's first encounter with the father also came in for criticism from Yu Yanfu, who found it too static: without any feelings expressed, it is not clear what they are thinking. Deng Baochen, on the other hand, saw the silence and length of this sequence as very appropriate. First, it effectively suggests the isolation and remoteness of the area; secondly, the local people are not in the habit of talking much, and before strangers are even more silent; third, Gu Qing is also unsure of himself and does not know what to say. Finally, the length of the sequence forces us to consider the significance of the silence (Deng Baochen here may be implying that it represents the distance between the peasants and the Party). He found the portrayal of Gu Qing too simplified and lacking depth, but it is not clear whether he is speaking of Gu Qing simply as a character in the film or Gu Qing as a symbol for the Party and therefore needing to be portrayed more positively.[50] Poor quality music and sound were mentioned by several speakers but no-one objected as such to the orchestral music.

The question of the film's audience was again very controversial. Xia Yan's attitude was the most uncompromising. Appealing to the slogan "seek truth from facts", he claimed that the facts were that films in China are made for an audience of "millions of people", so that film-makers must pay attention to what the masses like; film-makers must not depart from the masses.[51] Similar statements were made by many of the other speakers, but all contain an ambiguity that is at least partly deliberate. It is clear, for instance, that the directive "must not depart from the masses" as used by Xia Yan is a code for "must not depart from the accepted Party line". Some other speakers claimed that the film's message was acceptable, but being too subtle for most audiences to comprehend, it might leave an unfortunate and unintended impression on less sophisticated viewers. Huang Zongying twice tried to point out that artistic excellence and box-office appeal rarely went hand in hand,[52] but it seems that neither commercial nor artistic appeal was the major concern of the senior film officials.

Han Shangyi frankly found the film boring, and claimed that no-one would want to watch it.[53] No-one else took such an extreme view, but both supporters and detractors felt that the film would be beyond the reach of a mass audience. Yu Yanfu claimed that the film-makers had ignored the fact that people in the countryside could not possible cope with the subtleties of the characterization or cinematography.[54] Yu Min asked why the director, if he likes the peasants so much, did not make films which peasants actually like: comedies, war movies, kungfu movies and historical films: why give them something they can't understand?[55] Luo Yijun expressed doubt about Yu Yanfu's and Yu Min's references to the film as "experimental"; he pointed out that Western "experimental films" are simply experiments with form, have no social content and do not enter into the marketplace at all, whereas films like *The Yellow Earth* and *One and Eight* are not made for a small number of intellectuals but are intended for the cultural marketplace. Even more to the point, he stressed that these two films cannot be seen as simply a search for artistic form, but embody the film-makers' thoughts on life.[56] Nevertheless, the term "experimental" stuck, as did the consensus that the films were beyond the comprehension of a mass audience. Deng Baochen's comment that it would be especially popular among university students[57] was confirmed when the film was finally re-released.

On the question of giving the film an award, the panel was again divided, though not all speakers formally expressed an opinion. The famous actress Zhang Ruifang, emphasising the need to encourage young film-makers, suggested that it be given a prize for best first film, and even wondered if it might get an Oscar.[58] Huang Zongying disagreed with her first remark, saying the film was worthy of more, and rather caustically suggested it be given a prize for courage. She did not feel that the film should be given the main prize, however, but hoped it would get a mention, comparing it to a piece of uncut jade among a heap of jewels.[59] Deng Baochen was against giving it a major award, saying that he would not like the film-makers to become too satisfied with their achievement; on more general grounds, he felt it improper to give a Golden Rooster award to a film which failed to combine mass audience appeal with artistic excellence.[60] Making a fine distinction, Lu Zhuguo stated that of all the films entered for the award, *The Yellow Earth* was the one he liked the most and which moved him the most, but that was not to say it was the best; his reluctance to give the film a prize seems due to his fear that the film would not attract much of an audience despite its creativity and outstanding photography.[61] Luo Yijun recommended against giving the film an award on the grounds that it showed inexperience.[62]

In the end, a compromise was reached: the film was given an award for best photography only. This was in fact the only award that *The Yellow Earth* was ever given in its own country, although the English language press frequently claimed otherwise. Ling Zifeng, however, one of the panel adjudicators, was given that year's award for best director for his film adaptation of Shen Congwen's 沈從文 *Border Town* and Han Shangyi the award for best art director.[63]

Despite perceptive comments on the film as film, the panel as a whole saw the film's implied criticism of Party policy as its salient characteristic: those who saw some validity in that criticism praised the film for its courage, while those who took offence at it damned it under several labels. The panel concluded with an apt observation from Zhu Xijuan: the controversy provoked by the film is exactly what the film-makers had aimed for: to make people think.[64]

The Golden Rooster awards were announced on 9 March.[65] Rumours of the hostility towards *The Yellow Earth* shown by senior film personnel soon leaked out, and the panel report was published in the "internal" film magazine at the beginning of April.[66] Around the same time, *The Yellow Earth* opened at the Hong Kong Film Festival to rapturous and prolonged applause.

Notes

1. *DZDY*, March 1985: 2–3.
2. *HS HTD*: 5, 10.
3. *HS HTD*: 4–6.
4. *HS HTD*: 7–9.
5. *HS HTD*: 12–16, especially 13.
6. *HS HTD*: 16–18.
7. *HS HTD*: 18–20.
8. *HS HTD*: 21–22.
9. *HS HTD*: 22–23.
10. *HS HTD*: 23–24.
11. *HS HTD*: 24–26.
12. *HS HTD*: 26–27.
13. *HS HTD*: 27–31.
14. *HS HTD*: 20–21.
15. *HS HTD*: 31–32.
16. *HS HTD*: 12, 15.
17. *HS HTD*: 21, 24, 35.
18. *HS HTD*: 9.
19. *HS HTD*: 11.
20. *HS HTD*: 20.
21. *HS HTD*: 3, 3–4.
22. *HS HTD*: 2.
23. *HS HTD*: 32–34.
24. *HS HTD*: 35.
25. *HS HTD*: 1–2.
26. *HS HTD*: 3.
27. *HS HTD*: 11, 12.
28. *HS HTD*: 22.
29. *HS HTD*: 14–15, 16.
30. Han Shangyi, in *HS HTD*: 19.
31. Ling Zifeng, in *HS HTD*: 17; Han Shangyi, in *HS HTD*: 19. See also Wang Shushun, "Chuangxin chuyi", *DDDY*, February 1985: 54. Hao Dazheng, one of the film's supporters, disputes Han Shangyi's claim, saying that the peasants shown in this sequence are not fat, and that their depiction is realistic; see *HS HTD*: 146.
32. *HS HTD*: 33.

33. *HS HTD*: 15.
34. *HS HTD*: 20.
35. *HS HTD*: 22.
36. *HS HTD*: 28–29.
37. *HS HTD*: 30.
38. *HS HTD*: 9–10.
39. *HS HTD*: 16.
40. *HS HTD*: 27–28.
41. *HS HTD*: 18, 31, 35.
42. *HS HTD*: 18.
43. *HS HTD*: 4.
44. *HS HTD*: 19–20.
45. *HS HTD*: 28–29.
46. *HS HTD*: 32–34.
47. *HS HTD*: 35.
48. *HS HTD*: 3.
49. *HS HTD*: 4.
50. *HS HTD*: 15.
51. *HS HTD*: 6.
52. *HS HTD*: 23.
53. *HS HTD*: 18–19, 20.
54. *HS HTD*: 4.
55. *HS HTD*: 26.
56. *HS HTD*: 31–32.
57. *HS HTD*: 16.
58. *HS HTD*: 6.
59. *HS HTD*: 8–9, 26–27.
60. *HS HTD*: 12.
61. *HS HTD*: 20–21.
62. *HS HTD*: 31.
63. For a list of the awards see *DZDY*, April 1985 or *GMRB*, 10 March 1985: 1.
64. *HS HTD*: 35.
65. *GMRB*, 10 March 1985: 1; *RMRB*, 10 March 1985: 3. According to Chen Kaige, Zhang Yimou was informed of the cinematography award during the first week of February; see Chen Kaige, "Qinguo ren", *DDDY*, July 1985.4: 101–107.
66. See Chapter One, note 1, pp. 19–20.

5. *The Yellow Earth* in Hong Kong (April to July 1985)

On the night of April 12, 1985, a strange thing happened in Hong Kong. At the Kaoshan theatre in Kowloon a film had just finished. It was already past eleven o'clock, but almost all the more than two thousand people who had watched the film stayed in the theatre, wanting to hear the director and cinematographer speak. Nothing like this had happened at any film festival screening in Hong Kong before. Most of the audience stayed until past midnight, as the buses and ferries that keep Hong Kong moving began to shut up shop for the night. The film that caused all this interest was *Yellow Earth*.[1]

The Yellow Earth had a greater impact in Hong Kong than any film from the mainland before or since. Critics both for and against the Peking government for once joined hands in praising the film almost without exception.[2] Even more remarkable was the impact of the film on ordinary cinema-goers, not just festival film buffs but also the commercial audiences that followed. Its success in Hong Kong then led directly to its appearance in the international art film circuit, and to some extent also, the changing fortunes of the film within China. Getting the film to Hong Kong, however, together with its director and cinematographer, was not easily achieved.

The person mainly responsible for *The Yellow Earth*'s Hong Kong debut was Danny Yung, a member of the festival's Asian Cinema and Hong Kong Cinema '84 advisory panel.[3] Coming up to Peking in the autumn of 1984 to select films for the 1985 festival, he was urged to meet Chen Kaige and see his film by Tian

Zhuangzhuang 田壮壮 , whose *Hunting Ground* had already been released. Yung, who had liked *Hunting Ground* and wanted it for Hong Kong, was even more impressed by *The Yellow Earth*: "It was the first film I'd seen in China that was a film, that used film language." He had reservations about the film, mainly about the orchestral music and the clumsy dubbing, but in the rhythm he found a completely new style in Chinese film-making. Yung was also struck by the economy and significance of the dialogue. The question Cuiqiao's father asks, "If you're not happy or not sad, why sing?" seemed to him to suggest the director's own motive in making the film.

In order to get *The Yellow Earth* and its personnel to Hong Kong, Yung had to bargain with the Film Bureau and accept some of its recommendations. He was also obliged to abandon *Hunting Ground*, which other members of the panel found less convincing, but was able to substitute the same director's earlier film *September* (九月); it proved impossible to bring Tian Zhuangzhuang himself to the festival. The leaders of the official Chinese delegation were at first skeptical about the merits of *The Yellow Earth*, but couldn't help either being impressed by the film's reception, especially at the final screening and the seminar that followed. The official Hong Kong distributors for the Chinese Film Corporation, Southern [Nanfang] Film Company Limited 南方影業有限公司 , saw the possibilities for their first box-office success in an art film. In Hong Kong, commercial films generally require a return of eight to ten million HK dollars, whereas an art film usually only grosses at most one to two million, but on the basis of audience response at the festival, Southern Film Company Limited estimated a possible five million dollar return.

The Ninth Hong Kong International Film Festival ran from 29 March to 13 April. Since over a hundred films were scheduled, most were shown only once, a few twice. *The Yellow Earth* was shown three times, and each session was sold out in advance before the festival opened; an additional session was therefore arranged in response to popular demand. This response to a film from the mainland was unprecedented, according to festival organizers. Favourable reviews were carried in over a dozen local papers and magazines, and a series of interviews between the press and the two film-makers were arranged. Film festival organizers and critics from England, Switzerland, France, West Germany, Japan and the United States also called on the official Chinese delegation to offer congratulations on the film's success, and the film was invited to six film festivals on the spot: Cannes, Moscow, Montreal, Locarno, Edinburgh and Hawaii. The most moving tribute to the film, however, came after the final screening of the film at nine p.m. on 12 April, when Chen Kaige and Zhang Yimou stayed behind to answer questions from the audience. So many people had queued up to see the film that many had to be turned back. Out of the two thousand who did get in, all but a dozen people stayed for the discussion. Over thirty questions were asked, all in Chinese, and the questioners seemed to be from an ordinary Hong Kong audience, not critics or reveiwers. The discussion, which sometimes spilled over into the auditorium, lasted until the organizers closed the session at twelve-thirty. When a similar session had been arranged for the audience to meet the director of *Taxi Driver*, only about 20 per cent of the audience had stayed behind, and the session lasted only five minutes.[4]

The film's first commercial release began on 18 May. Six days later over a million tickets had been sold.[5] An advertisement on 26 May mentioned the Golden Rooster award and invitations to international film festivals, and its appeal both to the audience's visual/aural pleasure and its feelings of patriotism. It also listed favourable comments from eight dailies and a film magazine. The film was at this time showing in two cinemas, attracting a daily audience of several thousand, an unprecedented success for either an art film or a film from the mainland.[6]

The popularity of *The Yellow Earth* in Hong Kong was obviously related to its ability to draw forth different responses from different groups of people. The two main Chinese-language political weeklies both drew attention to the film's political controversiality. *Zhengming* 爭鳴 (Contention), the more radical of the two, stressed the contemporary relevance of the plot, citing the new Party policy that class struggle was no longer to be regarded as the main force in society. More daringly, it also described the film as an attack on the saviour mentality which mythified the role of the Party in Chinese life.[7] *Jiushi niandai* 九十年代 (The nineties) focussed on the lack of welcome the film received inside China, in contrast to Hong Kong, and included a brief summary of the Golden Rooster discussion (incorrectly claiming that the film did not receive any award).[8] The magazine also noted that Hong Kong audiences and critics on the whole paid little attention to the politics in *The Yellow Earth*, but welcomed its visual excellence. This was not entirely true, even for the more rightwing press. The film's honesty in presenting an unadorned picture of life in rural China was one quality which, in the opinion of the *Mingbao wanbao* reviewer, lifted it above even relatively good films like *Serfs* (農奴) from the 1960s and *Life* (人生) (a prize-winning film also from 1984).[9]

The patriotism aroused by the film's depiction of the grandeur and tragedy of China's land and people was also a dominating theme in the Hong Kong response, expressed, for instance, by the leading film critic Dai Tian 戴天 in *Xin bao* 信報 [10] and more emotionally by Ah Fan in *Da gong bao*.[11] (Some mainland filmmakers thought this reponse irrelevant to the film's true significance.[12]) *Da gong bao*'s film critic Bai Fei 白扉 showed gratification that the Chinese cinema had in this film reached international standards of excellence.[13] Tang Qiong 唐琼 , comparing the film with Pearl Buck's *The Good Earth*, conceded that the latter had the better title, but that the former was the more moving work of art.[14]

On 20 July the film opened in Macao under its original title, *Ecos do vale* (*Shengu huisheng* 深谷回聲), and ran for over a month.[15] At the same time it began its third run in Hong Kong.[16] This time round, several critics commented on the mixed reception the film received in China. One critic claimed, not quite accurately, that it was only after the provision of the experimental cinemas in Shanghai that *The Yellow Earth* would be able to open there, several months after its Hong Kong release. He saw the decision for the experimental cinemas, however, as a sign of the welcome change in cultural policy since the national writers' meeting in January.[17] A reporter on *Xin bao* noted caustically that despite the film's Golden Rooster, it had still not been publicly exhibited in Canton, so that critics in that city were not able to discuss the film convincingly with their Hong Kong colleagues.[18] A few days later, the same paper welcomed the news that *The Yellow Earth* had been shown on Chinese television.[19] Since only ten new films a year were allowed for television release, this was a considerable honour. The same report also mentioned the Shanghai experimental cinema, and justified special attention to films like *The Yellow Earth* by pointing out that by the end of June, more than 235 articles on the film had appeared in the Hong Kong press.[20] Comments from the Golden Rooster panel speeches were quoted in July by Xiang Zhuang 項莊 , critic for *Mingbao* 明報 ,[21] and reporting on the film's appearance in Edinburgh in August, the *Xingdao ribao* also mentioned the internal debate on the film and its temporary ban.[22]

Amid all the praise, only two discordant voices were heard. One feminist critic (inaccurately) complained that despite the central theme of Cuiqiao's tragedy, the director apparently shared the revolution's exclusion of women by failing to include women in the film's big set pieces such as the wedding feast; otherwise, she praised its honesty and originality.[23] A bolder attack appeared under the pseudonym Bai Tudi 白土地 (White Earth) in the reader's page of the August issue of *Contention*.[24] Bai Tudi's chief complaint was that the film did not in fact show the originality so often claimed for it, in particular in the television advertisements sponsored by the two cinemas where the film was being exhibited. For example, he claimed that folksong was used more richly in works by Li Ji 李季, Zhao Shuli, Zhou Libo and Liu Qing 柳青, while the relationship between Cuiqiao and Gu Qing was presented in the same clichés known from innumerable works since the 1940s. There is some basis for this criticism, but the latter half of the article descends into absurdity, the author apparently believing that Gu Qing was to be taken as a model hero.

Notes

1. Viewer's guide essay, "Yellow Earth" by Paul Clark, in *The Hawaii International Film Festival 26 November to 8 December, 1985*, The East-West Center (Honolulu), 1985, pp.43–44.
2. By June 1985 over two hundred articles on *TYE* had appeared in the Hong Kong press. I am most grateful to Stephen C. Soong for sending me a generous selection of them, which has been the basis of my generalizations about the Hong Kong reception. I have also consulted a selection of excerpts from the Hong Kong press printed in *DDDY* in April 1985, but since they are edited comments I have not included them within these generalizations.
3. The remarks that followed are based on an interview with Danny Yung in Peking, August 1986.
4. *DZDY*, June 1985: 11; description amplified by Danny Yung.
5. *Gong jiao bao*, 24 May 1985.
6. *Gong jiao bao*, 24 May 1985. The figure given in this account (50,000 daily) seems impossibly high.
7. Gu Er 古兒, "Dianying *HTD* guanhou gan" 電影《黃土地》觀後感 (Thoughts after viewing the film *TYE*), *ZM*, July 1985: 50–51.

8. Huang Bing 黃冰 , "*HTD, 'Rensheng'* ji qita"《黃土地》,「人生」及其他 (*HTD, Life* and others), *JSND*, July 1985: 11–12.

9. Shi Qi, "*HTD*, shang, xia" (*TYE*, I and II), *Mingbao wanbao*, 25–26 April 1985.

10. Dai Tian, "*HTD* guanhou"《黃土地》觀後(After viewing *TYE*) and "*HTD* zaji"《黃土地》雜記(Remarks on *TYE*), *Xin bao*, 15–16 May 1985.

11. Ah Fan, "Yumei heshi bian wenming" 愚昧何時變文明 (When will ignorance change into civilization), *Da gong bao*, 27 April 1985; see also Ah Fan, "Huanghe—huang tudi" 黃河——黃土地 (The Yellow River—the yellow earth), reprinted in *HS HTD*: 313–14.

12. See *HS HTD*: 207.

13. Bai Fei, "*HTD* ying jinkuai gongying"《黃土地》應儘快公映 (*TYE* should be publicly exhibited as soon as possible), *Da gong bao*, 27 April 1985.

14. Tang Qiong, "*HTD* guanhou gan"《黃土地》觀後感 (Thoughts after viewing *TYE*), *Da gong bao*, 27–28 April 1985; reprinted with deletions in *HS HTD*: 314–15.

15. *Gazeta Macaense*, 15 August 1985: 10.

16. Shang Yu 商宇 , "*HTD* zhongyu shangying"《黃土地》終於上映 (*TYE* finally shown), *Da gong bao*, 6 July 1985.

17. Ibid.

18. *Xin bao*, 5 July 1985.

19. *Xin bao*, 9 July 1985.

20. I am unable to verify this figure, but have been assured that it must be at least approximately correct. Other points in the article are not fully reliable. For example, it claims that Zhang Yimou went to Cannes in March or earlier, while my own diary clearly places his departure in April.

21. Xiang Zhuang, "Lishi de fanxing jingshen" 歷史的反省精神 (The spirit of enquiry on history), *Mingbao*, 6 July 1985: 14.

22. Ying Ren 影人 , "Di sajiu jie Aidingbao dianyingjie longzhong jiemu" 第卅九屆愛丁堡電影節隆重揭幕 (An exciting opening to the 39th Edinburgh Film Festival), *Xingdao ribao*, August 1985.

23. Gui Ying, "*HTD*" (*TYE*), *Gong jiao bao*, 24 May 1985.

24. Bai Tudi, "Dianying *HTD* bu zhide zanyang" 電影《黃土地》不值得讚揚 (The film *TYE* does not deserve praise), *ZM*, August 1985: 78.

6. Public Debates and Private Offensives (March to December 1985)

By the spring of 1985, *The Yellow Earth* and its director had become well known at least by reputation to movie fans and film buffs in China, as were also its companion films and their general unacceptability to the authorities. Articles in film magazines in the spring were generally favourable, and *The Yellow Earth* (to a lesser extent also *One and Eight*) became a common point of reference in general articles on recent films and new developments. None of the new films under discussion were on show in Peking at the time, though private screenings continued to be held.[1] Such circumstances were familiar and caused no particular comment.

The report of the annual meeting on the year's films at the end of 1984 published in the March issue of *Cinema Arts* shows that *The Yellow Earth* was one of the most talked-about films at the meeting.[2] One of the speakers, Li Xingye, followed up with an article in the same issue in which he praised *The Yellow Earth* as one of the four best films of a very good year; still very enthusiastic after three viewings, he compared the film to Luo Zhongli's painting "Father", Xian Xinghai's 冼星海 "Yellow River Cantata" (黃河大合唱), Lu Xun's short stories, and even Du Fu's poetry.[3] The April issue of *Cinema Arts* carried a report on the February seminar about the four new wave films, with a follow-up article from one of the participants, Kong Du. It also ran a short article by Chen Kaige (an expanded version of the article published under the names of Chen Kaige, Zhang Yimou and He Qun in *Popular Cinema* in September the previous year), and another short article on

The Yellow Earth's shortcomings (i.e. being too slow and monotonous for most viewers).[4]

The prize-giving ceremony for the Golden Rooster and Hundred Flowers awards brought *The Yellow Earth* into wider public focus in May (although still not into public view).[5] The May issue of *Cinema Arts*, covering the ceremony, featured stills from *The Yellow Earth* on the back inside cover, and an article by Zhang Yimou. The magazine *China's Youth* featured a short article on the film the same month, noting the director's youth and relative inexperience.[6] The success of *The Yellow Earth* in Hong Kong was conveyed to the mainland in the June issue of *Contemporary Cinema*, in the form of a collection of fourteen excerpts from reviews in the Hong Kong press.[7]

By this time, however, the criticisms from the Golden Rooster panel had become generally known within the film world. When the Ministry of Culture film awards were announced on June 11,[8] the absence of any of the new films from the list caused comment but little surprise. A few days later, criticisms of *The Yellow Earth* and the other new films began to appear in the daily press.

The campaign was led off by Wang Suihan 王歲寒 , a lecturer from the Peking Film Academy, and took the form of an open letter dated May 1985 in *Guangming ribao* 光明日報 (Enlightenment daily, a Party-controlled newspaper directed at intellectuals), addressed familiarly to [Zhang] Junzhao, [Chen] Kaige, [Wu] Ziniu 吳子牛 and [Tian] Zhuangzhuang.[9] A note by the editor explains that the controversy over the new films had led the newspaper to initiate a debate on their merits and faults. The impression made by this "open letter" on the reader, however, is of a campaign against the new films already in full swing. For instance, Wang's "letter" starts by recording his disagreement with those critics who consider the rain prayer scene to be over-conceptualized. There is little of substance in Wang's own criticisms, which amount to claims that the films do not follow

Marxist aesthetic principles and pay insufficient attention to a mass audience.

The Shanghai prong of the campaign began the following day, with an article in *Wenhui bao* 文匯報 chiefly on *The Yellow Earth*'s box-office failure: according to this, the film had been shown 41 times in Shanghai that March, but audience attendance averaged only 24.4% of cinema capacity. On the other hand, another article in *Wenhui bao* later the same month reported that a thousand people turned up to see the film at a special screening in Shanghai after the film's success in Hong Kong and Zhang Yimou's Golden Rooster award. The author, Chi Jinliang 池金良, also gave a factual and straightforward summary of the debate up to that time.[10]

One of the most severe criticisms of *The Yellow Earth* was meanwhile made in *Enlightenment Daily* by Ding Daoxi, another teacher from the film academy.[11] Accusing the director of "alienation" and lack of sympathy towards the characters in the film, he repeated the claim that the film "neglected content" and "lacked historical accuracy". "Neglect of content" (code for "neglect of correct content"), or "blind search for form" (meaning attention to "form" or "art" at the expense of correct content), was now one of the most frequent charges levelled against the film. (The vice-president of the film academy, Xie Fei 謝飛, was quoted in August as saying about the new films generally that "they are often criticized for paying too much attention to artistic form and too little to ideological content."[12])

The first response to Ding Daoxi's letter came from the film critic Hao Dazheng, who praised the new films for their "cinematic" nature, giving as an instance the substitution of gesture and movement for dialogue in *The Yellow Earth* as both true to life and cinematically effective.[13] Writing later the same month, he also tried to refute the charge of "coldness" made by Ding Daoxi.[14] Sun Naixiu's contribution to the debate, at the beginning of July, stressed the film's profound treatment of the complex national character of the Chinese people as well as the film's artistic break-throughs,[15] and a similar message was conveyed by Shao Mujun, a young critic from the Film-makers' Association, three weeks later.[16] This put an end to the *Enlightenment Daily* debate; possibly the directive to criticize the film had by this time been challenged and withdrawn.

In spite of the press campaign, film magazine comment on *The Yellow Earth* continued to be in its favour. *Cinema Arts* played a leading role: the June issue featured two articles by Wang Dehou and Yu Qian based on their speeches at the February seminar,[17] and one by Peng Jiajin, one of the new films' supporters in the 1984 meeting.[18] The pre-location statements by the director, cine-matographer and designer were published in the June issue of the journal of the Peking Film Academy,[19] together with a long appre-ciation of the new films by Ni Zhen, one of the more respected lecturers at the academy; these materials later proved very helpful to the film's supporters. The June issue of *Popular Cinema* ran a report about the Film Bureau delegation to the Hong Kong film festival and the unprecedented enthusiasm shown there to a film from the mainland, plus a short article summing up the domestic controversy surrounding *The Yellow Earth*.[20]

The response from Hong Kong seemed to make nonsense of the claim that the film was unacceptable to a mass audience, but some of the film's home critics seemed to become even more deter-mined in their hostility to the film. Writing in August, Shao Mujun notes that he became aware of criticism about the film "several months ago", before he had seen the film himself: some of these were trivial (i.e. that the violent music in the drum dance scene was "not co-ordinated" with the picture frame), but there were two important charges, that the film-makers took pleasure in por-traying peasant backwardness and that they had distorted the image of the Chinese peasant.[21]

When criticism of the new films faltered in the daily press, it was taken up in the Party's theoretical journal, *Hongqi* 紅旗 (Red flag), whose chief editor, Xiong Fu 熊復, was a follower of the orthodox ideologues Deng Liqun 鄧力羣 and Hu Qiaomu 胡喬木. *Red Flag, Enlightenment Daily* and *Renmin ribao* 人民日報 (People's daily) were all under the control of the secretariat of the Party's central committee, but the latter two were not at this point specifically associated with the more orthodox factions in the Party. In July a review of the films from 1984 by a teacher from the Peking Film Academy in *Red Flag* complained of three current problems in the film industry: the lack on films on current reforms and the mediocre quality of some which have tackled the subject; commercialization; and the weirdness of certain avant-garde films.[22] While he did not name names, it is easy to guess that in the last category he meant films like *One and Eight* and *The Yellow Earth*.

On the other hand, Xia Yan's hostility to *The Yellow Earth* became public in an interview, published in August, that he gave to the press after the ceremony for the Golden Rooster and Hundred Flowers awards in May. In answer to a question specifically about *The Yellow Earth* and its success in Hong Kong, he repeated his objections to the film, adding that Hong Kong audiences were attracted by novelty, and that it would have been better for the film to have had a good reception at home.[23] Another of the film-makers' former teachers reacted very sharply to these remarks, especially to the suggestion that they had deliberately aimed at a foreign audience. He pointed out that since the 1930s, Chinese films had in fact stuck very closely to a set of formulas that had originated in Hollywood, and that the "fifth generation" were trying to break through these "Western" conventions and create a genuinely native product.[24] He also defended the film-makers from charges of immaturity unsupported except by reference to the film-makers' youth, producing a three-page list of famous films made by people in their thirties or younger.[25]

What to do about *The Yellow Earth* remained unresolved during the summer of 1985. The film continued to receive praise in film magazines,[26] it was shown in July on Chinese Central Television and later in special cinemas in Shanghai and Canton, and it was allowed to embark on a swing through the international film festival circuit during August. Meanwhile, the debate on the new films widened in two related directions: the question of establishing special art cinemas, and the problem of declining cinema audiences generally.

The question of special cinemas for the "experimental films" came up in June 1985. The Shanghai branch of the Chinese Film Distribution and Exhibition Corporation took the lead, designating a number of city cinemas especially for showing the new movies. On 29 June a spokeswoman for the national corporation, Shi Meifen, told the New China News Agency of the decision to extend this move to other large cities.[27] Experimental films, according to Shi, often failed to attract the average viewer, who prefers stories told in a simple and straightforward way. As examples of experimental films she mentioned Chen Kaige's *The Yellow Earth*, Teng Wenji's 滕文驥 *The Beach* (海灘), Wu Yigong's *Sister* (姊姊) and Zhang Nuanxi's 張暖忻 *Sacrifice of Youth* (青春祭), singling out *The Yellow Earth* as the most controversial and mentioning its success in Hong Kong. (Teng Wenji and Wu Yigong are among the "fourth generation" directors who produced innovative work in the 1980s.) "Highly controversial as these films are", she continued, "they deserve to be seen, and the corporation will run the risk of financial loss to support them."

A report of this decision in the *China Daily* also featured an interview with Xie Fei, vice-president of the film academy.[28] According to Xie,

> The previous generations of film directors are basically followers of traditional techniques of expression taught by the Soviet experts in the 1950s. But the "fifth generation" has drawn much more on modern Western literature and Western schools of films since their horizons

were broadened through film exchanges with foreign countries after
the Cultural Revolution... But these films don't always appeal to the
average viewer who prefers a story told in a simple, straightforward
way.

He explained that the experimental films usually stress message
rather than plot, and use fast-paced imagery rather than dialogue
to convey their message. According to this article, *The Yellow Earth*
"began to attract audiences" after it won "the country's academic
film award and [*sic*] the Golden Rooster for best photography"
early that year. In fact, its distribution at that time was still extremely limited.

A report in the *China Daily* in September announced that the
Canton Film Distribution Company, in response to a request from
the film corporation that one or two cinemas should specialize in
"highbrow" films, had designated a cinema in the downtown area
for this purpose: *The Yellow Earth* was mentioned as an example of
such films. Not all of the "fifth generation's" films were too highbrow: during the summer, Wu Ziniu's modernized war film (with
elements of a thriller), *Bloodshed in Black Valley*, attracted both large
audiences and favourable reviews, according to a *China Daily*
reporter. Even the notoriously uncultured (in northern eyes) Can-
tonese flocked to see *The Yellow Earth*, which was described by
Hong Kong sources as a great box-office success in Canton.

The willingness of the authorities to provide special art cinemas
may have been at least due in part to their growing awareness that
the problem of poor box-office returns was not confined to the
new wave films. At the end of July, *Popular Cinema* organized a
symposium on declining cinema attendances, and published a
summary of the proceedings in its September issue.[29] According
to the editor Ma Rui, who led off the discussion, the decline had
already attracted considerable attention. The main report was
given by a spokesman for the film corporation, Fu Guochang
傅國昌 : the national cinema audience in the first five months of

1985 fell from over 15 billion in the same period in 1984 to over 12 billion, a decline of 20.8%; urban attendance fell by 0.7 billion, a decline of 26%.[30] Reasons for the lack of interest were the attraction of local and Hong Kong television serials (even foreign films were no match for Hong Kong television melodramas like *Shanghai City*), competition from home videos (i.e. illegal imports), the mediocre quality of domestic films and the new system of studio independence.

Other speakers put more blame on the quality of the films themselves, but only a few speakers singled out "highbrow" films as a cause of audience dissatisfaction. A table of the ten most popular and ten least popular films of 1984 accompanied the report: the only new wave film included in either category was Tian Zhuangzhuang's *September*. The report drew over a thousand letters from readers.[31] In September *Popular Cinema* and *Cinema Arts* joined forces to convene another meeting of film experts on the same topic, which remained a live issue through the end of the year.[32] One proposal, raised by Xie Fei and seconded by Shao Mujun, was for closer cooperation between film studios and television.[33]

The collapse of the cinema audience, especially in the cities, is obviously a factor in the low box-office returns for *The Yellow Earth*. Unfortunately, since total receipts for each film are not made public, we cannot compare relative audience numbers for the new wave films and the "best films" favoured by the authorities.

Meanwhile the daily press made brief reports on the progress overseas of *The Yellow Earth* (for details see next chapter). In July *Beijing wanbao* 北京晚報 (Peking evening news) reported that it had been chosen as the official Chinese entry for the Montreal Film Festival in August and that Chen Kaige was invited to attend; Ling Zifeng's *Border Town* would also be shown, and two of its actors would also be sent to Montreal.[34] According to some sources, the Chinese Film Bureau had originally wanted to enter

Border Town for the competition, but a Canadian participant at the Hong Kong International Film Festival who had seen *The Yellow Earth* insisted on its inclusion. Chen Kaige therefore hurried back from Guangxi to leave for Canada, but at the last moment the three-man delegation was cancelled. It was later reported that the Hong Kong film director King Hu 胡金銓, a member of the Montreal prize committee, had criticized the film as technically inferior, mainly in regard to the sound recording, and in consequence *Border Town* became the official entry after all. *Enlightenment Daily* noted in September that *Border Town* had won a prize and that *The Yellow Earth* had received good reviews.[35]

The China Daily continued its support for *The Yellow Earth* with a very favourable article in August.[36] The final paragraphs link the film-makers with the May Fourth generation of intellectuals and revolutionaries, and describe the film as attempting "to stimulate the nation to build a stronger and healthier body." It also featured prominently the film's Locarno award in mid-August[37] and its London award in December (but not Nantes).[38] *Enlightenment Daily* carried a favourable article on the music of *The Yellow Earth* and *The Beach* in August,[39] and though it failed to mention the Locarno prize in mid-August, it reported the London and Nantes prizes in December.[40] An article in *Xin guancha* 新觀察 (New observer) in September by Zhang Boqing was friendly,[41] and a hostile review by Meng Hongmei in *New Films* in October[42] was balanced by a favourable one by Huang Jianzhong in *Wenyi yanjiu* 文藝研究 (Studies in literature and the arts) the same month.[43] One can expect a certain amount of randomness in these reports, but it seems that on the whole, *The Yellow Earth* enjoyed a good press inside China in the latter half of 1985, and even limited public exhibition. It appeared in Nanking in November, and finally in Peking at the end of the same month.

The summer of 1985 had held a promise of new possibilities in the arts and ideology as economic reform seemed to recover the ground lost by fears of inflation earlier that year. To some extent, however, economic progress was illusory. Deeper economic irrationalities were highlighted by the first efforts in reform, as their unintended effects cast into relief the weakness of the economic mechanism in other areas.[44] The response of the reformers was to intensify the pace of reform; the alternative was to slow down or halt further reforms altogether. A new challenge to the reformist factions was mounted by orthodox Party leaders at an extraordinary national Party conference in September 1985, concentrating on falling grain production, economic corruption and lack of attention to Party ideology and Party work.[45] The disruption to the economy caused by reform was acknowledged by all sides, and old fears won the day. Central discipline was reintroduced as a national aim in the economy and in political control. By natural extension, the new cold wind was felt in the cultural world in November and December 1985.[46] Criticism of the new modernistic play *WM* (我們) was one of the most publicized examples; attacks on *The Yellow Earth* were made behind closed doors.

The nature of these attacks on *The Yellow Earth* was never made entirely clear. There was no doubt that many senior Party leaders had been seriously offended by the film's subtle yet devasting critique of the Yenan myth, and yet the story line was so innocuous that it was difficult to launch a campaign against it as had been done in the case of Bai Hua's 白樺 script for the film *Unrequited Love* (苦戀).[47] In the first instance, it was rumoured that the film's international awards had attracted the ire of both reformers and orthodox ideologues in the leadership as putting on show China's "backwardness"; it was even suggested that the film's greater success abroad than at home was in itself suspect, since it was well known that foreigners welcomed expressions of dissent from official policy.[48]

Beyond this chauvinistic defensiveness, however, there may be more serious reasons why the film managed to offend all groups within the leadership. The sharp decline in grain figures in 1985, after a period of continued steady rises in output from 1978 to 1984, was the single most important issue in the rural sector at the end of the year and a matter of extreme concern to Party and state leaders.[49] Its cause was officially related to natural disasters, but during intense internal debates, the orthodox accused reformers of market policies which undermined grain production, while reformers accused the orthodox of resistance to further price reform to encourage farmers to return to staple grains.[50] Whether by foresight or by coincidence, *The Yellow Earth* appeared at precisely this time, highlighting the problem of agricultural poverty in China. Orthodox Party leaders were put on the defensive by the film's implied criticism of the failure of Party policy in the past and its lack of reference to land reform or other forms of collectivization. Reformers, on the other hand, were displeased by the film's refusal to point to technological or market modernization as the solution to the problem (for example, by not employing more obviously "modernistic" film techniques such as split screens and zoom lenses). Both factions were irritated by the film's refusal to play to a mass audience and to offer clear and positive solutions. In addition, senior Party intellectuals objected to the strongly humanistic overtones in the film, to the effect that even in their backwardness the peasants must be respected, and that the solutions to their problems must come from themselves and not from an outside agency such as the élite intelligentsia. So remote was the film's combination of humanism and primitivism from the goals and methods of the reformers that even Hu Yaobang 胡耀邦 was said to have demanded its withdrawal.

Whatever the internal conflicts, the decision was taken to refuse the further participation of *The Yellow Earth* in international film competition while still permitting non-competitive showings and overseas sales. At the same time, the film disappeared again from local screens. A scheduled showing on Peking television on

Christmas Day was at the last minute cancelled and replaced by an American thriller on Nazism. The brief appearance of *The Yellow Earth* at downtown and suburban Peking cinemas, along with other new wave films such as *One and Eight*, came to an abrupt end.[51]

Notes

1. Hao Dazheng mentioned in June that young people from cultural circles in Peking had seen the film since its success among foreign viewers, although some, however, still found its main concepts hard to grasp; see *HS HTD*: 140.
2. Xiao Ou, "Duocaide xinxi".
3. Li Xingye, "Cong jinnian de jibu dapian shuoqi—jiu 84 nian dianying chuangzuo gei bianjibu de yifeng xin" 從今年的幾部大片說起——就84年電影創作給編輯部的一封信 (Speaking of some major films of this year—a letter to the editor about film-making in '84), *DYYS*, March 1985: 8–10.
4. Cheng Zhiwei 成志偉 , "Bu yao wangji dianying tedian he qunzhong—guan yingpian *HTD* you gan" 不要忘記電影特點和羣衆—— 觀影片《黃土地》有感 (Do not forget the special characteristics of and the audience for films—feelings on seeing the film *TYE*), *DYYS*, April 1985: 34–35; reprinted in *HS HTD*: 99–102.
5. *GMRB*, 24 May 1985: 1; *RMRB*, 24 May 1985: 3. The May issue of *DZDY* also mentioned the cinematography in passing (see p. 15).
6. Wang Zhongming, "Chu 'shou' bu fan", *ZGQN*, May 1985: 47; reprinted *HS HTD*: 118–20.
7. Xiao Shen 曉深 , ed., "Xianggang: *HTD* chongjibo" 香港：《黃土地》衝擊波 (Hong Kong: the shock wave of *TYE*), *DDDY*, 4 (June 1985); reprinted in *HS HTD*: 301–15.
8. *GMRB*, 12 June 1985: 1; *RMRB*, 12 June 1985: 3; *DZDY*, July 1985: 10. According to the latter, the awards were announced 14 June.
9. *GMRB*, 13 June 1985: 3.
10. Ye Zhou 葉舟 , "Cong dui *HTD* de zhengyi tanqi" 從對《黃土地》的爭議談起 (A discussion arising from the debate on *TYE*), *WHB*, 14 June 1985: 4; Chi Jinliang, "Yingpian *HTD* guanzhong you zhengyi" 影片

《黃土地》觀衆有爭議 (Audience debate on the film *HTD*), *WHB*, 26 June 1985: 2.

11. Ding Daoxi, "Dianying tansuozhong de xingshi meigan wenti—jian ping yingpian *HTD*" 電影探索中的形式美感問題——兼評影片《黃土地》 (The question of formal aesthetic perception in film exploration—together with a critique of the film *TYE*), *GMRB*, 20 June 1985: 3; reprinted in *HS HTD*: 155–58.

12. *CD*, 16 August 1985: 5.

13. Hao Dazheng, "Xin fengge dianying jianping" 新風格電影簡評 (A brief critique of the new style films), *GMRB*, 26 June 1985: 3; see also Hao's longer article of the same month, "*HTD* ru shi guan"《黃土地》如是觀 (*TYE* considered thus), *HS HTD*: 140–54.

14. *HS HTD*: 144–46.

15. Sun Naixiu, "*HTD* de meixue zhuiqiu"《黃土地》的美學追求 (The aesthetic search in *TYE*), *GMRB*, 4 July 1985: 3

16. Shao Mujun, "Huashuo *HTD*" 話說《黃土地》(Talking of *TYE*), *GMRB*, 25 July 1985: 3; see also the expanded version, dated the following month but under the same title, *HS HTD*: 256–63.

17. Wang Dehou, "Chenchen de *HTD*" (The deep *TYE*), *DYYS*, June 1985: 33–44; reprinted in *HS HTD*: 134–39; Yu Qian, "Faxian shenghuo yu fazhan yishu gexing—zai 'Qingnian daoyan sheying yingpian yantaohui' shang de fayan" 發現生活與發展藝術個性——在「青年導演攝影影片研討會」上的發言 (Discovering life and developing artistic individuality—speech at the Seminar on Films by Young Directors and Cinematographers), *DYYS*, June 1985: 41–44; reprinted in *HS HTD*: 121–27.

18. Peng Jiajin, "Bawo yu chaoyue—kan yingpian *HTD* he *Yige he bage*" 把握與超越——看影片《黃土地》和《一個和八個》(Grasping and transcending—seeing the films *TYE* and *One and Eight*), *DYYS*, June 1985: 36–40; abridged version reprinted in *HS HTD*: 128–33.

19. See Chapter One, note 1: 19.

20. *DZDY*, June 1985: 10–11.

21. *HS HTD*: 258.

22. Huang Shixian 黃式憲 , "Cong shenghuo de xuanliu zhong ningju shidai de shiqing" 從生活的漩流中凝聚時代的詩情 (From the whirlpool of life distill the poetic feeling of the age), *HQ*, 13 (1 July 1985): 44–47, esp. 47.

23. *DZDY*, August 1985: 2–3.

24. Zhou Chuanji, "*HTD*—chengshu de biaozhi"《黃土地》——成熟的標誌 (*TYE*—a sign of maturity), *HS HTD*: 209–21, esp. 210.

25. Zhou Chuanji, *HS HTD*: 219–21.

26. For example, articles by Li Jinsheng and Zheng Guoen 鄭國恩 in *DYYS* in July 1985: 13–17, 18–21; reprinted in *HS HTD*: 159–65, 166–75. Articles by supporters Li Xingye and Chen Maiping appeared in the relatively conservative *DYCZ* in July 1985; the latter was reprinted in *HS HTD*: 193–97; see also Chen Kaige, "Qinguo ren", *DDDY*, July 1985: 101–107. In September, *TYE* was also a major topic for discussion throughout most of that month's issue of *DDDY* and the subject of a readers' debate in *DYXZ*.

27. *Xinhua News Agency News Bulletin*, 30 June 1985: 44–45.

28. *CD*, 16 August 1985: 5.

29. Under the general heading "Dianying shangzuolü di de yuanin he zai?" 電影上座率低的原因何在？ (What are the reasons for the decline in cinema attendence), the report appears in *DZDY*, September 1985: 2–3.

30. For further statistics and analysis see Hu Jian 胡健 , "Weisuo: burong leguan de dianying shichang xianzhuang" 萎縮：不容樂觀的電影市場現狀 (Shrinking: the present situation in the film market which does not permit optimism), *DYYS*, November 1985: 11–16.

31. *DZDY*, October 1985: 2–3.

32. *DZDY*, October 1985: 2–3; *DZDY*, November 1985: 2–5; *DZDY*, December 1985: 5.

33. *DZDY*, November 1985: 5; see also *DYYS*, November 1985: 12–13.

34. *BJWB*, 16 July 1985: 4.

35. *GMRB*, 2 September 1985: 3.

36. *CD*, 6 August 1985: 5.

37. *CD*, 20 August 1985: 1 and 6 September 1985: 5.

38. *CD*, 6 December 1985: 3.

39. *GMRB*, 18 August 1985: 4.

40. *GMRB*, 5 December 1985: 4.

41. Zhang Boqing, "*HTD*—Chuang xin pian"《黃土地》——創新篇 (*TYE*—a trailblazer), *XGC*, September 1985: 6–8; reprinted in *HS HTD*: 241–46.

42. Meng Hongmei, "Yi cun bi xian—hua jin yi zai" 意存筆先 畫盡意在 (The concept precedes the writing, the concept remains at the end), *DYXZ*, 1985. 5; reprinted in *HS HTD*: 222–24.

43. Huang Jianzhong, "*HTD* de yishu gexing"《黃土地》的藝術個性 (The

artistic individuality of *TYE*), *WYYJ*, 1985. 5; reprinted in *HS HTD*: 234–40.

44. Andrew Walker, "Wage Reform and the Web of Factory Interests", *CQ*, 109 (March 1987): 22–41, esp. 22, 38.

45. *FEER*, 19 March 1987: 60.

46. *CQ*, 105 (March 1986): 189–90; *FEER*, 20 December 1985: 45–47.

47. For a brief account of this campaign see Paul Clark, "Film-making in China: From the Cultural Revolution to 1981", *CQ*, 94 (June 1983): 304–22, esp. 318–21.

48. China is not the only country in which the authorities take it upon themselves to doubt the motives of local film-makers and overseas audiences. The following dialogue was recorded by Salman Rushdie in his review of Andrew Robinson's *Satyajit Ray: The Inner Eye* (London: Deutsch, 1989), *London Review of Books*, 8 March 1990: 9. "The Bombay movie star Nargis (Nargis Dutt), star of the 1957 megaweepie *Mother India*, was by the beginning of the Eighties a member of the Indian Parliament, from which exalted position she launched an attack on Ray:

    Nargis: Why do you think films like *Pather Panchali* become popular abroad?… Because people there want to see India in an abject condition. That is the image they have of our country and a film that confirms that image seems to them authentic.

    Interviewer: But why should a renowned director like Ray do such a thing?

    Nargis: To win awards. His films are not commercially successful. They only win awards…"

    As a Russian film director remarked in a similar context, "Foreigners, in any case, know much more about us than we know ourselves." (Marina Goldevskaya, "The Making of Solovki Power", *Soviet Spring*, London: Channel 4 and the *New Statesman and Society*, 1989: 29.)

49. *CQ*, 106 (June 1986): 381, 386–88.

50. *FEER*, 19 March 1987: 78–80.

51. One instance of the new attitude towards *TYE* occurs in *DDDY*: whereas throughout 1985 it had received very favourable treatment in this magazine, it was hardly mentioned in the last issue for 1985, dated 8 November, although stills from *The Grand Parade* were featured in a special coloured inset.

7. *The Yellow Earth* Abroad (1985)

Official Chinese fears that the reason for the film's success in the West was its portrayal of Chinese backwardness are not only insulting to Western viewers but also far from the mark in their estimation of Western perceptions of its charm. Whatever the domestic reaction, it would have been more discreet not to have banned the film internationally, since Western film audiences, especially professional critics with no particular knowledge of Chinese history and politics, generally failed at first to probe the deeper layers of meaning in the film. The anonymous critic in *The Economist*, for instance, commenting in April 1985 on the film's extraordinary success in Hong Kong and its reputation as one of the best Chinese films since 1949, remarks, "Perhaps it is, but to Western eyes it belongs to a tradition of exoticism that often seems merely quaint.... How well *The Yellow Earth* stands up in international company will be tested when it goes to Cannes next month."[1] The critic also mistook the drum dance (a send-off for new recruits to the Eighth Route Army) for a wedding dance, and considered Gu Qing's mission, to collect folk songs, "as bizarre an assignment as can be readily imagined." Equally far from the mark is his assumption that the Chinese films that were shown at the festival were "carefully chosen to imply that, in Deng's new China, tracts are out and art is in." As shown above, the process by which these particular films reached Hong Kong was one of hard bargaining between parties with conflicting interests.

Western sinologists and experts on Chinese film, however, had already begun to create the film's international reputation. One of the most important judgements came from the Dutch director Joris Ivens, whose comment at the end of 1984 that *The Yellow Earth* was the best Chinese film since the 1940s became widely quoted. Another early supporter of the film, Geremie Barmé, was active in preparing the ground for the film's successful reception in Hong Kong. The fullest description of *The Yellow Earth* in 1985 came in August, from Paul Clark, a specialist on Chinese film at the East-West Center in Hawaii. In his program notes for the Hawaii International Film Festival later that year, he established himself firmly in the camp of those who claimed that *The Yellow Earth* was the best film produced in China since 1949. He bases his claim on three grounds. First, it is a film that knows it is a film rather than an imitation of a stage performance or the reverential adaptation of a short story or novel. Second, this film had gone further than any other in finding a Chinese style of cinematic art, exploring the possibilities in the native tradition; Clark comments that the road seems to have been via modern Western film: "Only from being familiar and comfortable with film art from abroad have the makers of *The Yellow Earth* felt free to explore the possibilities in their own tradition." In illustration he cites the film's deliberately slow pace as other Chinese directors try to speed up in imitation of the West. Thirdly, Clark points out that like all films made in China, *The Yellow Earth* is strongly political: "Its achievement lies in the use of film art to suggest its political points." Clark also mentions the inappropriate use of the "lush chords" of a full Western string orchestra, noting correctly that this may be more of a problem for Western than for Chinese audiences.

In Hong Kong *The Yellow Earth* had been invited to take part in six international film festivals. Zhang Yimou was sent to Cannes with only a videotape, and the European premiere of *The Yellow Earth* was at the Berlin Horizonte Arts Festival in May 1985. *The*

Yellow Earth then turned up for the 38th Festival Internazionale Del Film at Locarno, which began on 8 August and featured 17 films from 12 different countries. There it won the Silver Leopard award (the second prize), the citation mentioning "its original quest for a new national cinematographic language". It also received a special mention and an additional prize from the youth and ecumenical juries at the festival. From there the film went to the Edinburgh Festival, where it was screened on 14 August. Its appearance in Edinburgh, together with films from Hong Kong and Taiwan, was largely due to Tony Rayns. Rayns had tried to arrange for Chen Kaige to attend, as had also the organizers at Locarno, but both were informed by the head of the Film Bureau, Shi Fangyu 石方禹, that Chen Kaige was busy on his new film.

The Yellow Earth did not win an award in the official section at Edinburgh but the reviews were extremely favourable. *Variety* led off with a survey of festival showings from China, Taiwan, Hong Kong and a San Francisco director of Chinese descent, describing *The Yellow Earth* as "a pic that gets its points across in a subtle way, and furthermore shows a sophisticated visual style."[2] It also featured a review by David Stratton, describing the film as "the most impressive film from mainland China unveiled so far in the West ... Chen Kaige ... tells the story with great subtlety and delicacy, allowing silences, looks and gestures to convey the feelings of his characters. The compositions of cinematographer Zhang Yimou are outstanding, and the film's images are consistently rich and evocative. Only in the somewhat shaky post-synchronization of the songs does the film falter technically."[3] Ian Bell's review for *The Scotsman* describes *The Yellow Earth* as "a magnificent piece of film-making ... a politically daring film for a Chinese. It is a daring, breathtaking film for anyone, anywhere. An extraordinary debut."[4] Noting the political ambiguity of the film, he characterizes Gu Qing as becoming "confused in the face of a way of life which the party intends to change but which he cannot understand. Confronted with the arranged marriage of the farmer's 12-year old daughter, the soldier surrenders the responsibilities he has acquired." In a summary of the festival offerings as it came to an end, Bell gave as the example of the best art movie shown "the indubitable artistic triumph of 1985, Chen Kaige's *Yellow Earth*."[5] The *Guardian* reviewer Derek Malcolm introduced *The Yellow Earth* as the Chinese film "about which one had heard about all year as the best film from that source for many years, at least among those released to the West. And so it proved. This first feature film by Chen Kaige isn't interesting just because it comes from China but because it would look good in any company. The man has a real eye, and image after image shows he is potentially a world-class director…it is absolutely its own thing, beautifully composed, strongly plotted and acted out with great dignity."[6] In his survey article two weeks later, Malcolm includes *The Yellow Earth* as one of "the two or three movies which create a buzz of genuine excitement and surprise" at a film festival, and repeats the praise given earlier in his review.[7] Finally, Philip French for *The Observer* found *The Yellow Earth* less "accessible" than two other Asian offerings, but nevertheless "a visually bold and surprisingly subtle study."[8] The Chinese press ignored the festival altogether, but a short item appeared in the Hong Kong *Xingdao ribao*, mentioning briefly *The Yellow Earth*'s troubled history in its homeland.[9]

The Yellow Earth had been selected as the official Chinese entry at the Montreal Film Festival to be held 25 to 31 August, and Chen Kaige and two actors from a second film, *Border Town*, were invited to attend the festival. As described above, its entry in Montreal was a direct result of its appearance in Hong Kong the previous year. In the end it was withdrawn from the competition, the delegation stayed at home, *Border Town* was given a prize, and *The Yellow Earth* was reported as having received favourable reviews.[10] Also in August, a Chinese film retrospective was held in

Sydney and Canberra, but to the regret of the organizers, they were not able to obtain *The Yellow Earth*.

At the London Film Festival in November 1985, *The Yellow Earth* won further honours. The British Film Institute Award for the most original and imaginative film was given to *The Yellow Earth* by a panel made up of BFI staff, filmmakers, distributors and critics from a choice of 160 films, including again several from Asia, citing the film's "evocation of an isolated rural community" and "the striking use of landscape."[11] According to *The Economist* reviewer, the outstanding feature of the festival was the strength of the Asian contingent, with "superb" new films from Japan, Hong Kong, Taiwan, China and South Korea. On this second viewing, and perhaps with greater knowledge of the film's background, the reviewer's assessment of *The Yellow Earth* was more favourable but still reserved: "a lyrical pastoral saga that may conceal an incendiary political message.... Shot in a rich palette, with exotic local colour, *The Yellow Earth* is the handsomest Chinese film yet seen in the West."[12]

The British award was announced on 1 December. On 3 December *The Yellow Earth* won the prize for best photography at the Third World Film Festival in Nantes in southern France. From France the film then went to the Hawaii International Film Festival in Honolulu in December. This time Chen Kaige and Zhang Yimou were able to accompany the film, thanks mainly to persistent pressure from the festival organizers (including Paul Clark), and the film received both the Eastman Kodak Award for Excellence in Cinematography and the East-West Center Award for the film which "best promotes understanding among the peoples of Asia, the Pacific and the United States." Carmelita Hinton, an American documentary film-maker who grew up in Peking, and Paul Clark then arranged for Chen Kaige and Zhang Yimou to visit the mainland, where Hinton introduced them and the film to the Museum of Modern Art in New York.

In the United Kingdom, an article by Tony Rayns on Chen Kaige and the new wave films appeared in *China Now*, a friends-of-China magazine with limited circulation.[13] Rayns suggested it had been clear for two or three years that a new wave could break in Chinese cinema, given the combination of breakthroughs in Asian cinema in general, the "knock-on" effect these might have in China, the changes already taking place in the Chinese cultural scene, and the new generation of film-makers who responded to these changes. As Geremie Barmé and Danny Yung have both noted in this context, any evaluation of the tremendous success of *The Yellow Earth* in 1985 should also take into account the rising expectations of Western film critics in regard to Asian cinema, the great fund of goodwill in the West towards China so far lacking a substantial object for its expression, and the tendency of success to generate success especially in such limited circles as the art movies/film festival circuit.

Notes

1. *The Economist*, 20 April 1985: 84.
2. *Variety*, 21 August 1985.
3. *Variety*, 21 August 1985.
4. *The Scotsman*, 19 August 1985.
5. *The Scotsman*, 24 August 1985: 4.
6. *The Guardian*, 22 August 1985: 11.
7. *The Guardian*, 1 September 1985: 21.
8. *The Observer*, 25 August 1985.
9. *Xingdao ribao*, August 1985.
10. See Chapter Six: 100–101.
11. Quoted by *CD*, 6 December 1985: 3.
12. *The Economist*, 16 November 1985.
13. Tony Rayns, "Framing the future: a new cinema breaking through?", *China Now*, 115 (winter 1985–86): 9–12.

8. Reversals and Reappraisals (1986)

The international success of *The Yellow Earth* was only one of several problems upsetting the official film world. In an attempt to establish tighter state authority, the drastic step was taken in January 1986 of detaching the Film Bureau from the Ministry of Culture, where it had been since 1949 but where reformers were now in the ascendancy, and combining it with radio and television to form a new ministry for the audio/visual mass media. Since radio and television had traditionally been under stricter control than literature and the arts generally, and since neither radio nor television had any reputation for creativity, this move was generally seen by the film world as an ominous step towards greater regulation and restriction. Even some film bureaucrats regarded the step as retrograde: the head of the Film Board, Shi Fangyu (not hitherto seen as a reformist), commented that it might take film-makers one or two years to recover from the effects of the merger.[1] The praise given at the same time by an apparently united Party leadership (featuring Hu Qiaomu and Hu Qili 胡啓立 as spokesmen) to a potboiler called *The Fascinating Band* (迷人的樂隊)[2] increased the feeling of gloom among younger filmmakers in particular. An orthodox rural comedy about an amateur band seeking a higher standard of cultural life to complement their new material prosperity, it seemed almost like the leadership's answer to *The Yellow Earth*.

Despite leadership displeasure, however, the domestic controversy and overseas success of *The Yellow Earth* and other new wave films could not simply be ignored, and were noted in January as the ninth of the ten major events of 1985 in the film world.[3] The same issue of *Popular Cinema* also featured an article by the famous Japanese film critic Sato Tadao 左藤忠男 on three new wave films, *The Yellow Earth*, *Sacrifice of Youth* and *One and Eight*, and a note on the influence of traditional Chinese painting on the picture composition in *The Yellow Earth*.[4] The January issue of *Cinema Arts* featured a long article by the American George S. Semsel in praise of the new films, including *The Yellow Earth*.[5] In March, the Guangxi Studio felt bold enough to nominate *The Yellow Earth* and *One and Eight* for the Hundred Flowers Best Film award, along with Xue Bai for Best Actress and Tan Tuo for Best Supporting Actor.[6] The film was also shown on television during the spring but without prior announcement. It was also shown in Tientsin during the spring, and Paul Clark reports being shown by Zhang Yimou a huge billboard for the film outside a Xi'an cinema in April. Although attendances inside China were informally reported as good to excellent whenever it was shown in 1986 and 1987, the restricted number of showings generally added up to a poor box-office. By this time, however, it was clear that *The Yellow Earth* was earning a great deal of money in foreign currency.

The Chinese-language daily press had apparently exhausted its interest in *The Yellow Earth* (with the exception of an article in *Enlightenment Daily* on the film's spectacular failure in Poland in April 1986),[7] but the English-language press gave it even more coverage in 1986 than before. The weekly *Peking Review* featured a three-page article in February, listing the film's international awards and highlighting Ivens' now famous comment.[8] Despite a number of factual errors, the article gives a useful summary of the criticism and praise that the film received in 1985, coming down noticeably on the side of the film's supporters. Also mentioned in the final paragraph as part of the same trend are the films *One and Eight*, *Hunting Ground* and *Bloodshed in Black Valley*.

Next, after a brief note in February on *The Yellow Earth*'s London award,[9] the monthly *China Reconstructs* ran a two-page feature on the new wave films in June.[10] *The Beach* (海灘), *Hunting Ground* and *Wujie Mountain* (霧界) are mentioned, but the main focus is on *The Yellow Earth*. Unfortunately almost every detail in the account of the film's history as well as the plot summary is inaccurate (the film is described, for instance, as the winner of the Golden Rooster Best Film Award, its title is described as coming from the original essay, and the director is described as a graduate of the National Film Academy—a non-existent institution; some but not all of the incorrect detail could have come from the *China Daily* article of 16 August 1985). The article also picks up the question of the foreign praise given to the film. Zhong Dianfei 鍾惦棐 , described as a famous movie critic, is quoted as saying "The four prizes won by *The Yellow Earth* abroad demonstrate that Chinese movies can also win respect in the international film world." Xia Yan, however, is quoted as having said as a press conference, "Chinese movies should be for Chinese audiences, not foreign ones." The truly remarkable idea that Chen Kaige at the height of the campaign against spiritual pollution had been planning his first film with a foreign audience in mind is given without further comment. What is clear from this exchange, however, is that the film's international success had by 1986 become an integral part of its controversial nature.

The temporary banning of *The Yellow Earth* from the film festival circuit did not have much effect except as an additional source of frustration to sinologists, Asian film specialists, festival organizers and, of course, the film-makers themselves. The film had become so well known that Chinese embassies in Western countries were frequently asked to show or lend it, but even before the ban the embassies frequently possessed only a videotape at most. Nevertheless, the film was not to be easily forgotten over the cold winter. In Britain, the BBC and ITV negotiated with the Chinese for its purchase.[11] *The Yellow Earth* was shown at the Fifteenth Rotterdam Film Festival and on Dutch television at the end of January: it did not win an award but received good reviews and was rated fifth out of a hundred films by the festival audience of more than a hundred thousand.[12] Huub Bals, the festival director, who had seen the film at the Ninth Hong Kong International Film Festival, reported that he had no trouble in obtaining it, but that he had no response to his invitation to the director to attend.[13] Huang Jianzhong was present, however, along with his two films, *As You Wish* (如意) and *A Woman of Good Family* (良家婦女).[14]

In 1985 there had been plans to enter *The Yellow Earth* at the Moscow Film Festival but in the end it was not shown. It first reached Eastern Europe at the beginning of April 1986, at the Polish International Film Festival in Warsaw. According to the Chinese press, however, the film was given a very cold reception. At the evening session on 8 April, the 1000-odd seats at one cinema were all vacant; even more telling, at the afternoon session the following day, the small handful of people who did turn up began to leave ten minutes after the start of the film. At the evening performance the same thing happened, so that at the end of the screening only a dozen or so people remained in the auditorium. Critical reception was also poor, the reviews commenting unfavourably on the simplicity of the plot, the blandness of the content, the slowness of the action and the general lack of artistry.[15] There is no reason to doubt the accuracy of the Chinese report, but it would have been interesting to hear the uncensored responses of the few who did sit through the whole film. The film was also reported to be a failure when it was shown commercially (i.e. in Chinatown cinemas) in the United States in April–May.

Nevertheless *The Yellow Earth* continued to command respect in Hong Kong, Japan and Western Europe. It overshadowed the Chinese offerings at the 1986 Hong Kong International Film Festival in April, reminding viewers that the second film by Chen

Kaige and Zhang Yimou, *The Grand Parade*, completed the previous summer, had still not been released: *The Economist* report on the festival was headlined "Yellow dearth".[16] In April–May Chen Kaige returned to the United States for the New Directors, New Films Festival, organized by the Museum of Modern Art and the Lincoln Center Film Society; however, a proposed screening at a festival in Dallas was cancelled over a contretemps involving a Taiwan flag and national pride. *The Yellow Earth*'s first appearance in Japan had been in October 1985, along with five other Chinese films in a Sino-Japanese film seminar,[17] and had attracted attention from Japanese critics.[18] Chen Kaige was invited to Japan in July 1986 for pre-release publicity for the commercial distribution of *The Yellow Earth*, and the subsequent season was reported to be very successful. The Japanese release was organized by the sinologist Karima Fumitoshi, who also acted as Chen Kaige's interpreter during his visit. Sato and Karima had earlier collaborated on a book on contemporary Chinese cinema in which *The Yellow Earth* was given favourable mention.[19]

The summer of 1986 witnessed an intellectual, artistic and social boldness almost unprecedented in contemporary Chinese history. At the time it seemed that the constraints of the previous winter had been miraculously abandoned, and old inhibitions were being shed at a startling pace.[20] Though no longer centre stage, *The Yellow Earth* was a part of the general euphoria. In July, it even made a showing in the Hundred Flowers awards for best film, coming fifth with 43,900 votes as against 225,530 for the prizewinner, *Juvenile Delinquents* (少年犯), and 93,600 for *The Fascinating Band* in fourth place.[21] Chen Kaiyan, compiling for the Chinese Film Press a book on the controversy surrounding the film, made little attempt to balance the articles in its favour with those against it. Chen Kaige, interviewed by two French film students while magnificently attired as captain of the Qing imperial guard (see below), was uncharacteristically unguarded on the issue of audience response to his film. With a nice mixture of candour and dishonesty, he replied that he knew that some of the peasants who had acted as extras had seen the film, but that he did not know what their response to it was nor did he think it very important. (According to studio gossip, of which Chen Kaige must have been aware, the Shaanbei peasants who saw the completed film were not particularly impressed, commenting that it "just showed their ordinary lives—that was just the way they lived.") His aim was not a representation of reality, nor was the film made for any specific purpose. The important thing was not other people's opinions but what he himself wanted to say.[22]

The Yellow Earth returned to London in August for a triumphant season at the Institute of Contemporary Art (ICA), under the rubric "The Most Acclaimed Chinese Film Ever Made".[23] The original subtitles provided by Chinese Film Import and Export Corporation had been widely criticized, and for this showing a new set of subtitles had been prepared, based on the translation by Bonnie McDougall and adapted (albeit inaccurately) for the film by Tony Rayns and Dominique Brasseur. Rayns also supplied an interview with Chen Kaige and a review of the film for *Time Out*,[24] quoted in part in the ICA brochure. In this interview, exaggerating slightly about his fellow-students at the film academy, Chen Kaige claimed that all of them shared two convictions:

> First, the older generation of Chinese filmmakers could be dismissed as propagandists, and second, film itself was an artistic medium that should be used personally. All of us hated what was passing for cinema in China—all that didacticism, all those dated, theatrical styles—and we started out determined to do something different and better... What interested us most was the challenge of exploring a purely Chinese aesthetic—an aesthetic with peasant roots, whose growth had been cut short by the Cultural Revolution. We've learned a lot from Western films, and we wanted to combine that with something distinctively Chinese. We didn't look to Chinese films to find it so much as to painting and folk arts. Our main visual inspiration was

> a school of peasant painters in Shensi province. We tried to capture the
> character of a people and their relationships. We aimed for subtlety.

In the accompanying review, Rayns describes briefly the political undercurrents that caused trouble for the film in China, but claims that what really stirred up the old guard was "the film's insistence on going its own way." More details were provided in two follow-up articles in the October *Monthly Film Bulletin* (published by the BFI).[25] The availability of background information about the film and its already considerable reputation may have exercised an inhibiting as well as a positive influence on audiences.

On the third appearance in Britain of *The Yellow Earth*, the reviews tended to be better-informed about its political history but more cautious about its artistic excellence. Derek Malcolm's second-time-round review for *The Guardian*[26] warns the audience against expecting some "cinematic miracle":

> *Yellow Earth* isn't that, though it is certainly very beautiful to look at and has an atmosphere about it that only the Japanese cinema can match. But Chen Kaige is certainly an exceptional filmmaker, and the least you can say is that his debut is as promising as anyone else's in the world last year... The film is only 89 minutes and the compression adds to its force. I've seen no other Chinese film like it, since even the gentlest hint of propaganda or polemic is subjugated to the demands of pure cinema, laid out before us with a kind of intensity that's much more eloquent than words. It seems a very private, personal film to have come out of China, made by a director with a natural eye for relevant detail. No one should fear that they will be bored, or that critics writing well about it are being merely patronising. This, by any standards, is a first class film.

In their assessments of the plot, Rayns and Malcolm focus on the relationship between the villagers, or Cuiqiao and her family, and Gu Qing: Rayns describes their mutual disappointment, and Malcolm describes Gu Qing as leaving the village as "a chastened man." Similarly, *The Observer* critic, Adrian Turner, finds him "a placid, sensitive hero" who becomes "disheartened" by the fatalism shown by Cuiqiao's father.[27] Turner notes the ballad-like construction of the film, with scenes initiated and closed by songs, and the director as having "a painter's eye for composition and perspective, turning the landscape, with its single tree perpetually and symbolically on the horizon, into a fully fledged character." The review ends with a perception of one of the director's most central and deliberate paradoxes, Cuiqiao "swallowed up by the swirling waters which she has so dutifully gathered. It is the final irony in a haunting and provocative film." Nigel Matheson, reviewing in *City Limits*,[28] gives little space to Gu Qing, "Red Army cadre and Right On Maoist Man," but comes closest to the central problem of the film in his description of the conflict between the new philosophy of change and "an ancient way of life and the intransigence of the yellow earth itself." He goes on,

> Were the subject matter closer to home you might question this film's purity. But it's hard not to be disarmed by such unfamiliar faces, the hardships and poverty they endure and the truthfulness of tone. The actors are charismatic, the framing constantly takes you by surprise, the visual integrity is outstanding, and long, quiet passages open out into noisy colourful ceremonial scenes—right up to the brilliantly bizarre finale.

To my knowlege, Matheson is the only Western critic to raise in print, however indirectly, a question on the film's basic philosophic outlook, hinting at the potentially huge ideological gap between the new generation of post-socialist intellectuals and artists in China and Western intellectuals whose humanist outlook is strongly coloured by Marxism or other leftwing philosophies.

The *Times* reviewer, David Robinson, while praising the film in general, also notes its technical shortcomings:[29]

> A second viewing exposes weaknesses—moments of somewhat self-conscious artistry, shaky post-synchronization of the very taking folk music, and some inappropriate passages of background music quite

inconsistent with the skilful manipulation of sound elsewhere in the film. They are slight faults in such an encouraging first work.

Robinson also comments at length on the film's political background and history, presumably borrowing from pre-release publicity by Rayns. Gabriele Annan, writing for *The Sunday Telegraph*,[30] takes up both problems in technique and taste, delivering a sharp jab at the kind of political pretentiousness in the film that other critics tend to shrug off, patronizingly, as being "Chinese" and therefore beyond reproach:

> *The Yellow Earth* is an experience farther out than any space movie. It comes from China. Like travel there, it has seriously boring stretches, but they are worth enduring for the sense of a world previously unimaginable. One needs a new drawer in one's filing cabinet of mental images... One can't help seeing the film partly as a travel documentary. The beauty of the photography is seductive, the colour particularly rich and soft. And then there are all the folk songs. The little boy sings a jolly ditty... All the other songs are sad, perturbing, haunting—and strangely un-strange. The Yellow River towman's song sounds just like the Volga boatman's; all the more, alas, because it is backed by sobbing Western strings. This artistic faux pas is typical of the film. A sensitivity and refinement not often seen in the Western cinema alternate with naive ineptitude and corn... The emotional impact is strong, and achieved by great subtlety of direction, photography and lighting. The pace is as slow and patient as the peasants themselves. Nobody seems to mind repetition. A good shot—like the figure coming up over the horizon—is serenely recycled over and over again. Soviet films have taught one that nothing raises the audience's boredom ceiling as much as a Communist regime... The army, when he gets back to it, is busy recruiting with the aid of a peasant waist drum troupe doing their number in such numbers that they might almost be the pioneers at their May Day drill in Moscow's Red Square. Was this sequence compulsory? Is it meant to be taken seriously? Would it make a sophisticated Chinese audience giggle? The film invites a lot of suspicious questions like these, and still manages to bowl one over with a kind of disarming innocence reflected in the girl's unforgettable little face. But it's not exactly entertainment.

Despite its flippant tone, this review may be said to represent the attitude of Western viewers who are favourably impressed by the film without being blind to its shortcomings. Annan's speculation about the genesis of the drum dance sequence is probably closer to the truth than all the defensive comments in the Chinese press or even Clark's inspired guess that it represents Cuiqiao's fantasies of Yenan (not to be identified with the film-makers' vision of that place). Echoing Matheson's use of the world "disarming", Annan also pinpoints a major source of the film's appeal to Western audiences: not, as Chinese conservatives assured themselves, the spectacle of Chinese backwardness, but of an innocence now so outdated in the West that its appearance in this film has a new freshness about it. Given its association with utterly real hardship and tragedy, it is indeed hard not to be moved. The tug of conflicting responses is perhaps even better conveyed in the unlikely pages of *Fashion/Lifestyle* by Paul Mathur,[31] a critic evidently under no obligation to pay tribute to film-criticism jargon:

> Your Foreign Film Correspondent finds himself and his overnight bag on the banks of a Chinese river watching another film with a plot as enticing and clear as the thick mud sludging around his ankles. An hour and a half later he is once more in raptures and knows it can't be too long before he is despatched to give the Siberian Film Industry the once over. Before he goes, he attempts to explain why every last one of you ought to go and see this film despite the basic plot which is about to unfold… Not exactly the sort of thing to tempt you away from the telly, but watch out, it's a brilliantly filmed and exquisitely executed drama, gaining everything from its quiet understatement. The acting, particularly that of Cuiqiao, the young girl, is superb and the environment is communicated so effectively that you leave the cinema with fine yellow dust deep beneath your finger nails. The film also features a number of extremely fine haircuts. Your correspondent went ape.

Despite information on the political controversy surrounding the film, most Western critics still failed to perceive the subversive meanings that had so bothered the Golden Rooster panel. Instead they were more conscious of the remaining surface features typical of the orthodox Chinese cinema, praising the director for toning them down.

Western sinologists tended to be more critical of these remnants of orthodoxy. Especially to those who first saw the film in 1986, when its reputation for artistic excellence and political daring was at its peak, first viewing tended to be something of a let-down. Even for specialists on modern China, the film's symbolism and references were frequently obscure, while at the same time this audience's greater familiarity with Chinese cinema made the film's conventionality even more irritating. For example, many viewers who were impressed with the rugged appearance of the male peasants felt disappointed precisely because Cuiqiao was so delicate and appealing. One repeated shot that attracted criticism was of figures silhouetted along the slope of a hill against the sky. This kind of silhouetting was so mercilessly discredited in the 1930s that it has remained absent from Hollywood ever since, so that its appearance here also had an odd freshness about it; nevertheless, it was felt by some viewers to be an easy effect. The orchestral music was much criticized, and many viewers felt that the film as a whole was marred by a lingering sentimentality that seems inevitable in even the best Chinese cinema. On the other hand, some film critics were more able to perceive the artistic innovations in *The Yellow Earth* than sinologists with no particular knowledge of film art.

Autumn and early winter brought no apparent change to the arts in China, though behind-the-scenes preparations for a new campaign had begun as early as September. A criticism of the new wave films, for instance, was made in the September issue of *Cinema Arts*, with *The Yellow Earth* starring as main culprit.[32] Writing oddly enough in the context of the film's unexpectedly good showing in the Hundred Flowers awards, Ma Rui concentrates his attack on the film-makers and their supporters for ignoring the

Chinese mass film audience. Without unfortunately giving the source of his information, he quotes a recent survey of university students in north and south China which showed that apart from members of the Chinese and film departments, students did not particularly commend the film.[33] The balance was restored the following month in a thoughtful discussion of audience appreciation of the new wave films which places *The Yellow Earth*'s Hundred Flowers citation in the context of traditional aesthetics in regard to Chinese film.[34]

Two books brought the year 1986 to a triumphant end for *The Yellow Earth*. The first was Chen Kaiyan's *Huashuo "Huang tudi"* 話說《黃土地》(Talking of *The Yellow Earth*), published in October. It contains the report on the Golden Rooster debate, plus thirty-one articles, most of them published in film magazines or the newspapers in 1985, and an appendix with contributions from Chen Kaige, Zhang Yimou and He Qun, and a selection of short comments from Hong Kong. The second was *Seeds of Fire: Chinese Voices of Conscience*, edited by Geremie Barmé and John Minford, published in Hong Kong in November. This collection of translations and comments from and about contemporary Chinese literature also included a section on *The Yellow Earth*, consisting of a two-page introduction by the editors, a synopsis of the script by McDougall,[35] and excerpts from the Golden Rooster debate with additional comments by Chen Kaige and Zhang Yimou. In the editors' words, the film reflected the vision of the dispossessed young people sent to be re-educated in the countryside during the Cultural Revolution:

> The director as well as most of his film crew belonged to this group, and the understanding of Chinese realities that their exile afforded them is in striking contrast to the distorted and blinkered vision of the older Party and cultural leaders. Although critics made much of the tragic fate of the heroine, Cuiqiao, it is perhaps in the character of her younger brother, Hanhan, and the deceptive silence with which he

preserves his individuality, that we can find the most striking message of the film.

The cover of the book features a medium close-up of Hanhan in his tattered jacket, his mouth open bawling his song. *Talking of "The Yellow Earth"*, in contrast, features Cuiqiao dressed in red for her wedding.

The Yellow Earth continued its peregrinations overseas with successful commercial runs in Stockholm in November 1986,[36] at the Sydney Opera House in December 1986,[37] in Canberra in March 1987 and in Singapore in January 1987. In July and August 1987 it was performed as a dance-drama by the Hong Kong Dance Company in Hong Kong's City Hall, with choreography by Shu Qiao 舒巧 and Ying Eding 應萼定 and music by Tan Dun 譚盾. In a season on Recent Chinese Cinema at the Harvard Film Archive in the autumn of 1987, it was billed as "a sensitive love story" in which "people lead a quiet, isolated existence occasionally punctuated by local ceremonies" and was described in *The Harvard Independent* as "directed by Huang Tu Di".[38] In its fifth year, it was still being shown at festivals and in commercial cinemas, and is widely acknowledged as the best film to have come out of China in more than thirty years.

Notes

1. See Geremie Barmé, "Bureaucrats and zealots stifle Chinese cinema", *FEER*, 13 March 1986: 40–41.
2. *CD*, 14 January 1986: 3; see also [Chen] Huangmei, "Zamen de xin tiane zhi ge" 咱們的新天鵝之歌 (Our new swan's song), *HQ*, 4 (16 February 1986): 26–29.
3. *DZDY*, January 1986: 1–2; see also *DYXZ*, January 1986: 69.
4. *DZDY*, January 1986: 30–31 and 9–8.
5. See Qiaozhi S. Saimusaier 喬治 S · 塞姆塞爾 [George S. Semsell], "Jinqi Zhongguo dianying zhong de kongjian meixue" 近期中國電影中的空

間美學 (Spatial aesthetics in recent Chinese films), *DYYS*, January 1986: 49–56.

6. *DZDY*, March 1986: 6–7.
7. *GMRB*, 28 May 1986: 2
8. *BR*, 10 February 1986:30–32.
9. *CR*, February 1986: 62.
10. *CR*, June 1986: 26–27.
11. *The Guardian*, 3 January 1986.
12. *Klassekampen* (Oslo), 20 February 1986 and other clippings compiled by the Festival.
13. I am grateful to Garrie van Pinxteren, one of the two translators into Dutch of *TYE*, for supplying me with the official collection of press clippings and other information from the Fifteenth Rotterdam Film Festival.
14. *Klassekampen*, 20 February 1986.
15. *GMRB*, 28 May 1986: 2; see also *DYXZ*, October 1986: 94.
16. *The Economist*, 12 April 1986: 96–97.
17. *DYYS*, February 1986: 3; see also the subsequent report in *DYYS*, May 1986: 51–54, 14.
18. See for example *DZDY*, January 1986: 30–31, and note 19 below.
19. Sato Tadao and Karima Fumitoshi, *Shanghai: kinema poto. Yomigairu Chugoku eiga* (Shanghai: cinema port. Reviving Chinese film), Kaifusha, Tokyo, 1985.
20. For a description of this summer and the events around it, see McDougall, "Breaking Through: Literature and the Arts in China, 1976–86", *Copenhagen Papers in East and Southeast Asian Studies*, 1 (1988): 35–65.
21. *DZDY*, July 1986: 2–3.
22. Summarized from my own notes of this interview.
23. My thanks to Jamie Lehrer, managing editor of *2PLUS2*, for sending me a copy of the ICA brochure. I am grateful to Tony Rayns for a selection of press clippings from the ICA season.
24. *Time Out*, 833.
25. *Monthly Film Bulletin*, 633 (October 1986): 295–96, 296–98. The account includes a few minor errors of dating.
26. *The Guardian*, 7 August 1986.
27. *The Observer*, 10 August 1986.
28. *City Limits*, 7–14 August 1986.

29. *The Times*, 8 August 1986.
30. *The Sunday Telegraph*, 10 August 1986.
31. *Fashion/Lifestyle*, n.d.
32. Ma Rui, "Baihua jiang pingxuan de qishi" 百花獎評選的啓示 (An inspiration to the public choice in the Hundred Flowers awards), *DYYS*, September 1986: 14–18, esp. 16–18.
33. Ma Rui, "Baihua jiang pingxuan de qishi": 17.
34. Zhang Wei 張衞 , "Panni chuantong ye shi minzuhua de neirong; jian tan ben minzu de xiandai dianying" 叛逆傳統也是民族化的內容；兼談本民族的現代電影 (Rebelling against tradition is also part of sinification; together with a discussion of our modern films), *DYYS*, October 1986: 32–38; see also the favourable mention by Peng Jiajin in *DYXZ*, 1986.6: 86.
35. Wrongly attributed in the first edition of the book (Hong Kong: Far Eastern Economic Review, 1986) to Zhang Ziliang. The synopsis was compiled in May 1985 for a screening of *TYE* at the British Embassy in Peking under the sponsorship of the International Society at the initiative of the Swedish Embassy, and later distributed privately.
36. I am most grateful to the Swedish Film Institute for supplying publicity materials and press clippings.
37. I am most grateful to Jean Wakefield and Geremie Barmé for supplying publicity materials and press clippings from the Australian release, which the latter also helped very largely to arrange.
38. From programme notes, Harvard Film Archive (September to October 1987; see also *The Harvard Independent*, 29 October 1987: 13. Better documentation for *TYE* was provided at the Boston Museum of Fine Arts "New Chinese Cinema: The Revolution of Style" season in May 1988).

9. The Director
(1952 to the Present)

The extraordinary success of his first film transformed Chen Kaige into a national celebrity within a few months and within a year to an internationally known art film director. *The Yellow Earth*, however, was not the only film of the Chinese new wave, nor the only controversial work in the arts. It is possible that part of the reason for the publicity given to the film has to do with Chen Kaige's personality and eloquence, his network among his contemporaries in literature and the arts, his family's standing in the film world, and their connections within the cultural bureaucracy. While it remains difficult to assess the weight of these factors, this chapter is an attempt to give a brief sketch of the director's background and present circumstances. Except where otherwise credited, it is based on my own observations and conversations with Chen Kaige and his family since 1982.[1]

Chen Kaige's family comes from two very different traditions in China. His father, Chen Huaikai 陳懷皚 [Chen Huaiai], came from a small village of about eight hundred families outside Fuzhou 福州 . Following Chinese custom, Chen Kaige's "place of origin" is still formally given as Shouzhan 首占 village, Changle 長樂 county, Fujian. Changle had always been a poor area, and one in every two families had a relative who had left China to seek a better living overseas. Chen Huaikai's father was a carpenter, and his mother grew vegetables for market; both were illiterate. Huaikai, born in 1920, was the eldest child and was able to attend school. There were two younger brothers, of whom one died young; the other went to Taiwan, and a younger sister went to Malaysia as a bride to an Overseas Chinese. The younger children helped support the family.

Official accounts stress Chen Huaikai's humble background, as do his own family. Chen Kaige has also been known to claim, however, that his father's family were high officials under the Qing dynasty. There is not necessarily a contradiction here, since social mobility was probably more common in traditional China than in the last forty years.

Chen Kaige's mother, Liu Yanchi 劉燕馳, came from a very different background. Her family was originally from Yinjiazhuang 殷家莊 in Shandong 山東, and Chen Kaige has inherited the big frame typical of the Shandongese; he also likes to tell his friends that his mother's family is descended from the Yin, one of the ruling dynasties (or tribes) in ancient China. Liu Yanchi was born in Nanking in 1928. Her family was engaged in the construction business and was quite wealthy. Every day she was driven to her exclusive girls' school in the family's motor car, but some of the more adventurous of her fellow pupils had formed a communist cell, and Yanchi became a member of the Party in 1946. Other members of the family joined up with the Nationalists, and withdrew with them to Taiwan after 1949.

In the early period of the war of resistance Chen Huaikai took part in theatrical work in Fujian, and in 1941 he was accepted in the National Drama School in Nanking. Among his teachers at that time were the famous leftwing dramatists Hong Shen 洪深 and Cao Yu 曹禺. After graduation, he was kept on as a teacher, but he was dismissed in 1948 for taking part in the student movement. By this time he had met Liu, already a Party member. Threatened with immanent arrest for their leftwing activities, Chen and Liu left Nanking in October for Shijiazhuang 石家莊, capital of one of the Liberated areas in north China. Chen became the head of the drama group in the Third Cultural Troupe of the

College of Art in the Huabei 華北 (North China) University, where he also taught stage direction. Liu tried her hand at scriptwriting and occasionally performed as a singer.

Chen and Liu went to Peking in 1949, just before the capital was taken over by the PLA, and were married the same year. In 1950, now in the Film Bureau in the Ministry of Culture, Chen began work as an assistant director. Over the next few years, he was co-assistant director in films like *Family* (家) and *New Year's Sacrifice* (祝福). He was eventually posted to Peking Film Studio, and given his first independent directing opportunity in 1957. Meanwhile, Liu was first made responsible for organizing scripts in the Film Bureau and later transferred to the scriptwriting department of Peking Film Studio. In the early 1960s her health began to deteriorate, however, and although she continued to work at home, she was obliged to rest most of the day.

Chen Huaikai has been involved in some of modern China's best-known films. In the 1950s and 1960s he was director or co-director on films such as *Song of Youth* (青春之歌) and *Women Generals of the Yang Family* (楊門女將). *Women Generals of the Yang Family* is a film of a traditional Chinese opera, and Chen Huaikai became an expert in this genre. In 1974, during the latter half of the Cultural Revolution, he was co-director of *Haixia* 海峽 , and in early 1976 he was given responsibility for filming a series of famous performances of traditional Chinese opera (requested, according to rumour, by Mao Zedong for his private viewing). In 1977, immediately after the fall of the Gang of Four, he was co-director of *The Great River Rushes on* (大河奔流), and continues to direct a variety of modern, historical and opera films.[2]

Chen Kaige, their first child, was born in Peking on 12 August 1952, and his sister, Chen Kaiyan, on 29 July 1954. Kaiyan recalls clearly that the children were brought up to believe that achievement was the main goal in life, far more important than one's personal well-being. During the 1950s, the family lived in a courtyard house in Xinjiekou 新街口 , in the west city. Kaige went first to a nursery-kindergarten in 1954, and then to primary school in 1959. The primary school was attached to Peking Normal University and therefore one of the better primary schools in Peking. In 1965 he was admitted to his local school, Number 4 High, also one of the key high schools in Peking. Many of the pupils were from families of leading members of the Party and government, and Kaige, formally classified as coming from a cadre family, could also be counted as having a solid background: with his mother's pre-Liberation Party membership and the glamour of his father's position as a well-known film director, his social status seems desirably high. Nevertheless, he felt he was not on equal terms with his even more highly placed schoolmates, and did not have close friends among them. Two years senior to him at the school were two boys who later became his friends, Zhao Zhenkai 趙振開 and Zhong Acheng 鍾阿城 . (Zhao Zhenkai, under the penname Bei Dao 北島 , became one of the best-known of the new poets; Zhong Acheng, under the penname Ah Cheng 阿城 , became one of the best-known of the new fiction writers.) Like Chen Kaige, they were from very respectable but not top-level families.

The Cultural Revolution began with preliminary skirmishes in the literary and art world in late 1965, and schools throughout the country were virtually closed down, at least for ordinary educational purposes, by the end of the school year in July 1966. For Chen Kaige, finishing his last year in junior middle school, it put an end to his formal education for the next twelve years, and he has since felt he has never really made up for the two years of senior middle school that he missed. In retrospect, he also considers that the educational system of the 1950s and early 1960s was very poor, and he was lucky in a way to have escaped from its stultifying influence. His sister, who had only one year at junior middle school, regrets her lack of formal education more keenly.

134

As the schools became taken over by revolutionaries and rebels, Chen Kaige at first became an enthusiastic Red Guard. Later, because his father had been a member of the Nationalist Party, the son was not permitted to continue in the increasingly factionalized movement, and for the better part of two years, 1966 to 1968, he spent his time either reading or playing basketball. Although the books and the basketball were to play unexpectedly influential roles in his later life, the isolation must also have had an effect on his personality, leading him to develop a strong sense of the social injustice which had been visited on him, to feel self-doubt about his own social standing and personal worth, and to devise, consciously or unconsciously, methods of self-protection.

Chen Kaige recalls that at this time his morale was low and that he would often feel depressed. Mostly he would read the history books he found at home, returning again and again to the Han dynasty *Records of the Historian*.[3] He was also very fond of the eighteenth century novel *Dream of Red Mansions*,[4] in which he found a rich cultural life almost unknown to his generation. He claimed later that these books taught him to realize that people's troubles and joys are very small, and that this awareness deeply affected his attitude towards life, so that he was unable to be either extremely happy or extremely sad, knowing how transitory these emotions are. He also came to feel that there was a very great difference between the Chinese of Sima Qian's time and the present. The men of the past seemed to be much braver, to have a greater ability to live and more self-knowledge than the adults he saw around him, and he attributed this to the fact that civilization in those days had not developed far enough to suppress a more natural and instinctive response to life.[5]

In the spring of 1968, following the intense urban violence of the summer of '67, the great movement of youth from the cities and towns to the countryside began. Whole schools and neighbourhoods were organized into teams and sent down to more or less desolate areas of the country, and trains carrying two or three thousand EYs steamed across the length and breadth of China. In the two years 1968 to 1970 some five million junior and senior school students, ages ranging from thirteen to eighteen, were sent to the countryside, especially from the major cities.[6] One destination marked out for the EYs was the sub-tropical jungle of south-west China, especially the so-called Dai Autonomous Zhou of Xishuangbanna 西雙版納傣族自治州 in the south of Yunnan 雲南 , where an ambitious scheme was underway to grow rubber in defiance of foreign belief that the Chinese mainland was unsuitable for tropical crops. By the mid-1970s, about four hundred thousand EYs had settled in Yunnan, about one-quarter of them on state farms.[7]

In the first months of this movement, many of the participants, including Chen Kaige, were volunteers, believing that it would mean only a spell of one or two years.[8] In this early period of dispersal, it was also possible for some students to choose their own destination, especially volunteers.[9] Instead of going with his classmates, therefore, Chen Kaige teamed up with a few friends to go to Xishuangbanna in June 1968 to live and work on a state farm in the mountains planting rubber. He has written about this period in the filmscript *We Called It Hope Valley* (我們叫它希望谷) (originally entitled *Opium Valley*).[10]

Again, we can only speculate about the effects of this period on Chen Kaige's development. Presumably it gave him a long awaited chance to exercise the kind of social leadership he was initially trained in and which later he employed in his work as a director. It also taught him the invigorating effects of hard work and intense concentration on the task at hand. More importantly still, it showed him, at least in hindsight, that life pushed to the edges did not resemble the abstract political entities he had been brought up to believe in. Some EYs sent to rural areas found at least an area of personal freedom away from the control of school and Youth

League supervision, but life on the state farms for Chen Kaige and his friends was more strictly disciplined and privation more intense.[11] Friendship was some kind of consolation. In 1969 he met Zhong Acheng, who was in the neighbouring team of the same state farm in Jinghong 景洪. Like the characters in the latter's short stories, he came to realize in a very personal and practical way that hunger was man's most basic emotion, and food his most basic need.

According to Chen Kaige in 1986, it was his early training as a basketball player that rescued him after two years as a rubber planter. He was lying on his bed one day at noon resting when a soldier came in looking for a Chen Kaige. When he identified himself, he was asked if he'd like to join the army. In those days, joining the army was regarded as a very special privilege, and as a rule one needed both connections and a special talent to qualify. It turned out that he had attracted attention because of his height, and when he admitted being a player he was told to report to army barracks the next day at six a.m. According to Chen Kaige, a request to enrol him in the PLA was forwarded to Peking but rejected because of his father's background; by this time, however, the new team member had apparently become too valuable an acquisition to lose, and the rejection was ignored. Some romanticism may have crept into this account as it was related to me in 1986. Chen Kaiyan also spent part of the Cultural Revolution in the PLA, and it is possible that strings were pulled for both brother and sister.

Chen Kaige spent five years in the army, stationed outside Kunming 昆明. Life in the army was not all basketball. In the spring of 1971, for instance, there was intense activity along the Laos border, and the area remained a very sensitive one throughout the seventies. In the autumn of 1971, following the defection of Minister of Defence Lin Biao, there was a substantial purge in army personnel. Leadership changes, however, did not affect

Chen Kaige's life at this stage, and photographs of him as a soldier show him looking strong, confident and happy. In several ways the army was a good unit to belong to in those days. For a start, it gave a basis for Party membership, and Chen Kaige was admitted into the Chinese Communist Party in 1974. Again, it was relatively easy to get out of, at least for people in his position.[12] In 1975 he was transferred back to Peking, where he was first assigned work in an airconditioning factory. It was at the factory he met Sun Jialin 孫家林, his future wife. Later he got a better job at the Film Processing Factory, across the road from the Peking Film Studio. About the same time, he got to know Zhao Zhenkai, who was gaining a reputation (in limited circles) as an underground poet.

Like other cultural units, the film industry in 1975 was re-establishing itself with modified Cultural Revolution policies.[13] The first true feature film since 1966 (i.e. not based on a model opera or ballet) was made in 1973, and several new feature films came out in 1974. As Chen Huaikai and other directors from the 1950s and 1960s were set to work again, the studios began to realize that new blood would also be needed. As a young man, Chen Kaige had not necessarily always had the ambition to become a film director, despite his film background and the tendency still in China for children to follow their parents' profession. Nevertheless he had always felt that film-making was very suitable for him. "Films are a kind of dream, and since I've been young I've been a dreamer. Sometimes—often—in real life I don't know how to reach people; through films I can."[14] In his three years back in Peking, the chances of his becoming a film-maker advanced and receded with the waves of factional struggles that governed all forms of public life. Finally, after the death of Mao in 1976, new policies were put into effect in education and the arts. His chance had come.

In 1978, Chen Kaige sat for the entrance examination for the Peking Film Academy. Like other colleges and universities throughout the country, it was throwing open its door to those whose education had been interrupted, holding competitive exams for the first time since the mid-1960s. The first session took the form of an interview about the candidate's views on literature and art. Chen Kaige found out later that he nearly failed this interview. The five teachers sitting behind a desk at the front of the room had so unnerved him that (very typically), he adopted such an aloof air that the examiners thought he was looking down on them. Fortunately, five days later, he had an opportunity to assure them that this was not so. By the second session, the number of applicants had been reduced to one thousand.

Chen Kaige was applying to enter the directing department, and on the second day of the examinations, he found himself competing against a hundred people for this department. At the first session this day, the candidates were asked to watch a film and then write an analysis and evaluation. The film was *Heroic Sons and Daughters* (英雄兒女), which he, like most of the others, had seen many times before. He had, however, his own ideas on the film, and wrote very fast in the ninety minutes allotted. At the next session, which took place the following day, the candidates were given twenty minutes to prepare stories, which they were then to relate to the examiners. Chen Kaige found this very easy: he knew many stories from his life in the army, and as he related them, he himself felt very moved by them. He saw that the teachers were impressed, and knew that he had won.

Finally there was an exam in acting. For this he felt very nervous, and for several days he was coached by the director Xie Jin 謝晉 , practising every night. In the examination room this time he was able to control his nervousness, and faced the teachers relatively calm and relaxed.

The successful candidates entered the academy in September 1978. There were only 153 of them altogether, but the atmosphere within this small group was highly competitive. Everyone wanted to be posted to Peking upon graduation, but only one half of them could hope for such good luck (or had the right connections to ensure it). As a result, there was not much sense of mutual help: the students did not discuss their studies much, nor go to watch each other's student exercises.[15] The good side of this was that students like Chen Kaige became very independent in their outlook. Not all of the students were in fact looking forward to careers as active creative artists, but hoped to become officials or critics in the film world. Such students may have been more interested in holding forth, but Chen Kaige felt that to be a director it wasn't necessary to talk a lot about films. The head of the directing department at the academy recalls that Chen Kaige took rather little part in student life, and was not considered an outstanding student among the 23 budding directors in his class. He was very studious, however, and always reading. Compared to others in his age group, he was serious about his education and eventually reached a fairly high level by sheer application.[16] Interviewed in his third year at the academy, he said that he had particularly enjoyed the scriptwriting class in the first year.[17]

Chen Kaige confirms that he spent most of his spare time reading. At that time students at the academy were normally four to a room, but after some time his three roommates moved out, and every night he would read till very late. He does not regard his heavy reading then as a virtue; it was just that there were few other amusements. In the late 1970s there was a sudden craze for dancing, which the authorities at first permitted, and many of the students at the academy were always arranging dancing parties. Chen Kaige, however, because of his size, felt clumsy on his feet and though he knew how to dance, rarely went to these parties. His conflicting feelings at this time are depicted in his short story, "Jiamian wuhui" 假面舞會 (The masked dance), where there is something of him in both the successful protagonist, who gets the girl, and the clumsy antagonist, who loses her.[18] He comments that at that time, many people had learnt the need for self-protection.[19]

His first independent work was the television film "Xiang zuotian gaobie" 向昨天告別 (Say goodbye to yesterday), which was completed in 1980. It was made for Fujian television at the suggestion of some classmates from Fujian, and counted as part of his pre-graduation work experience. After graduation he was first given a temporary assignment to the Youth Film Studio in Peking, from September 1982 to September 1983. He was then given his permanent assignment to Peking Film Studio as an assistant director, and worked on two films, both directed by Huang Jianzhong: *A Small Boat* (一葉小舟) and *Twenty-six Girls* (二十六個姑娘). Neither film pleased him. He also spent some time in Yunnan again working on Wang Junzheng's 王君正 *Brother Echo* (應聲阿哥). At this time there were already seventy directors on the books at Peking Film Studio, many more than necessary to complete the studio's quota of about twenty films a year. In the normal course of events, Chen Kaige would have been in his fifties before he had a chance to direct on his own. He had an income (at that time, about ¥50 a month), but nowhere to live except in a room in his parents' apartment (now in studio housing behind the adminstration buildings and sets). After his marriage to Sun Jialin in January 1983, they lived in this same small room, their two desks side by side. Sun Jialin had also entered college to become a civil engineer specializing in solar power, and at this time was working on the design of solar panels for a new luxury hotel in Peking.

Chen Kaige's participation in *The Yellow Earth* came with a phone call in September 1983 from Zhang Yimou in Guangxi. From November 1983 to August 1984, Chen Kaige then concentrated all his energies on the film. Between November and January he shuttled betwen Guangxi, Shaanxi and Peking. In January he was briefly in Peking to see off his wife on her departure to take up a scholarship in Canada, and returned in February to work on the revision of the script. Although the script was not his original idea, a comparison of the different versions in its transition from essay to screenplay to finished script reveals the extent to which Chen Kaige transformed it into a highly personal creation. He left Peking in mid-March and apart from brief visits did not return until late August.

After finishing *The Yellow Earth*, Chen Kaige had little time to rest. First the delay in releasing the film gave him the opportunity to make further minor revisions. The cloud hanging over the film and his own private uncertainties also prevented him from relaxing. At the same time he was already wondering about his second film. Then in the autumn of 1984 he was asked to make a television film for the air force. The air display that had been planned for the grand parade to commemorate the 35th anniversary of the People's Republic in 1984 had been a failure because of the heavy pollution which obscured the planes as they flew in formation over Tiananmen. The film was called "Qiangxing qifei" 强行起飞 (Forced takeoff). Zhang Yimou was the cinematographer. A brief note in *Enlightenment Daily* in February notes its completion and explains the circumstances under which it was made;[20] a review by Zheng Dongtian appeared in *Literature and the Arts* in April.[21] The Flying Asparas (National Television Drama Awards) were announced in June: two first class awards, no second class awards, and three third class awards, including one for "Forced takeoff".[22] It was shown on television several times in 1985 and 1986.

A major event in Chen Kaige's career was the invitation for him and Zhang Yimou to visit Hong Kong in connection with the screening of *The Yellow Earth* at the 1985 Hong Kong International Film Festival. Danny Yung had come up from Hong Kong in the latter half of 1984 to make selections for the following year's festival, and was very favourably impressed by several films made by members of the class of '78, including *The Yellow*

Earth. The final selection was made in mid-December. In order to get *The Yellow Earth* plus Chen Kaige and Zhang Yimou to Hong Kong, Danny Yung was obliged to make some concessions, but in early April all three turned up in Hong Kong to a rapturous reception.

The film had already received a great deal of praise in Peking from younger colleagues and foreign critics, but the overwhelming response it met with in Hong Kong dispelled any last doubts Chen Kaige may have had about the fundamental truth of his vision. It also brought him and Zhang Yimou into an international circle of film-makers and critics. Henceforth, what happened to *The Yellow Earth* and its creators was no longer just of interest to the Chinese themselves and a small band of China-watchers, but also to an ever-expanding world audience. Chen Kaige's confidence and eloquence in the late night seminar on *The Yellow Earth* and in his interviews with the Hong Kong press and foreign film festival organizers certainly added to his stature in Hong Kong and abroad. In a more personal way, Chen Kaige was also deeply moved by the opportunity to meet with young film artists in Hong Kong and talk with them with complete freedom and informality about film-making, art and life.

Chen Kaige began working on his second film, *The Grand Parade*, in the spring of 1985. It was to be produced by Guangxi again, and filmed again with Zhang Yimou and He Qun. Again he rewrote the script himself, in his usual fashion holing up in a small hotel in the west city for long uninterrupted sessions of intense concentration in May and June. In July the crew moved to Hubei 湖北 for shooting on location. Working conditions were in some ways even more frustrating and arduous than for *The Yellow Earth*. Chen Kaige admits to losing his temper several times, and on his birthday was battling against a bout of influenza. At the back of his mind was always the problem of living up to *The Yellow Earth*: he felt that no matter how good his second film was, it would automatically be considered inferior to his first. He and Zhang Yimou agreed it had to be different, with the emphasis on motion, where *The Yellow Earth* was static; with a lot of dialogue, where *The Yellow Earth* was sparing; with many characters, where *The Yellow Earth* had few; and with the small hills and rolling plains of Hubei instead of the mountains and gullies of Shaanxi.

Chen Kaige returned to Peking at the end of August, expecting to join a film delegation to Montreal for the showing of *The Yellow Earth* and *Border Town*. At the last moment the delegation was cancelled. Other invitations to the Locarno, Edinburgh and Rotterdam festivals were refused on his behalf by the Film Board. However, Chen Kaige and Zhang Yimou were allowed to accept invitations to Hawaii for the East-West Center Award competition in December 1985. After collecting their awards, they went on to the United States mainland, where they stayed for almost two months in New York and Philadelphia before returning to Peking. As on his earlier visit to Hong Kong, Chen Kaige found the experience very exhilarating.

The Grand Parade was first screened in autumn 1985. Despite rumours that this time Chen Kaige was playing safe, the official film world was not happy with it. The film was then shown to the army, which was even less pleased, senior officers complaining that the PLA was portrayed like the Japanese army. Chen Kaige himself was not satisfied with some of the effects, especially the sound, and spent most of the spring and summer of 1986 reworking it. The new version was completed on 10 August 1986, and privately screened several times over the next few days. On 14 August, he left for Yunnan to look for sites for his third film.

Since the completion of *The Yellow Earth*, Chen Kaige had often thought about going overseas to study—not as a student but as a director "between films." However, his plan was always to make three films before taking an extended leave of absence, since the second film was bound to be unfavourably compared with *The Yellow Earth*. (It was in fact generally regarded as a flop except for Zhang Yimou's cinematography.[23]) At one point he favoured Zhang Xianliang's 張賢亮 *Lühuashu* 綠化樹 (Mimosa), and over the spring he had several discussions with Xi'an Film Studio on this and other ideas.

In April–May he took time off from *The Grand Parade* to go to the United States for the second time, travelling to the west coast and Texas as well as to New York and Philadelphia, and at the end of June, he was invited to Tokyo for pre-release publicity for *The Yellow Earth*. On his return to Peking, he left almost immediately for one of several visits to Xi'an to discuss plans for the third film. In July, he and his wife, who had returned briefly from Canada, filed for divorce. Later the same month, Chen Kaige played the role of captain of the imperial guard in the opening scenes in Bernardo Bertolucci's *The Last Emperor*. The two directors had met early in July and expressed admiration for each other's work. Bertolucci was also struck by Chen Kaige's physical appearance and presence, and pressed him to act in his film. Chen Kaige learnt to ride a horse and overcame the effects of a heavy cold to play his part.

During these summer months he made the decision to base his third film on "Haizi wang" 孩子王 (The king of children), a story written by his old friend Ah Cheng;[24] another old friend, Chen Maiping, was pressed into preparing a filmscript that could be shown to the people at Xi'an. Xi'an Film Studio finally agreed to produce it in August, and work began immediately afterwards. While on location in Xishuangbanna at the end of 1986, Chen Kaige heard the good news that *The Grand Parade* was finally approved for public release.

At the end of 1986, Chen Kaige was making ¥92 a month and still lived in his overcrowded room in his parents' apartment, where he continually mislaid important letters and materials for lack of space. With a constant stream of phone calls and visitors, his father, who had no office either, found himself acting as his son's secretary. His main possessions were a bicycle, a stereo set, a good Japanese camera that was presented to him that summer, and a videocamera and recorder. Although fame had brought him little material benefit except the chance to travel abroad, he received his salary regularly every month, whether or not making a film and even whether or not his work was acceptable to the authorities.

In August 1986, Chen Kaige commented in answer to questions from an American researcher on Asian cinema that in some ways a Chinese film director is better off than an American.[25] On visits to Universal Film Studio and Paramount in the spring of 1986, he saw for himself the commercial pressure under which directors in the United States have to operate, and wondered if the superiority of European films over United States films might be due to comparative lack of such pressure. Even more important was the influence a director could have in China. Precisely because the authorities pay so much attention to literature and the arts, the artist's life is potentially of much greater import than in the West. If *The Yellow Earth* had been made outside China it would not have had anything like the same impact. Unfortunately, he added, most writers and artists in China lack the courage to defy the authorities and exercise their tremendous social influence.

Asked about the difference between Chinese films now and in the past, Chen Kaige replied that in the past, Chinese directors regarded the cinema as a profession: if you asked them why they made such and such a film they would not know how to answer. Today's directors use films to express themselves. Films are a thing in themselves, not a vehicle for something else. For example, *Wreath under the Mountain* (高山下的花環) was made to show what war was like, but if you take away this purpose, there is no film left. The Chinese directors who have most influenced him were Wu Yonggang 吳永剛 and Fei Mu 費穆 from the 1930s and 1940s.

In the past, Chinese directors used realism to represent dreams; he wants to use dreams to represent reality. He wants to make films that can communicate things that move him, so that other people can be moved. In *The Yellow Earth* he was able to say some things that he wanted to say. Not everyone understands his films. He is not a teacher. Therefore his films can teach something.

The most important failure of contemporary Chinese films is that though they stress content, they are not always honest in the way they show human relationships. This needs to be changed. For example, the position of women is shown in a feudal way in most Chinese films, as for instance in the film *Autumn in Spring* (春天裏的秋天) (1985). When the young man leaves the woman in this film, he obviously has the director's approval although his behaviour is very feudal.

The most important message of *The Yellow Earth* is that people should live a human life, not a life based on illusion. Whether rich or poor, people still have their human dignity. He also wanted to show through Cuiqiao that to do what no-one else has done before is always a risk, but that this risk must be undertaken. The static shots, which signify the stasis in Chinese history as well as showing the beauty of the landscape, express the need for change in China.

The Yellow Earth was a film about food; *The King of Children* is to be a film about culture.

The King of Children was completed in the summer of 1987 and given immediate permission for general release. Though praised by some local and foreign critics and entered at the Cannes Film Festival that year, it failed to make the impact of *The Yellow Earth*.[26] More obviously didactic than the earlier films, it contains a relatively finite critique of traditional Chinese culture but delivers it in obscure images, in contrast to the wonderfully clear images in *The Yellow Earth* which evoke a range of intellectual and emotional responses even in the director's own mind.

In the autumn of 1987 Chen Kaige left for New York, where he has lived to date except for a brief visit home when his mother died in 1988. He continues to be identified chiefly as the director of *The Yellow Earth*.

Notes

1. I first met Chen Kaige in 1982. From then until January 1986, when I left China for Oslo, we would meet usually at least once a week except when he was on location in the summer of 1984 and 1985 or when one of us was out of the country. I returned to Peking for two months in the summer of 1986, spent five weeks in the winter of '86–'87 in Peking, Xishuangbanna (on location with *Haizi wang*) and Xi'an, and seven weeks in the summer of 1987 in Peking and Xi'an (during post-production processing on *Haizi wang*). During these periods we met frequently, sometimes every day. I also interviewed Chen Kaige in New York in August 1988. Especially after leaving for New York in 1987, Chen Kaige has been interviewed many times, the longest interview appearing in the Chinese edition of *Playboy* (May 1988: 42–50). Since these accounts of his life and work differ in some ways from earlier versions, I have not incorporated into the present text any such material published after 1986.

2. The biography of Chen Huaikai (he prefers this pronunciation to Huaiai, and used the same character in the original versions of his children's names) as given in *Zhongguo yishujia cidian* 中國藝術家辭典 (Dictionary of Chinese artists) (Hunan renmin chubanshe 湖南人民出版社, Changsha 長沙, 1981: 262–63) is in several details inaccurate and incomplete. The above account is based on corrections to the dictionary entry made for me by Chen Huaikai in 1987 and several interviews with him in 1986 and 1987.

3. *Shi ji* 史記 by Sima Qian 司馬遷 (c. 145–c. 86 B.C.), a comprehensive history of pre-Han China.

4. *Hong lou meng* 紅樓夢 by Cao Xueqin 曹雪芹 (1716?–1764).
5. Conversations with the author in summer 1986. Chen Kaige's experiences and reactions at this time bear a striking resemblance to the case studies in Anita Chan's *Children of Mao: Personality Development and Political Activism in the Red Guard Generation* (London: Macmillan, 1985): the pressure at high school for students to become politically active, intensifying during 1962 to 1966 (p. 52); the tendency for children of professionals to be under heavy pressure also from their families (pp. 120–21); and the tension that resulted from conflicting demands for activism and self-abnegation (pp. 63, 128). The following passage is worth quoting in full:

> Several interviewees, to prove that their inner integrity and revolutionary devotion were far superior to the petty activism around them, copied the harsh physical tempering to which the young Mao had subjected himself. They practised exercise routines that required austere, stringent self-discipline, and cultivated a self-image that through this self-tempering they were different, tougher, more genuine than the rest of their classmates, especially the league members. They told themselves that they were toughening their willpower for a 'revolutionary' moment that would come one day; and that when it came they would be able to achieve something truly great, unlike those 'docile tools' such as Lei Feng who limited themselves to being no more than a screw. The Cultural Revolution would soon provide them with their long-awaited opportunity to act out their dreams on a grand violent scale. Violence, and the risk of death, would become to them a liberating experience. (p. 69)

6. Thomas P. Bernstein, *Up to the Mountains and Down to the Villages; The Transfer of Youth from Urban to Rural China* (New Haven: Yale University Press, 1977): 31.
7. Bernstein, *Up to the Mountains*: 69.
8. Bernstein, *Up to the Mountains*: 89.
9. Bernstein, *Up to the Mountains*: 115.
10. Chen Kaige, Liu Qing and Peng Xiner, "Women jiao ta Xiwanggu", *DYCZ*, no. 3, 1984; reprinted in *DYXK*, no. 4, 1984 (August 1984): 2–27.
11. Bernstein, *Up to the Mountains*: 113.
12. Bernstein, *Up to the Mountains*: 243.

13. See Paul Clark, "The Film Industry in the 1970s", in McDougall, *Popular Chinese Literature and Performing Arts*, 177–96.

14. From a conversation with Chen Kaige in January 1986.

15. From a conversation with Chen Kaige, July 1987; cf. interview with Rayns quoted above, pp. 120–21.

16. Interview with Zheng Dongtian, August 1986.

17. In an interview by Paul Clark, November 1980 in Peking.

18. Xia Ge 夏歌 (pseud.) "Jiamian wuhui", *Jintian* 今天 , 9 (no. 3, 1980): 11–19; English translation by McDougall in *2PLUS2* (Lausanne), 1986: 219–27.

19. Conversation with Chen Kaige, November 1985.

20. *GMRB*, 3 February 1985: 2.

21. *WYB*, April 1985: 63–64.

22. *GMRB*, 18 June 1985: 1.

23. See for example the review in *New York Times* by Walter Goodman, 15 March 1988, where it was shown as part of the New Directors/New Films Festival at the Museum of Modern Arts, and Derek Malcolm, *The Guardian*, 13 August 1987.

24. For my English translation of the original story, see Ah Cheng, *Three Kings*, London: Collins Harvill, 1990; for my English translation of the filmscript, see Chen Kaige, *King of Children*, London: Faber and Faber, 1989 (the latter contains unauthorized and erroneous changes to my manuscript).

25. Interview with Chen Kaige by Gina Marchetti, August 1986. Working from my own notes of the interview, I have rearranged the sequence of questions and answers. See also Gina Marchetti, "Two from China's Fifth Generation: Interviews with Chen Kaige and Tian Zuangzhuang", *Asian Cinema* (Murdoch, W.A.), II. 1 (1988/89): 128–134.

26. This is not the place for an appraisal of *The King of Children*, which has already gathered its own substantial bibliography. Western press reports to date suggest that like *TYE*, it can be mistaken for a charming rural idyll by Western audiences; see, for instance, Thomas Quinn Curtiss characterizing it as "an engaging novelty" in *International Herald Tribune*, 21–22 May, 1988: 7.

10. Conclusions

The controversies and the evaluations are now part of the history of *The Yellow Earth*. The controversies and the evaluations are also part of the further evaluation of the film: the fact that it has meant so many different things to so many different kinds of people is also a testimony, to Western eyes at least, to the artistic subtlety and philosophical depth of the film, just as its appeal to audiences unconscious of or uninterested in the film's political messages is testimony to its cinematic skill. In turn, the evaluations have become part of the controversies, as the film's conservative detractors suspect the praise heaped on it by both domestic and foreign reviewers, while veiling their own rejection of the film with misleading criticisms of its authenticity.

With such a wide range of responses it is difficult to sum up the impact of *The Yellow Earth* at home and abroad. A few central positions are clear. At home, senior film directors and critics, other high-ranking cultural figures and top Party leaders attacked the film primarily for its implied criticism of Party policy in regard to the peasants during the Yenan period, and by natural extension, its implied critique of the Party's economic and political policies from the 1930s up to and including the present. It was said that the film-makers were too young and inexperienced to pass comment on the crucial issues of the Party's relations with the peasants at that time or since. The fact that the film managed to offend both orthodox and reformist factions within the leadership, however, indicates the significance of its critique and the unlikelihood of its being merely superficial. A second cause for offence was the film's departure from conventional film aesthetics, the open-ended nature of its symbolism and its deliberately limited appeal to a cinematically sophisticated audience. However, I know of no case where the film was attacked on the latter grounds where the primary target was not in fact the former. On the other hand, a common description of the film by the more defensive of its critics was that the film-makers paid too much attention to the "artistic form" of the film to the neglect of its "content." This is probably the most seriously deceptive of all the many inaccurate and mis-leading remarks made about the film since its appearance.

The critics of *The Yellow Earth*, however, were reluctant to draw public attention to the film's implied attacks on Party policy, so that much of the hostile criticism was necessarily oblique. The film's supporters in the public media were obliged to be equally discreet, so that their enthusiasm for the film's political messages and artistic breakthroughs was also expressed in code words such as "deep reflection" and "search". Since the evaluation of the film was a political commitment, many of the film's supporters pro-tected themselves in print by acknowledging, without being spe-cific, that "of course" the film had its faults. Vagueness here sometimes appears to be a convenient cover, giving possible refer-ence either to the film's technical shortcomings or to its ideological independence. In contrast, some radical interpretations circulated by word of mouth attributed to the film very concrete political messages. The film-makers themselves of course were not respon-sible for all the interpretations imposed on the film, but as the film moved into its "second life",[1] these interpretations became part of its meaning.

As the film itself and information about it became more famil-iar, it became easier to identify the film's technical shortcomings (e.g. clumsy postsynchronization). On the other hand, it became more difficult for critics to claim that the rain prayer scene or other details of the plot were inauthentic. The film's supporters also had a strong emotional appeal in their arguments that the film-makers were, in fact, well qualified to comment on peasant life, having spent a large part of their youth in the countryside during the Cultural Revolution. One member of the older generation noted that although Chen Kaige had spent only a brief time in Shaanbei, he had captured the life there better than the Yenan writers of the period. Statements by the film-makers themselves about the value of their Cultural Revolution experiences (in contrast to the "scar" school of writers, who emphasised only the waste and suffering of those years) also helped to give the film respectability and were widely quoted.

At the beginning, the film's supporters were very much on the defensive about the film's apparent lack of audience appeal. It was not until the summer of 1985 that film officials admitted that the cinema audience in general was rapidly declining, so that *The Yellow Earth*, in fact, was not trailing far behind the more conventional type of film favoured by the authorities.[2] When special art cinemas were finally established in Shanghai and Canton in the summer and autumn of 1985 and *The Yellow Earth* and other new wave films were exhibited there and in other big cities, these films finally found their audience. It is impossible to establish precisely who this audience included, but it is generally believed that it consisted of urban intellectuals, especially the young and those engaged in literature and the arts. It is equally difficult to say what this audience appreciated most about the film. On the basis of random conversations with such people, my impression is that Shao Mujun's comments from August 1985 may be taken as representative. He thought that the film itself was not to blame if its audience was initially small; it had its faults, but a "blind search for form" was not one of them. The significance of *The Yellow Earth* was not in its breakthroughs in technique or imagery, all of which have been used before in world cinema, but is rather in its deep reflections on Chinese history and in its search for new meaning in the Chinese national character.[3]

The question of derivation from Western cinema was a rather touchy one. Chinese and Western interviewers and critics constantly speculated on the influence of foreign films on *The Yellow Earth*.[4] It has been compared to classics like Eisenstein's *Viva Mexico!* and Flannery's *Nanook of the North*,[5] and also to Shindo Kaneto's *The Island*,[6] Antonioni's *Red Desert*,[7] Renais' *Last Year at Marienbad*[8] and Fellini's *La Dolce Vita* and *Amacord*.[9] (I would add to this list Pasolini's *Porcile*.) Among Chinese critics (with some exceptions), and to some extent among Western critics also, there is somehow something slightly derogatory in acknowledging foreign influence, and Chen Kaige and Zhang Yimou have always denied substantial debts to foreign films.[10]

On the other hand, and with a wonderful consistency, all parties seem to believe that the influence of traditional Chinese aesthetics, from either high or popular culture, was highly commendable, and Chen Kaige and Zhang Yimou both claim this line of descent (in due union, of course, with life itself). One might therefore suspect the film-makers' dismissals of foreign influence and claims for native inspiration as being somewhat disingenuous. However, in Zhang Yimou's statements we can find evidence of genuine commitment to the principles of traditional Chinese painting and a workable understanding of Taoism; and while Chen Kaige does not quote as freely as Zhang Yimou, his writing is witness to his familiarity with the classical tradition. In their private life, both men shared the passion of their generation for a kind of Western trendiness in clothes and manners, yet both were more at ease at any level of Chinese society than in Peking's foreign enclaves. Intellectually, both felt that they were undereducated in Chinese culture but through private study had managed to compensate for the deficiencies of their schooling (or lack of it). In contrast, while both had extensive knowledge of

Western cinema and were familiar with questions of conflicting values of Chinese and Western civilization, their knowledge of the latter was so patchy that their understanding of Western cinema must necessarily also have been uneven.

There is, of course, an undoubted gap between the new professional film personnel, who had at least limited opportunities to see a range of films from different countries and times, and the majority of the Chinese film audience, which has been restricted to a very limited number of films, from a very limited number of countries, on a very limited number of topics, filmed with a very limited range of techniques. Not all film personnel were cinematically literate in terms of contemporary world film. At times one suspects that the obtuseness shown by certain critics is not to be taken literally; it is apparently never held against orthodox critics that their expressed opinions are simply stupid, and stupidity like vagueness can be a convenient cover. Nevertheless, forms of expression that are now taken for granted in some countries are not necessarily regarded as axiomatically excellent by people unfamiliar with the idiom. Thus, Hao Dazheng feels obliged to argue that concepts may have different layers of meaning; that the plot and external form of *The Yellow Earth* are simple, and if people don't understand it is because they are unaccustomed or lack patience; and that if they get impatient in the cave scenes that's fine, because they should indeed get impatient at the slowness of the peasants' life.[11] Corresponding to the indeterminateness of the imagery, the film can be interpreted as being "about" a range of subjects: again, this was a feature that pleased some, puzzled many more, and irritated most of the authorities.

Evaluation in the Western press was a very different matter altogether. For a start we need not look beyond critical terminology for coded meanings, nor need we assume a wide gap between critical and audience response. Up to the end of 1986, *The Yellow Earth* was rarely shown to a straight commercial audience in the

West but at film festivals, in art cinemas, or for student groups, where opinion was overwhelmingly in its favour. Some British critics were almost ecstatic in their praise on first viewing, but second time round tended to be more critical of technical and artistic lapses in the film. Despite available material about the controversy over the film, they were not particularly interested in or perceptive about its political implications. Some reviewers were sensitive to the remaining political clichés in the film, but only one critic attempted, and at that very indirectly, to take issue with its implied pastoral utopianism and negativism in regard to political reform. In general, the attitude of Western critics could be summed up as that as long as the film-maker's point of view was presented convincingly and did not offend basic human decencies, it was not a matter of concern in a film review.

From this point of view, one could say that the film was a greater success in China than in the West, despite the more lavish praise it received abroad: in other words, if the film-makers' aim was to provoke deeper reflections on Chinese tradition and contemporary history, it achieved this goal to a remarkable degree in China but only partially outside. Inevitably, outside responses were simpler: while many Chinese viewers and sinologists were deeply impressed with the father and son, non-sinologist Western critics tended to be more taken with the charm of Cuiqiao. Western sinologists were otherwise among the film's severest critics abroad, especially after 1985, though some the film's early champions (such as Paul Clark) remained its strong supporters even after many viewings.

The film's reception in Hong Kong fell predictably between domestic and foreign responses. The film's commercial succcess indicates that its artistic sophistication presented no particular problem and that its messages of concern for China's past and present could be understood and welcomed. More familiar with productions from the mainland than their foreign counterparts,

Hong Kong reviewers were quicker to realize the unconventionality of both plot and treatment; they were also less restrained than mainland critics in describing them. An important element in the Hong Kong response was the feeling of patriotic pride aroused by the film's excellence, and the credit then given to the Chinese authorities for permitting such a film to be made and then released outside. In this sense, the film was unintentional propaganda for the Chinese government in its desire for support from the people of Hong Kong in its continuing negotiations with Britain over details on the return of the colony. The ban on the film cancelled out some of this credit which its eventual lifting could not restore.

Returning to the domestic scene, we may consider what impact *The Yellow Earth* may have on film-making and cultural activity in general in China. In the very broadest sense, its international success may have encouraged young film-makers to have more confidence in their ability to produce films of world standard, given the opportunity to prove themselves, and to know that the outside world is waiting for their films. More timid film-makers might shrink from the controversy caused by *The Yellow Earth*, but since nothing very dreadful happened to anyone directly concerned with the film—except notoriety itself—its domestic reception could be seen as stimulating rather than the opposite.

In a narrower sense, the film's influence should be seen in context with the other works it is usually grouped with, the new wave/experimental/fifth generation films such as *One and Eight* and *Hunting Ground*. Most of the critics of *The Yellow Earth* were equally hostile towards all the films in this group, to the extent that some senior film personnel even refused to acknowledge the young film-makers as the "fifth generation" in a legitimate line of descent. By most accounts, the new wave films shared a range of innovative techniques, themes and motifs. Most notably, these include photographic techniques borrowed from Western and

Japanese cinema, more variation and subtlety in lighting and rhythm, more realistic characterization and acting, the introduction of traditional folk customs and the re-examination of the historical period immediately before or after Liberation. *The Yellow Earth* seems to be the only film to have combined all these characteristics, though this in itself is not especially significant. Beyond the new wave, a number of other films made about the same time also featured scenes of peasant rituals and a similar historical setting, such as *Border Town*, *A Woman of Good Family* and *Life*. (*Life* is set in the present but also in Shaanbei, and included a traditional wedding ceremony similar to *The Yellow Earth*'s.[12]) As all of these films appeared within one or two years, it may not be a question of copying but rather a common response to a new atmosphere in Chinese cultural life.

Within this common response of course there were differences. The film *A Woman of Good Family*, from the fourth-generation director Huang Jianzhong, was made at the same time as *The Yellow Earth* and has broad similarities in basic plot and cinematography. In south China on the eve of Liberation, a young woman is married to a small boy (in the south, a woman's labour value was more important than her fertility value, hence the reversal of the northern practice of marrying young girls to grown men). Tormented by sexual longings, she eventually takes a lover and is punished for it by the villagers. The opening scenes in particular are strikingly similar, with both close detail and sweeping shots of the eroded terrain accompanied by roughly-sung local folk song. Despite these common features and some daring erotic images, however, the film leaves an impression of conventionality and superficiality. Ingredients alone do not constitute the excellence of a film: it is the way they are put together. For example, there are several scenes in *A Woman of Good Family* where the child-husband pees; these scenes are prolonged and the camera focusses on the child's penis. The result is a kind of coy sensationalism which draws titters from the audience. The scene with Hanhan singing about the "wetabed husband", on the other hand, is one of the most moving episodes in *The Yellow Earth*.[13] In another scene, Cuiqiao's father goes outside to relieve himself before going to bed; this must be one of the first instances in a Chinese film when an adult urinates at all, yet it is done so simply and naturally that many foreign viewers do not even notice. In details such as these, it seems that the director of *A Woman of Good Family* is manipulating the audience in a way that is either cynical or shallow, so that though these scenes evoke a positive response, it is to the surface meaning and does not lead to further reflection. In the case of *The Yellow Earth*, on the other hand, the surface detail is presented as ordinary and natural (except in occasional moments of melodrama, such as Cuiqiao's wedding night, and in the deliberately stylized drum dance and rain prayer sequences), so that the audience is drawn unobtrusively into sympathy with the characters at the same time as being confronted with powerful descriptive passages with profound and subtle implications.

Primitivism (as it was called by critics) or neo-traditionalism was a new trend in the first half of the 1980s which extended also into the theatre, painting and fiction.[14] In this respect Chinese critics have set *The Yellow Earth* in the context of fiction by Ah Cheng, Shi Tiesheng and Zhang Chengzhi 張承志 , and the paintings of the Sichuan school.[15] Briefly, primitivism or neo-traditionalism may be defined as a search for meaning in neglected areas of traditional Chinese culture, which has its origins in the rustication of urban youth and intellectuals during the Cultural Revolution, and its appeal in its alternative to the bankruptcy of orthodox or Maoist communism, the crass materialism of the "four modernizations" and the alienation of Western literary modernism. The best of the underground writing of the 1970s and the "scar" literature of the immediate post-Mao period, for instance by Bei Dao and his fellow contributors to the unofficial magazine *Today*, represent a return to urban intellectual values such as humanism and modernism after the anti-intellectual wasteland of the Cultural Revolution. It is significant that Ah Cheng, despite his experience as a storyteller in the countryside, did not write fiction for publication in this period.

By 1983 and 1984, disillusionment with modern urban life began to make itself felt among former sent-down youth and intellectuals. Under the impact of this disillusionment, some writers and artists began to re-examine their experiences during the Cultural Revolution and reassess the knowledge they gained at that time of village life and traditional customs. Since this trend seemed to give a more positive view of recent Chinese history, the authorities initially welcomed it, and its potentially subversive nature became apparent only gradually. Ah Cheng and Zhang Chengzhi were both awarded literary prizes in 1984 while *The Yellow Earth* was being greeted with suspicion, but if one may speak of two strands within the neo-traditionalist trend, they came together in 1986 with Chen Kaige's decision to make his third film on Ah Cheng's third story.

An even broader context for *The Yellow Earth*, if one is to assess its future influence more systematically, is the general renaissance in the arts which started as an underground movement in the 1970s. Despite the difference suggested above in outlook between Bei Dao and Chen Kaige, for instance, what they had in common was more significant, both artistically and philosophically, than the common ground shared by Chen Kaige and Huang Jianzhong. Bei Dao's poems and fiction are distinguished by a sense of inevitable tragedy. To a certain extent, the personae of the poems and the characters in the stories are oppressed by a cruel or uncaring society, and their fate is also connected with flaws in their own temperament. Beyond this, however, there is a sense that the whole society in which they exist is doomed, that the fate of the Chinese people is to suffer. The society in which they exist, after all, is created by their fellow humans, so what hope is there for escape when everyone around them suffers from the same wounds? It is this sense of tragedy, despairing and fatalistic, which marks off the more powerful works of the period from representative "scar" stories such as "The Class Teacher" 班主任 and "The Scar" 傷痕 . The Yellow Earth, similarly, is not a socialist tragedy of feudal oppression nor a bourgeois tragedy of personal flaws, but a portrait of the two sides of the Chinese national character in a conflict that seems irresolvable. The fatalism in Bei Dao's story "Waves"[16] 波動 is suggested in images and structures of waves; in The Yellow Earth it is given form by repetition in imagery, structure and cinematography.

The sense of tragedy in recent Chinese writing and art is often marred for Western audiences by what is seen as excessive sentimentality and self-indulgence. The distancing techniques of recent Western literature, theatre and cinema have gone largely unregarded in China, where the artist in his earnest grappling with life urgently demands the similarly dedicated engagement of the audience.[17] In The Yellow Earth, the film-makers wish us to sympathize with Cuiqiao, and so the delicate, sensitive face of the young actress reflects every emotion a fourteen-year old heart can feel, and the same half-calculated sentimentality is echoed in the romantic music with its folk-tune theme. The life of the peasants is arduous, but it is still picturesque; the "warmth" that Zhang Yimou tried so hard to invoke softens the impact of their poverty and even imparts the glamour of simplicity to their circumstances.

Even more alarming is the film-makers' awareness of their weighty responsibilities; rarely breaking through in the film itself, it sometimes becomes ponderous in their statements to the press. Portentousness indeed is a common failing of even the better works of the underground or post-Mao period. Its historical precedent is in the May Fourth period, a period very similar to the 1970s and 1980s in many ways. Lack of humour—of a sense of self-critical irony as well as a sense of fun—is a major character-istisic of the literature of the early 1920s to the end of the 1930s.[18] But for the example of Lu Xun, we should be tempted to believe it is an essential component of courage and independence in modern Chinese society.

For courage is what we must most admire about these writers and artists: Bei Dao writing during the Cultural Revolution and its immediate aftermath, Chen Kaige embarking on his first film when the campaign against "spiritual pollution" was underway. There was a closer, stronger link: as early as 1979, Chen Kaige was contributing to *Today* 今天 , the unoffical magazine edited by Bei Dao and his fellow-poet Mang Ke 芒克 . One critic describes the director of *The Yellow Earth* as having drawn his experience from the Cultural Revolution, the April Fourth movement (referring to the Tiananmen demonstrations of 1976) and the spirit of the Third Plenum in 1978.[19] The question of Chen Kaige's actual involvement in the underground or unofficial movement is unimportant: what is significant is their common ground of emancipated thinking in culture and society.[20]

Any assessment of the impact of *The Yellow Earth*, therefore, must start from the premise that it was not unique: either as experimental cinema, as a founder of a new artistic trend, or as a part of a new emancipation in literature and the arts generally. It should also be kept in mind that even by the end of 1986, the film had very restricted exposure in its homeland. Since films in China are only made within the official film world, the lack of a broad public audience is not particularly significant in term of future film-making; it is, however, a limitation on the film's possible impact on film-goers as distinct from film-makers.

If *The Yellow Earth* is not unique, however, and has had only limited circulation in its own country, the question of its fame becomes more complex: given all the other examples of the new wave in the cinema and the renaissance in literature and the arts generally, why has *The Yellow Earth* achieved such eminence? The political controversy and short-lived bans undoubtedly helped publicize the film tremendously, both at home and abroad. (A total ban, of course, such as held back *One and Eight* for a long time, would have been disastrous.) Nevertheless, *The Yellow Earth* was not the only film to have had problems with the authorities, and writers and artists in other genres have suffered much worse abuse in the Chinese press. Film itself has a much greater claim on public attention, both at home and abroad, than less popularistic arts such as painting. Not being purely verbal, it also suffers less from problems of translation internationally. The international film festival circuit is an excellent showcase for new directors from third world countries, and, unlike the Nobel Prize for Literature, offers a generous portion of its rewards to the young. For several reasons, it is inherently more likely for a Chinese film rather than poetry or sculpture to reach a world audience.

Some observers believe that Chen Kaige's written and spoken statements about the film played a significant part in its success. His statement and interview of 1984, which were widely read and quoted in 1985, were expressed with great power and lyricism, but were at the same time politically very cautious. In 1985, as his fame with the general public grew, he became in demand as a speaker to student audiences and was interviewed many times. By the end of the year his family was becoming concerned with his rashness on such occasions, but he became even more outspoken in 1986. His reputation for arrogance dates back at least to the end of 1984, but by late 1986 many of his friends and colleagues were trying to warn him against a kind of recklessness in his behaviour. Nevertheless, his early training in self-protection was not so easily forgotten, nor was he always as confident as his public image appeared. Known around the studios as a *xiucai* 秀才 [21] for his literary ability (rare among film professionals), none the less he found it hard to write the kind the article about his work that was constantly being demanded of him in 1985 and 1986. The folk songs in *The Yellow Earth*, which he substantially rewrote, and even more the film itself, show such attributes of lyric poetry as emotion, suggestion, imagery, repetition, stillness, slowness and space, but he himself admits he is not a poet. The combination of confidence and vulnerability, of boldness and caution, of eloquence and reticence, creates an image that press and public find immensely appealing.

Giving full weight to all the factors mentioned above, we are nevertheless obliged to recognize that they are not sufficient in themselves to raise the film to such heights; we still need to assess the qualities that are unique to the work itself. Briefly, *The Yellow Earth* is an unusual combination of excellences.

In the first instance, its theme, the relationship between the peasants, the Party and the land, is among the most fundamental and most sensitive questions in modern Chinese history, and the unorthodox handling of this theme in the film is one of the most politically daring acts in contemporary Chinese literature and art.

Secondly, the theme is presented in a framework of artistic innovation, based on traditional Chinese aesthetics but using Western cinematic techniques to create an authentically Chinese product. Not all innovation is necessarily successful, nor are all attempts to synthesise two very different traditions, but in this regard opinion is almost unanimous (with minor reservations) on the film's triumph.

Thirdly, the film creates a series of images that are both visually powerful and thematically suggestive. The multiple associations developed by these images gave the film a quality of open-endedness that was so unusual in Chinese films that it needed to be defended. Even disregarding as specious a large portion of the Chinese discussion of the film, there is still a considerable body of evidence pointing to the many levels on which the film establishes its appeal.

Finally, and in my own opinion most importantly, this is the first film in the post-1949 Chinese cinema to present a personal vision of life and society. This phenomenon was already familiar in literature and painting from as early as the 1970s, but not in the cinema for several reasons. Films represented both a heavy investment from the state and one of the Party's most far-reaching and powerful propaganda media; access to production facilities was severely restricted, with four years training and several years apprenticeship as the minimum requirement; censorship of the finished product was both in form and practice more rigid than in the other arts. Although one can distinguish levels of quality in film-making between 1949 and 1983, all products reflected an aspect of current political policy. Even the controversy over *Unrequited Love* in 1981 can be seen as a quarrel between two factions within the Party leadership: one which offered further emancipation to intellectuals as part of modernization and political reform, the other still highly suspicious of challenge to Party authority in any field.[22] The difference between such films and *The Yellow Earth* is not one of depth in political commitment or personal risk; it is the ability of the director, in close consultation with the cinematographer, to develop and formulate his private convictions, based on experience and reflection, and to express these convictions with the courage and confidence of a true creative artist. To do so in the framework of an utterly conventional storyline makes its achievement even more poignant.

Perhaps it is still too early to come to a final assessment of *The Yellow Earth*. The film itself, however, the controversy surrounding it, its success, and the controversy about its success, constituted altogether such an event in Chinese film history that the Chinese film world has never been the same since. Internationally, its creativity and maturity demand that Chinese films no longer be judged by patronizing double standards but against the best the rest of the world has to offer. In the development of a new Chinese culture, it contributed new ideas, a confidence engendered of its success, a synthesis of widely different artistic traditions, a presentation of a political philosophy as an aesthetic perception, and a truly creative work of art.

Notes

1. Montale's term for the public identity of a work of art as distinct from its identity as its author's creation. See Eugenio Montale, *The Second Life of Art* (New York: Ecco Press, 1983): 22–23.
2. Shao Mujun, *HS HTD*: 257–58.
3. Shao Mujun, *HS HTD*: 257–58.
4. Apart from the references given below, see also John Minford, "Picking up the Pieces", *FEER*, 8 August 1985: 30–32, esp. 31.
5. Li Tuo, *HS HTD*: 51–52 *et passim*; Huang Jianzhong, *HS HTD*: 234.
6. Huang Jianzhong, *HS HTD*: 234–38.
7. Ni Zhen, *HS HTD*: 75; Han Xiaolei, *HS HTD*: 87; interview with two French students, July 1986.
8. Ni Zhen, *HS HTD*: 75.
9. Han Xiaolei, *HS HTD*: 87.
10. Chen Kaige has mentioned his admiration for Japanese directors to several interviewers (e.g. for Kurosawa to Paul Clark as early as 1980, and to me several times around 1984–86); see also the interview by Sato Tadao in *BYDY*, December 1986: 28–30. Zhang Yimou acknowledges the influence of Oguri's *Doro no Kawa*; see above, Chapter 2, p. 41.
11. *HS HTD*: 146–47, 149–50, 153. Chen Maiping also felt obliged to defend the openness of the imagery; *HS HTD*: 200.
12. See for instance Wang Shushun, *DDDY*, February 1985: 54.
13. See for instance Wang Dehou, *HS HTD*: 134, and SoF: front cover.
14. For a more detailed discussion of neo-traditionalism, see McDougall, "Breaking Through: Literature and the Arts in China, 1976–86", *Copenhagen Papers in East and Southeast Asian Studies* , 1 (1988): 35–65.
15. Ni Zhen, *HS HTD*: 67. For Ah Cheng see also above, pp. 134, 137, 145; for Shi Tiesheng and Zhang Chengzhi see also Zheng Dongtian, *HS HTD*: 41, Li Chao, *HS HTD*: 111 and Chapter 2, p. 40.

16. "Bodong" in Zhao Zhenkai, *Bodong* (Hong Kong: The Chinese University Press, 1985): 1–138; English translation by Susette Ternent Cooke and Bonnie S. McDougall in Zhao Zhenkai, *Waves* (Hong Kong: The Chinese University Press, 1985): 1–146.

17. Perhaps because of the personal reputation of Brecht, who is acceptable as a socialist playwright, the contemporary theatre in China is to some extent an exception in this respect, with examples ranging from *Jiaru wo shi zhende* 假如我是真的 (If I were real) in 1979 and *WM* in 1985. It may not be a coincidence that both of these plays came under attack by the top Party leadership.

18. See for instance McDougall, "The Importance of Being Earnest in China: Early Chinese Attitudes towards Oscar Wilde", *Journal of the Oriental Society of Australia*, IX. 1, 2 (1972–1973): 84–98, esp. 98.

19. Kong Du, *HS HTD*: 96; also Huang Jianzhong, *HS HTD*: 239.

20. Chen Maiping, who knew both men well, was one of the first to draw public attention to the common ground shared by Chen Kaige and Bei Dao; *HS HTD*: 200–1.

21. A graduate under the traditional system of classical education; a term used generally to refer to a person for a talent for writing, not necessarily but usually literary.

22. Hu Yaobang's attacks on *Unrequited Love* and *TYE* are consistent with his pronouncements on the arts generally in the 1980s, whatever his views on economic reform and his scapegoating in 1987. See McDougall, "Breaking Through".

Glossary

1. Film Titles*

As You Wish	Ruyi 如意 (1984)
Autumn in Spring	Qiutian li de chuntian 秋天裏的春天 (1986)
Beach, The (On the Beach)	Haitan 海灘 (1984)
Bloodshed in Black Valley	Diexue heigu 渫血黑谷 (1984)
Border Town	Biancheng 邊城 (1984)
Brother Echo	Yingsheng age 應聲阿哥 (1982)
Camel Xiangzi (Rickshaw Boy)	Luotuo xiangzi 駱駝祥子 (1982)
Family	Jia 家 (1953)
Fascinating Band, The	Miren de yuedui 迷人的樂隊 (1985)
Grand Parade, The (Big Parade)	Da yue bing 大閱兵 (1985)
Great River Rushes on, The	Dahe benliu 大河奔流 (1977)
Haixia	Haixia 海峽 (1974)
Heroic Sons and Daughters	Yingxiong ernü 英雄兒女 (1964)
Hunting Ground (On the Hunting Ground)	Liechang zhasa 獵場扎撒 (1984)
Juvenile Delinquents	Shaonian fan 少年犯 (1985)
King of Children, The	Haiziwang 孩子王 (1987)
Life	Rensheng 人生 (1984)

* The English titles supplied by the Chinese Film Import Export Corporation are often as clumsy as their subtitles. These versions are given in brackets after the title I use in the text.

Memories of Southern Peking (My Memories of Old Beijing)	Chengnan jiushi 城南舊事 (1983)
New Year's Sacrifice, A	Zhufu 祝福 (1956)
One and Eight	Yige he bage 一個和八個 (1983)
Red Detachment of Women	Hongse niangzi jun 紅色娘子軍 (1961)
Sacrifice of Youth (Sacrificed Youth)	Qingchun ji 青春祭 (1984)
September	Jiuyue 九月 (1984)
Serfs	Nongnu 農奴 (1964)
Sister	Jiejie 姊姊 (1984)
Small Boat, A	Yiye xiao zhou 一葉小舟 (1983)
Song of Youth	Qingchun zhi ge 青春之歌 (1959)
Twenty-six Girls	Ershiliuge guniang 二十六個姑娘 (1983)
Unrequited Love	Kulian 苦戀 (1980)
Woman of Good Family, A	Liangjia funü 良家婦女 (1984)
Women Generals of the Yang Family	Yangmen nüjiang 楊門女將 (1959)
Wreath under the Mountain	Gaoshan xia de huahuan 高山下的花環 (1984)
Wujie Mountain (In the Wujie Mountains)	Wujie 霧界 (1984)

2. Film and other personnel mentioned in the text (with their positions as of 1984 to 1986)*

Ah Cheng 阿城 (Zhong Acheng 鍾阿城)	writer
* Ai Mingzhi 艾明之	scriptwriter, Shanghai Film Studio
Bei Dao 北島	dissident poet

* Member of the Golden Rooster adjudication panel 1985

* Chen Huangmei 陳荒煤   senior writer, critic, cultural bureaucrat

Chen Kaige 陳凱歌   assistant director, Peking Film Studio

Chen Kaiyan 陳凱燕   editor, Chinese Film Press

Chen Maiping 陳邁平   teacher, Central Drama Academy; dissident writer

Cheng Zhiwei 成志偉   critic

* Deng Baochen 鄧寶宸   science documentary director

Ding Daoxi 丁道希   teacher, Peking Film Academy

Fei Mu 費穆   film director pre-1949

* Gu Xiaoyang 顧曉陽   editor, *Cinema Arts*

Han Shangyi 韓尚義   art director; former head of Shanghai Film Studio

Hao Dazheng 郝大錚   film theorist

* He Zhongxin 何鍾辛   documentary director, Xi'an Film Studio

* Hu Bingliu 胡炳榴   director, Pearl River Film Studio

Huang Jianzhong 黃健中   director, Peking Film Studio

* Huang Zongying 黃宗英   writer, actress, film director

Jin Sheng 晉生   see Li Jinsheng

Kong Du 孔都   teacher, Peking Film Academy

Li Jinsheng 李晉生   editor, *Cinema Arts*

Li Tuo 李陀   fiction writer

Li Xingye 李興葉   research worker, Federation of Writers and Artists

* Liang Xin 梁信   scriptwriter, Guangdong Film Studio

* Ling Zifeng 凌子風   director, Peking Film Studio

Liu Yanchi 劉燕馳   scriptwriter, Peking Film Studio

* Lu Zhuguo 陸柱國   scriptwriter, August 1st Film Studio

* Luo Yijun 羅藝軍   critic, Film-makers' Association

Ma Desheng 馬德生   dissident painter

Ma Rui 馬銳	editor, *Popular Cinema*
Mang Ke 芒克	dissident poet
Ni Zhen 倪震	associate professor, Peking Film Academy
Peng Jiajin 彭加瑾	literary critic, *Literature and the Arts*
Shao Mujun 邵牧君	critic, Film-makers' Association
* Shen Songsheng 沈嵩生	deputy director, Peking Film Academy
Shi Fangyu 石方禹	film administrator
Wang Dehou 王得後	Lu Xun research scholar
Wang Junzheng 王君正	director, Peking Film Studio
Wang Shushun 王樹舜	film production administrator
* Wang Suihan 王歲寒	lecturer, Peking Film Academy
Wu Yonggang 吳永剛	1930s film director
* Xia Yan 夏衍	senior scriptwriter, director, critic
* Xie Fei 謝飛	vice-president, Peking Film Academy
* Xie Tian 謝添	actor, director, Peking Film Studio
* Yu Min 于敏	scriptwriter, editor, *Cinema Arts*
Yu Qian 余倩	professor, Peking Film Academy
* Yu Yanfu 于彥夫	director, Changchun Film Studio
* Zhang Ruifang 張瑞芳	actress, Shanghai Film Studio
Zhang Yimou 張藝謀	cinematographer, Guangxi Film Studio
* Zhao Huanzhang 趙煥章	director, Shanghai Film Studio
Zhao Yuan 趙園	professor, Peking Film Academy
Zheng Dongtian 鄭洞天	head of directing department, Peking Film Academy
Zhou Chuanji 周傳基	associate professor, Peking Film Academy
* Zhu Xijuan 祝希娟	actress; producer, Shenzhen Television

The Yellow Earth*

A Film by Chen Kaige
Screenplay by Zhang Ziliang
Translated by Bonnie S. McDougall

Translator's Introduction

The film is set in Shaanbei, the northern part of the province of Shaanxi. Yenan, the headquarters of the Communist Eighth Route Army, is in south Shaanbei, and the main action of the film takes place in central Shaanbei.

The Eighth Route Army, formerly known as the Red Army, changed its name for the sake of the United Front with the Nationalist Party (Kuomintang) during the War of Resistance to Japan (1937–1945). It established its base areas away from cities and towns, along provincial boundaries usually marked by rough terrain. The most important of these was the Shaanxi-Gansu-Ningxia Border Area with its capital in Yenan.

In the early period of the resistance, the Eighth Route Army used local folk culture in mobilizing the peasants. One of the most popular and distinctive forms of folksong in Shaanbei was the *xintianyou* 信天游 (roughly meaning "following the natural flow"): it consists of a series of rhymed couplets, in which the first line generally presents an image and the second carries the narrative. There is normally a caesura in the middle of each line.

Although not acknowledged in writing, the script was extensively revised by the director before and during filming.

Mistakes in the printed text have been corrected on the advice of the director or with reference to the final screen version.

BMcD

---

* The copy of the original Chinese filmscript is held by Chen Kaige and it is translated with his permission.

Abbreviations

BE: Big establishing shot   LS: Long shot
CU: Close-up   MC: Medium close shot
ECU: Extreme close-up   MS: Medium shot
ELS: Extreme long shot   OS: Off screen
ES: Establishing shot   SE: Small establishing shot
EXT: Exterior   TPL: Telephoto lens
INT: Interior

The Yellow Earth

Reel I

1   **1. STUDIO LOGO**

Guangxi Film Studio

2   **2. MAIN TITLES**

The Yellow Earth

3   *The Yellow Earth*: adapted from "Echo in the Valley", an essay by Ke Lan.

4   *The Yellow Earth*: screenplay by Zhang Ziliang.

3. INSERT TITLES

5   INSERT TITLES slowly roll up against a black field:

"In September 1937, the establishment of the United Front against Japanese aggression forced Jiang Jieshi to acknowledge the status of the Shaanxi-Gansu-Ningxia Border Area. Because of the persistence of Nationalist local government in parts of central Shaanbei, despite the cooperation between the Nationalists and the Communists, feudalism was still deeply entrenched and the people still suffered under heavy oppression."

(BLACK SPACE) Then:

"In this ancient land, the melodies of *xintianyou* drift the year round …"

(ANOTHER BLACK SPACE) Then:

"Members of the literature and arts troupe of the Eighth Route Army formed into teams and fanned out in different directions. They hoped to find the origins of Shaanbei folksong …"

6   The following words then appear against a black field:

EARLY SPRING, 1939

4. A Sequence of DISSOLVE SHOTS
(DUSK, EXT)

7   BE   Countless gullies and ravines at sunset, steeped in a solemn silence.

8   BE   (DISSOLVE) The same solemn, silent gullies and ravines.

(PAN FROM LEFT TO RIGHT)

9   ELS   (DISSOLVE) GU QING slowly walks along a bare ridge.

10 BE   (DISSOLVE) From a sheer cliff, TILT UP to the moon.

11 LS-ES (DISSOLVE) The distant figure of Gu Qing comes along the ridge.

12 ES   (DISSOLVE) (PAN FROM LEFT TO RIGHT) A cross section of the hillsides cut by deep gullies.

13 ES-MS (DISSOLVE) Gu Qing gradually descends the ridge.

14 BE   (DISSOLVE) (PAN FROM LEFT TO RIGHT) Countless gullies and ravines at sunset, steeped in a solemn silence.

5. The Hillside (DUSK, EXT)

15 MC   Gu Qing crossing in right halts mid-screen. He is wearing the padded cotton uniform of the Eighth Route Army, and has a small backpack and satchel.

He turns his head towards the right, listening intently to something.

The drawn-out note of a *xintianyou* ballad, resonant and plaintive, is heard in the distance: "Ai—"

6. A Distant View of the Hillcrest (DUSK, EXT)

16 BE   The hillcrest is bleak and bare. There is no sign of human habitation except for a white path winding up against the brown earth and disappearing over the crest. A solitary wild pear tree stands at the top.

The long drawn-out note of the *xintianyou*, resonant and plaintive, seems to leap up, as if rising from the depths of the earth: "Ai—"

7. The Hillside (DUSK, EXT)

17 ES   Gu Qing listens intently, standing on the hillside.

8. A Distant View of the Hillcrest (DUSK, EXT)

18 BE   The solitary wild pear tree stands on the crest.

The song, distant but clear:

"The towman's life // is hard and drear,
Ai-yo, the towman's life ..."

9. **The Hillside** (DUSK, EXT)

19 MS   Gu Qing takes out a pen and a small notebook.
The song:
"… is hard and drear,
Work and toil // ten months of the year."
Gu Qing writes something down and waits, his
head bent. The lingering notes fade, and the
gullies and crests sink back into silence. Gu
Qing slowly raises his head …

10. **A Distant View of the Hillcrest** (DUSK, EXT)

20 BE   The wild pear tree stands in silence on the crest,
stripped to its last leaves.

11. **Gullies and Ravines** (DUSK, EXT)

21 ES   (TILT UP) Gullies and ravines, eroded by time.

12. **The Ridge** (DUSK, EXT)

22 ES   (FOLLOW FROM LEFT TO RIGHT) A wedding
procession comes down from the ridge.

23 BE   The procession, which includes several musicians, the "receiving" and "dispatching" female attendants astride donkeys, and a red
bridal palanquin, comes down the ridge along
the winding path. There are about several
dozen people altogether.

24 BE   (FOLLOW) The procession forms a group along
the ridge.

13. A Riverbed (DUSK, EXT)

25 ES   (TILT DOWN FROM THE HILLCREST) The bridal procession goes along a riverbed.

26 CU-ECU   The suona in the bridal procession, blaring vigorously into the camera, their red silk streamers fluttering ...

27 CU   The gongs in the bridal procession, struck with their sticks ...

28 CU   The donkeys in the bridal procession, bearing red rosettes ...

29 CU   One side of the bridal palanquin in the bridal procession, hung with red silk.

30 CU   The top of the palanquin in the bridal procession.

31 ECU   The red shoes worn by the receiving attendant, embroidered with a pattern of red pomegranate flowers, swaying from side to side with the movements of the donkey.

32 CU-ECU   Ań old man playing a suona in the bridal procession walks towards the camera.

(ECU on the suona, FOCUS on the old man's face.)

33 CU   The top of the palanquin in the bridal procession comes towards the camera.

34 ES   People stand around the riverbed watching the excitement, talking and laughing among themselves. Some young boys slide down the hillside to the bottom of the gully and stand among the crowd watching the excitement.

35 MS   The musicians pass across the screen from the right. Hands tucked into the sleeves of black padded jackets, the farmers grin.

36	ECU	The dazzling red clothes chest in the bridal procession, with a red bundle on top.
37	MC	Astride her donkey, the receiving attendant passes across the screen from the left. On the hillside, the farmers grin.
38	MC	On the hillside, the seated farmers grin.
39	ES	The procession walks along the riverbed. The crowd stands on all sides watching the excitement.
40	MC	The grinning farmers sit on the hillside. The music reverberates across the screen.
41	ECU	The curtain on the palanquin, screening off the bride, sways slightly, slowly filling the screen.
42	MS	A farmer crosses in from right. (FOLLOW) He walks through the crowd and over to CUIQIAO, who is standing among the spectators, then crosses out to the left.
		Cuiqiao watches the procession approaching.
43	MS-CU	The curtain on the palanquin, swaying to the steps of the chair bearers, moves to the right.
44	MC	Cuiqiao's impassive face can be seen through the farmers in the foreground, her eyes following the palanquin.
45	ECU	From the curtain of the palanquin FOLLOW to ECU of the palanquin window.
46	MC	The red palanquin moves across from the right. In centre screen, Cuiqiao, who is standing among the grinning crowd, dodges and runs out left.

14. The Wedding Courtyard (DAY, EXT)

47	ECU	A memorial tablet to heaven and earth, with a red door-curtain in the background.
48	MS	The red door-curtain hangs down from the top of

the screen. At the bottom of the screen are peasants, like immobile puppets. The band strikes up. The crowd suddenly moves and scatters. Only the red door-curtain is left in centre screen.

49 CU   The bridal procession approaches.
            The MASTER OF CEREMONIES grasps a handful of "drops of gold" and throws them towards the camera.

50 BE   To the sound of firecrackers, the courtyard is filled with farmers coming to watch the excitement. The band plays energetically, the young men escorting the palanquin come forward, and the attendants standing at either side step forward and lead the bride out. The bride's head is covered with a red cloth.

51 MC-ES   To the sound of firecrackers, scattering "drops of gold", the Master of Ceremonies steps back, mumbling a chant:
            "First sow the bran ..."

52 BE   The Master of Ceremonies (OS):
            "Second sow the grain ..."
            The bride, escorted by her attendants, walks along the red matting towards the camera. A crowd of young children scramble for the peanuts and other food scattered by the Master of Ceremonies.

53 BE   To the sound of firecrackers, scattering "drops of gold", the Master of Ceremonies steps back, mumbling a chant:
            "Down steps the bride // from her palanquin.
            First sow the bran ..."

54	BE	The bride, escorted by her attendants, walks along the spread-out red matting towards the camera.

The Master of Ceremonies (OS): "… second sow the grain …"

55	BE	To the sound of firecrackers, scattering "drops of gold", the Master of Ceremonies steps back, mumbling a chant:

"Down steps the bride // from her palanquin."

56	BE	The bride, escorted by her attendants, walks along the spread-out red matting towards the camera.

The Master of Ceremonies (OS):

"Man and wife // a match for life,
Harmonious days // all free from strife.

A match for life // man and wife …"

57	ECU	The tablet to heaven and earth is set off against the red door-curtain. In centre screen the incense smoke curls up …

The Master of Ceremonies (OS):

"Happy days // all free from strife.

Man and wife // together one life,
Happy days // all free from strife.

Man and wife // together one life,
Happy days // all free from strife."

58	MC	The bottom of the screen is filled with the wooden faces of the black-clad farmers, set off against the cave door.
59	CU	The expressionless face of the Master of Ceremonies against the red door-curtain in the background.

60	CU	(FOLLOW) The red-covered head moving through the crowd …
61	MC	The black-clad farmers move slowly to the right.
62	CU	(FOLLOW) The red-covered head moving slowly through the crowd …
63	MC	The impassive black-clad farmers.
64	CU	(FOLLOW) The red-covered head moving through the crowd …
65	CU	The expressionless face of the Master of Ceremonies.
66	BE	In front of the table with the tablet to heaven and earth, the bride crosses in left screen, is pushed by her attendants. She comes up to the table. Next the bridegroom, with a red silk sash crossed over his chest and back, is pushed up to the table.
67	MC	The black-clad farmers as before.
68	CU	The Master of Ceremonies shouts: "Kneel!"
69	ES	Their backs to the camera, the inexperienced bride and groom are almost pressed down in front of the table by their relatives.
70	MC	The impassive faces of the black-clad farmers fill the screen, with the cave in the background.
71	MC	The bottom of the screen is filled with heads, with the cave in the background. A blast from the suona …
72	MS	Backs to the camera, the black-clad farmers fill the foreground. Through the spaces between them, the bride and groom can be seen kneeling. The Master of Ceremonies (OS): "First kowtow!"
73	MC	The puppet-like black-clad farmers face the camera, with the cave in the background …

The Master of Ceremonies (OS): "Second kowtow!"

74 MS   The black-clad farmers are still in the foreground,
            their backs to the camera. Between them the
            candles can be seen burning ...
            The screen is filled with a sense of mystery.

75 MC   The bottom of the screen is filled with the heads
            of the puppet-like black-clad farmers, facing
            the camera with the cave in the background ...
            The Master of Ceremonies (OS): "Third kowtow!"

76 MS   From a back view of the kneeling bride and
            groom, TILT UP to the tablet to heaven and
            earth against the red door-curtain.
            The Master of Ceremonies (OS): "Rise!"

77 MC   At the entrance to the courtyard, Cuiqiao leans
            against the door, watching.
            The Master of Ceremonies (OS):
                "Bring up sons // to be good lads,
                 To wear blue gowns // and officials' hats.
                 Bring up daughters // to be quick lasses
                 ..."

78 ECU   A male relative's bent shoulders and linked
            hands.
            The Master of Ceremonies (OS):
            "Skilled in sewing...."

79 MC-ES   With the cave door in the background, the male
            relative, back to camera, has linked his hands
            to form a step. The bride kneels on his hands,
            her own hands leaning across the man's back,
            her red covered head towards the camera. Car-
            rying the bride, the man walks quickly to-
            wards the wedding chamber. (ES) A crowd of
            children follow behind ...

The Master of Ceremonies (OS):
"… peony patterns.

Bring up sons // to be good lads,
To wear blue gowns // and officials' hats."

80 MC Cuiqiao leaning against the door as before. (Someone crosses out.)

81 MS The man carrying the bride goes quickly into the wedding chamber, to which the door-curtain has been lifted, and disappears from view.

The red door-curtain, now lowered, sways slowly …

82 MS Cuiqiao stands at the entrance. Gu Qing is ushered into the courtyard by the Master of Ceremonies.

The Master of Ceremonies smiles. "Come in, please come in."

A farmer accompanying him turns and looks at Cuiqiao, who lowers her head …

83 MS (PAN) All is noise and bustle. Gu Qing follows the Master of Ceremonies up to a square table. The farmers around the table stand up.

A young lad shouts out: "Hey—here comes the food!"

Several young lads bearing red trays start setting the food out.

84 MS Standing at the head of the table, the Master of Ceremonies introduces Gu Qing to the farmers: "Kinsmen, here is His Honour the Government Official from Yenan in the south. He has come to this small village to visit our homes."

85 MS Standing around the table, the farmers respond blankly: "Er, er."

86 MS   Standing at the head of the table, Gu Qing intro-
            duces himself: "My name is Gu Qing. Just call
            me Gu."

87 MS   It's not clear whether the farmers have under-
            stood what Gu Qing has said. Responding
            only with "Er, er," they dare not look at him
            directly.

88 MS   At Gu Qing's side, the Master of Ceremonies
            pours a cup for Gu Qing, saying, "Please have
            something to drink, please sit down." He then
            turns around and crosses out.
            The farmers stand there.
            Gu Qing smiles. "I'm disturbing you, why don't
            we all sit down." As he speaks he sits down.
            The farmers don't move.
            Gu Qing stands up again, but the farmers sit
            down.

89 MC   Bewildered, Gu Qing looks at the farmers. He
            slowly sits down, a baffled expression on his
            face.

90 BE   Back to the camera, Gu Qing looks at the farmers
            in silence. The farmers lower their heads, only
            interested in the big pieces of fat pork, bean-
            starch noodles, turnips and shredded potatoes
            piled high in big earthenware bowls on the
            table ...
            An old man at Gu Qing's table points with his
            chopsticks at the table, saying, "Eat ..."
            Gu Qing: "Er, er."
            He picks out a piece of fat pork and eats it.
            The old man: "Drink ..."
            Gu Qing: "Er, er."
            Throwing back his heads, he empties the cup.

91	MC	Gu Qing's reaction to the raw alcohol.
92	MS	The children sitting on the courtyard wall are laughing, looking at A POOR MAN standing off screen who has accepted a drink.
93	MS	A poor man in his thirties standing among a crowd of people eating has accepted a cup from the Master of Ceremonies. With the ease of long practice, he empties it in one go.
94	MC	Suddenly a burst of song attracts the attention of Gu Qing at his table. The poor man has begun to sing a local ballad:

94 MC ... The poor man (OS): (sings)
> "They put down the cash // for twice-brewed wine ..."

95 MS The poor man, standing in front of the tables, is absorbed in his song:
> "And invited their kinsfolk // and neighbours to dine.
>
> The same wine // the same things to eat,
> The same friends // the same kind of treat."

96 MC Gu Qing, his attention caught by the song, hurriedly takes his notebook out of his pocket and puts it on the table, getting ready to write.
The poor man (OS): (sings)
> "Pairs of ivory chopsticks // are set out on the table ..."

97 MC The farmers at the same table as Gu Qing look at him suspiciously.
The poor man (OS): (sings)
> "The sieved wine from the silver pot // is poured with a golden ladle."

98 MS   ·   The poor man, who is a little drunk, is absorbed in his song:

> "Coloured platters are set out in fours // to invite the guests to dine,
> The bride's attendants are all served with // big cups of well-sieved wine."

The song comes to an end. The poor man is given a drink from off screen, which he swallows in one gulp.

99 MS   The children sitting on the courtyard wall stare impassively at the poor man off screen.

End of Reel I (892.3 feet)

Reel II

100 MC   Between the farmers eating and drinking in the foreground, Gu Qing can be seen writing. He lifts his head in excitement and says to the old man at the same table, "He sang that so well!"

The old man, not regarding it as anything special, agrees. "True. This lad, you know, his family's been dead poor for generations, he's over thirty already and he still can't afford a wife. All he's good for is singing our local songs."

Gu Qing looks for a long time at the poor man (OS).

101 MS   One of the lads: "Here comes the fish!"

(FOLLOW) The lads thread their way through the crowd. Reaching Gu Qing's table, one of them sets down the fish.

	The old man at Gu Qing's table taps the fish with his chopsticks, making a hollow sound.
	The old man: "It's wood, it's just for the meaning."
	The farmers at the table start chuckling.
102 ECU	A wooden fish is set on one of the other tables.
103 ECU	Another wooden fish is set on a table.
104 ECU	Yet another wooden fish is set on a table.
105 ECU	The red door-curtain.
106 BE	The bride and groom come out from the bridal chamber. The bride curtseys to the crowd from time to time. The crowd greets them with smiling faces.
	The band plays even more energetically.
107 MS	(FOLLOW) The bride and groom walk up to the tables, gradually getting nearer to Gu Qing. The Master of Ceremonies leads them up to Gu Qing.
	The Master of Ceremonies smiles. "Your Honour, here are the bride and groom …"
	Gu Qing smiles. "Congratulations …"
	Suddenly Gu Qing gives a start.
108 MC	The bridegroom's face—the face of a man close to forty.
	The Master of Ceremonies (OS): "Here is the bridegroom."
109 MC	From behind the groom's back, Gu Qing, startled, doesn't know what to say.
110 CU	The bride, dressed in a red printed padded cotton jacket, slowly lifts her head—she is only thirteen or fourteen.
111 MC	From behind the groom's back, Gu Qing, shocked by the great difference in age between bride

	and groom, still doesn't know what to say ...
112 CU	The bride, wearing a red printed padded cotton jacket, slowly lifts her head ...
	An old man next to her says in a low voice, "She's from Shuanniu's family ..."
	Another old man smiles and says, "That's right."
113 MC	From behind the groom's back, Gu Qing is still startled.
114 MS	An old man (OS): "Bow!"
	The bride curtseys to Gu Qing.
	The Master of Ceremonies (OS): "This way!"
	Supported by her attendants, the bride crosses out left.
115 CU	The bridegroom's face.
116 CU	Cuiqiao, who has been watching all the wedding rites, slowly lowers her head ...
	From off screen comes the voice of the poor man: (sings)
	"Paired off in twos // carp swim in the rills, ..."
117 BE	The bridal pair go towards the bridal chamber, where the door-curtain hangs down.
	It is still the same celebratory music, but in it there is a note of sadness—deep and indirect ...
	From off screen comes the voice of the poor man: (sings)
	"Paired off in twos // goats leap in the hills ..."
118 ES	The bride enters the bridal chamber and disappears from view ...
	The music still blares forth ...

119 ECU	The red door-curtain looks as if it will never be lifted again ...
120 CU	Standing in the crowd, his face covered in sweat, the poor man concentrates on his song:

> "Paired off in twos // pigs root in the trough,
> Fortune smiled // as they pledged their troth."

121 CU	Cuiqiao's face again. When the song comes to an end she turns and crosses out.
122 CU	Gu Qing gazes at the poor but cheerful farmers ...

15. The Bank of the Yellow River (DUSK, EXT)

123 BE	The stately flow of the Yellow River ...
124 BE	(PAN FROM LEFT TO RIGHT) A group of towmen are going along the bank, hauling upstream a flat-bottomed boat laden with goods. From deep in their chests comes a work chant. They cross out. (CAMERA STOPS) In front is an open beach, a path which has been trodden solid, and brown mud inundated by the tide, stretching up to the river's edge. In the setting sun, Cuiqiao's small figure crosses in right. Carrying two water buckets balanced on a pole, she walks to the river's edge.
125 BE	... The work chant gradually fades.
	Cuiqiao stands at the river's edge, her eyes following the towmen into the distance ...
126 MC	... The work chant fades away.
	As Cuiqiao's eyes follow the towmen into the distance, her glance gradually falls on the river water.

127 CU	The Yellow River current.
128 CU	A blackened wooden bucket dips into the water with a plop and the water splashes in. TILT UP to Cuiqiao's meek face. Absorbed in filling the bucket, she seems to have nothing on her mind, but a *xintianyou* ballad, sung in a low, light voice, pours forth:

(The sound of Cuiqiao singing to herself:)

> "Sixth Month on the river // the ice has not yet thawed …"

129 LS	The muddy river water fills up the wooden bucket. A girl's hand picks it up, and a string of drops fall away. (PAN) The bucket is set on the bank and the water inside settles, spreading ripples …

> "It's my own father forcing me // towards the wedding board.
>
> Of all the five grains // the green pea is the roundest …"

130 CU	The Yellow River current. (sings)

> "Of all us poor folk // daughters are the saddest …"

131 CU	Again the muddy water fills up the other bucket. Again the same hand, again a string of drops. TILT UP to Cuiqiao's face. Straightening up, she crosses out left. (sings)

> "Daughters are the saddest, o daughter o …"

132 MS-CU	With the river current in the background, Cuiqiao carries the water home, the buckets suspended from a carrying pole …

Cuiqiao sings to herself:

"Pigeons fly high above // one with the
other,
The one I long for // is my own dear
mother."

133 ES   The surging muddy river water …

16. The Hillside Leading to Cuiqiao's
Home (DUSK, EXT)

134 MC-BE   Cuiqiao comes over the hillside from far off, carrying water. The sun sinks behind the hills, the
path gleams white, the twilight gathers, the
carrying pole creaks.
HANHAN (OS): "Sister—"
Cuiqiao stops, raising her head.

135 ES   On the side of the path appears Hanhan's skinny
figure, wrapped in a man's old sheepskin jack-
et. His features are obscure in the twilight. A
small flock of sheep surround him, bleating.

136 ES   Cuiqiao, carrying water, crosses in left and walks
up to Hanhan.
Cuiqiao: "Hanhan, coming home so late? Oh,
Hanhan's a good boy, he's been waiting for his
sister."

17. The Exterior of Cuiqiao's Cave Home
(DUSK, EXT)

137 ES   A small, five-foot square yard. By the light of
the lamp from the main cave can be seen the
stone roller for crushing grain and a side-cave
for firewood—a poverty-stricken "one family
village".
The Master of Ceremonies (OS): "Comrade Gu

has said that he wants to stay with a poor family, so I have brought him here to you ..."

CUIQIAO'S FATHER (OS): "Ah ..." He coughs twice.

Gu Qing (OS): "Elder uncle ..."

The Master of Ceremonies (OS): "Yes, you two have a chat, I'll be on my way."

Father (OS): "Ah ..."

18. The Hillside Leading to Cuiqiao's Home (DUSK, EXT)

138 ES   In the deepening twilight, Cuiqiao carrying water and Hanhan leading the sheep walk down the hillside.

19. Inside Cuiqiao's Cave Home (NIGHT, INT)

139 CU   The father's face, his eyes lowered, silent.

140 MC   Gu Qing's enquiring face. Wanting to say something, he deliberates.

141 MC   The father, still silent.

    Gu Qing (OS): "Elder uncle ..."

142 MC   Gu Qing: "... I'm putting you to a lot of trouble, staying here."

143 ES   The father has his back to the camera, Gu Qing faces it. The two men are sitting on the *kang*.

    Father: "Er." It seems as if he acknowledges that fact, but also as if he basically has not heard what Gu Qing has said. He slowly places his sheepskin vest under his buttocks. He tucks his hands in his sleeves and doesn't say any more.

The two men face each other.

Gu Qing leans forward: "How old are you this year?"

The father shifts his buttocks. After a while he says, "From the year of the Dragon; forty-seven."

144 CU   Gu Qing lifts his head in surprise. He gazes at this old man in front of him, so slow in his movements and sparing with his words.

145 CU   The father looks at least sixty. The wrinkles etched in his face seem in the dim lamplight like ravines. The white towel around his head has already become indistinguishable in colour from his dark brown skin. The old man lifts his eyes, but they seem to look straight through Gu Qing as if seeing nothing, with neither sorrow nor joy. Looking at his dull gaze, one can know his past and present life.

146 MC   Gu Qing's reaction.

147 ES   Gu Qing is uneasy. He simply doesn't know what more to say. The two men remain silent as before.

Preceded by the creak of the carrying pole, Cuiqiao comes in the door, carrying water. Gu Qing exclaims and is about to jump down from the *kang* to help. He feels very pleased because someone else has come back home.

The father coughs twice, as if to check Gu Qing. Gu Qing is obliged to sit down again. Cuiqiao puts down the wooden buckets.

148 MC   Cuiqiao lifts her head and looks at Gu Qing.

149 MC   The father lowers his eyes.

150 CU   The water in the buckets is poured into the small

water vat. TILT UP to Cuiqiao's face. She lowers her eyes but it seems that she has already used the remaining light to look at Gu Qing and can't control an inner tension. Fortunately, the dim oil lamp cannot illuminate her face.

151 MC   Smiling, Gu Qing watches Cuiqiao.

Cuiqiao, filling up the basin, disappears from the screen.

152 ES   Gu Qing and the father are sitting on the *kang* in the background.

Carrying the basin of water, her head lowered, Cuiqiao hesitates, then steps quickly over to the stove. She pours the water into a pot, then sits down cross-legged and begins to get the fire going.

153 MS   With Cuiqiao in front of the stove in the background, the father is still sitting silently on the *kang* like a clay figure.

154 ES   With Cuiqiao tending the fire in the foreground, Gu Qing is sitting on the *kang*. "What's your name, lass?"

The father, his back to the camera, shifts his body. Just at this moment Hanhan pushes open the door and comes in.

Cuiqiao, sitting by the stove, says shyly, "Cuiqiao."

155 ES   Gu Qing, in the background, repeats: "... Cuiqiao!"

In the foreground, in the firelight, Cuiqiao's head is bent very low.

156 MC   Gu Qing suddenly feels that someone is staring at him. He turns his head around.

From Gu Qing, PAN slowly left to Hanhan standing in the doorway. Gu Qing doesn't know when Hanhan has come home. He stands in the doorway, not coming in. His old sheepskin jacket reaches down to his knees. He stares blankly at Gu Qing.

Gu Qing (OS): "And you, what's your name?"

Hanhan doesn't answer. He stares at Gu Qing with his mouth half open, as if he hasn't heard.

157 MC	Gu Qing turns his face round.
158 MC	Cuiqiao seems to have opened her mouth and then closed it again. She starts pumping the bellows.
159 MC	Gu Qing's reaction.
160 ES	With Cuiqiao tending the fire in the foreground, it is silent in the cave. No-one speaks, and the only sound to be heard is the bellows.

Gu Qing is sitting on the *kang*. "On this trip, a few of my comrades and I up from the south want to roam the hills collecting the folksongs of our Shaanbei …"

The bellows in Cuiqiao's hands stop pumping.

Gu Qing: "… so that our Eighth Route Army troops can pass on the ones that are easy to sing."

"Er," responds the father, back to camera.

Gu Qing: "Can you sing, uncle?"

"Er." It is not clear what the father's answer means.

Gu Qing: "Can you sing, lass?"

Cuiqiao hurriedly pumps the bellows again.

161 MS	The father sits right screen.

Gu Qing: "They say that there's a girl in one of the

villages around here that's a really first-rate singer. Do you know who she is, uncle?"

162 MC The father gives a covert sidelong glance at the notebook in Gu Qing's hand.

End of Reel II (753 feet)

Reel III

163 MC Hanhan is still looking woodenly at Gu Qing in right screen. (PAN RIGHT) Gu Qing, notebook in hand, looks silently at Hanhan.

164 MC Cuiqiao, sitting in front of the stove, seems to have opened her mouth. She shuts it again and begins pumping the bellows.

165 ES Steam from the pot of boiling water spreads through the dimly lit cave. The father, apparently relaxing, lifts his buttocks.

The water boils. In the foreground Cuiqiao pours out a bowl of water. She walks over to Gu Qing, and lowering her eyes, hands it to him.

Gu Qing quickly shuts his notebook and takes the bowl. "Ah …"

Cuiqiao turns round and walks towards the camera.

Gu Qing: "At noon today I was in the next village, I saw a wedding … I …"

Cuiqiao slowly walks over to the stove, listening intently.

The father suddenly breaks in. "Ah, that was the ninth daughter of Shuanniu's family,

from Mud River Gully behind the crooked hill
…"

Cuiqiao slowly sits down.

Gu Qing: "The girl was still pretty young, wasn't she?"

Cuiqiao, distracted, starts pumping the bellows.

166 MC   The father, sitting on the *kang*: "How do you mean, young!—Her father often drives his animals past our cliff, he told me that she'd be fourteen after Sixth Month … how do you mean, young!"

It seems as if here is a topic that is of interest to the old man. He tucks his hands into his sleeves and shifts his body in some satisfaction.

167 MC   In the far background Cuiqiao tends the fire. Hanhan stands by the door, his face apparently expressionless, but the young boy's silence seems to imply something …

Gu Qing (OS): "Uncle, in the south we don't go in for this."

168 MC   The father finally raises his eyes: " Don't go in for girls getting married?"

169 ES   Gu Qing: "Getting married, yes, but we have to …"

The father listens intently.

Gu Qing: "… change the form. Our girls in the south have made up a new folksong—'Sheep and goats // always walk apart, To the man of my choice // I'll give my heart.'"

Father: "—What?"

Gu Qing: "That means, finding your own husband."

Father: "No matchmaker?"

199

Gu Qing: "No."

Father: "No wedding gifts?"

Gu Qing: "No."

In the foreground Cuiqiao tends the fire.

170 MC   Gu Qing's smiling face.

171 MC   In the background Cuiqiao tends the fire. The father suddenly seems to be a little ill at ease. He looks around as if seeking support.

Father: "... Well, what does that amount to then?"

There is a touch of sarcasm in his words. Afterwards a swift fear appears in his eyes. "Those women are worthless, if they go with a man they just run off like that?"

172 CU   Cuiqiao's face in the firelight. Her body rocks lightly as she pumps the bellows. In the presence of strangers, Shaanbei girls use their ears rather than their eyes.

Gu Qing (OS): "Our women aren't worthless ..."

173 MC   Gu Qing: "... but we don't sell them. Uncle, this society ..."

174 MC   Cuiqiao's face in the firelight.

Gu Qing (OS): "... must be changed. It's already changed in the south, and it must be changed in the north too, it must be changed all over China!"

175 MC   Gu Qing's earnest face.

176 MC   The father looks confused. He mutters: "We farmers have our own ways." Then he says again: "We farmers have our own ways," as if not addressing Gu Qing. "This blasted girl, still pumping away at the bellows: there's no "face" on kindling ..."

	In the far background Cuiqiao tends the fire.
177 MC	Father (OS): "... so it's not money!"
	Hanhan's apparently expressionless face.
	Cuiqiao (OS): "—Oh."
	The sound of the bellows stops.
	Gu Qing(OS): "Uncle ..."
178 ES	In the foreground Cuiqiao tends the fire.

The father interrupts, unwilling for him to continue: "Give His Honour the Official some water
to wash his feet in. It's time to sleep."

As he finishes speaking, he gets down from the
kang and walks out to relieve himself.

Gu Qing pulls over his satchel and starts to take
out his towel.

Cuiqiao hurriedly pours out some water. The atmosphere in the cave seems suddenly different.

179 MS	Gu Qing takes out his toothbrush, towel and a sewing kit embroidered with a five-pointed red star, and lays them on the *kang*. (PAN LEFT)
	Hanhan, still standing by the door, looks blankly at the things Gu Qing puts on the *kang*.
180 MC	Gu Qing, who is unwrapping his leggings, lifts his head and looks at Hanhan with a smile.
181 MC	(PAN) Hanhan hesitates a little, then cautiously walks over to the *kang*.
	Cuiqiao crosses out to pour out some water.
	Gu Qing smiles affectionately at Hanhan.
182 MS	Cuiqiao watches Hanhan from the side.
183 MC	Gu Qing looks affectionately at Hanhan, who is seen in partial view.
184 MC	Hanhan looks at Gu Qing, and silently puts out

his hand. (TILT DOWN) He strokes the star and then withdraws his hand.

185 MS   Rolling up his trouser legs, Gu Qing asks with a smile: "How old are you?"

Not speaking , Hanhan touches the red star again.

186 ES   From far back, Cuiqiao comes up to the *kang*, carrying an earthenware basin.

Gu Qing hastily gets up from the *kang*: "Oh, let me." He sets the basin in front of the *kang* and gets ready to wash his feet.

Cuiqiao: "My brother doesn't like talking. He's a Tiger, he's called Hanhan. He herds sheep for people."

Steam rises, warming up the cave.

Gu Qing looks at Hanhan, who is standing by the edge of the *kang*.

Cuiqiao: "Wash …"

"Mm." Gu Qing takes off his shoes and puts his feet slowly into the water.

Gu Qing: "My name is Gu Qing. You can call me brother Gu."

Cuiqiao thinks it over and nods her head.

Gu Qing washes his feet with great relief, and asks: "You drink well water?"

Cuiqiao: "River water."

Gu Qing: "You bring it from the river?"

Cuiqiao nods her head.

Gu Qing: "Is it far?"

Cuiqiao: "No, three miles."

"Oh!" When Gu Qing hears this he immediately draws his feet out of the water.

187 ES   The father comes in, hitching his trousers. He peers at Gu Qing.

He asks Cuiqiao, who is standing in front of the *kang*: "Eh! What, isn't the water hot?"

As he speaks he walks over to the *kang*, grabs the ladle and pours out the last drops of hot water into the basin.

188 CU   Cuiqiao averts her eyes and lowers her eyelids.

189 ECU   Gu Qing's feet slowly enter the warm water.

190 ECU   The lamplight is the size of a pea as the last drops of oil are used up ...

191 ECU   The father's head is outlined against the light cast on the dark wall behind him. As the last drops of oil are used up, the halo of light gradually disappears, merging with the huge silhouette of the father's head into the darkness.

20. Exterior of Cuiqiao's Home (NIGHT, EXT)

192 BE   Night. Inside the main cave it is dark, but there is a light in the side cave. The low hum of a spinning wheel and the sound of a light ballad issue from this cave.

21. Inside the Side Cave (NIGHT, INT)

193 BE   A spinning wheel turns in the light of a single lamp. The light falls on Cuiqiao's calm face.

The spinning wheel is ancient and creaks, sounding several thousand years old. The white threads are pulled through without a break, forming a round ball.

To the sound of the spinning wheel, Cuiqiao sings:

> "Pigeons fly high above // one with the other,

> The one I long for // is my own dear mother.
>
> Melons on the hillside // gourds on the plain,
>
> For not wanting to wed // I was beaten again,
>
> I was beaten again, o daughter o!"

She sings lightly, spinning slowly, and it doesn't seem as if she suffers any great grief. Perhaps her grief has already become part of her normal life. She stops the spinning wheel and listens carefully. All is silent on the other side of the wall and she relaxes. No-one can hear her sing, she is singing for herself. Nevertheless, her song gets louder, as if she is hoping anyway that someone besides herself will hear.

> "The embroidered purse // is round and neat,
>
> As long as I don't marry // hardship is sweet."

Tonight she feels especially like singing. A poor girl who has grown up in these barren hills, her songs are her dreams ...

194 ECU   The moving spinning wheel.

Cuiqiao's song (OS):

> "Up on the window-sill // the cock lies sleeping ..."

The spinning wheel stops.

22. The Exterior of Cuiqiao's Home
(NIGHT, EXT)

195 ES   PAN RIGHT from the white path on the hillside to the door of the side cave.

Cuiqiao's song (OS):
> "Who can I turn to // when I get a beating,
> When I get a beating, o daughter o!"

The only sound and light in the still night are the creak of the spinning wheel and the warm lamp light. This is one of Cuiqiao's countless nights ...

23. The Yard of Cuiqiao's Home
(MORNING, EXT)

196 MS	Gu Qing is sweeping the small yard.
197 BE	A view from the hillside facing Cuiqiao's home. The sun has just appeared, and a white mist flows along the earth, stained red by the sun, and along the winding white path. Cuiqiao appears from the foot of the hill, carrying water ...
198 BE	Cuiqiao, wearing a red jacket, walks with her back to the camera along the white path towards the small yard carrying water. Gu Qing goes down from the small yard to meet her.

24. Inside Cuiqiao's Cave Home
(MORNING, INT)

199 ECU-MC	The muddy Yellow River water flows slowly into the water vat. PAN UP to Gu Qing's face.
200 ES	Beside the door, Cuiqiao's red face. She is panting slightly, peeking silently at Gu Qing pouring out the water.
201 MC	Gu Qing deftly pours out the water into the vat. The carrying pole leans against the wall. The

buckets land on the floor. His breathing completely normal, he turns his head and catches sight of Cuiqiao standing blankly in the doorway.

202 CU   Cuiqiao hastily lowers her eyes.

203 ES   (FROM INSIDE LOOKING OUT) Her braid swinging, Cuiqiao goes to the stove, lights the fire, ladles out water and pours in some millet, then sits down and pumps the bellows, as swift as a breeze in order to disguise the joy in her heart.

Gu Qing stands by the vat, his sleeves rolled up. He would like to help Cuiqiao with something. He goes outside. Sunlight comes in from outside the cave.

Cuiqiao pumps the bellows a few times, then stands up again. She carries the basin over to the window. Gu Qing comes in through the door, carrying a bundle of firewood.

204 MC   Cuiqiao carries the basin over, holding it level with her chest. She averts and then lowers her eyes, not saying anything.

205 ES   (FROM INSIDE LOOKING OUT) Gu Qing puts down the fire-wood, takes the basin and pours the water back into the vat. He picks up his towel from the previous night and wipes his face. Cuiqiao carries the firewood over to the stove, hastily kneels down and puts the lid on the pot, then takes up the bellows again. Gu Qing walks over to the *kang* and starts mending his clothes.

Gu Qing: "Cuiqiao, last night, was it you singing?"

Cuiqiao's hands stop pumping. "… Who says so?" It is not clear whether she is pleased or startled.

Gu Qing does not ask further, and smiles.

206 SE　　Cuiqiao sits in front of the stove pumping the bellows, ears alert. For some time she doesn't stir, then, unable to keep still any longer, she silently turns her head. When she sees what he is doing she gives a start.

207 MC　　Gu Qing is sitting on the edge of the *kang* mending his clothes.

208 MS　　Cuiqiao's dumbstruck face.

209 ES　　Gu Qing calls out to Cuiqiao: "Look! What do you think of my stitching?"

210 MC　　Cuiqiao dumbly stands up.

211 SE　　(ONE ACTION AFTER THE OTHER) Cuiqiao slowly goes over to the *kang* to look.

Gu Qing: "Hm!"

Cuiqiao: "… Nice … You officials … grown men, can you sew too?"

Gu Qing: "It's nothing. Our women comrades in the army are the same, they can swing an axe, and they can fight the Japs behind the lines. They cut off their braids and crop their hair. They've got such spirit!"

Cuiqiao, blankly: "Oh …"

212 SE　　Cuiqiao walks quietly back to the stove. She takes the cover off the pot. The water inside is boiling. Using a bowl as a ladle, she takes out some millet gruel and walks slowly over to the door.

On each side of the door is pasted a strip of red paper for good luck couplets. One edge has been torn loose by the wind. She sticks it back on with the millet gruel. Her eyes are lowered and she doesn't speak.

Gu Qing sits to the right on the *kang* sewing.

213 MC   Gu Qing looks at Cuiqiao, not understanding.

End of Reel III (932 feet)

Reel IV

214 MS   (FROM OUTSIDE THE CAVE LOOKING IN) Gu Qing walks up to the door and looks at the strips of paper. He is taken aback. Instead of matching couplets, there are only two rows of black circles, printed with the bottom rim of a bowl.

Gu Qing: "What's this?"

Cuiqiao lowers her head. Flatly, "It's a poor area here, there's nobody who can write ..." As if suddenly happy again, she points at one strip of paper. "This bit's been torn by the north wind,—I've stuck it back on again. Doesn't it look nice! When we put them up at the end of the year they were much redder."

Gu Qing: "Oh ..." He doesn't know what to say.

215 CU   (FROM INSIDE THE CAVE LOOKING OUT, WITH A PARTIAL VIEW OF GU QING'S RIGHT BACK) Cuiqiao smiles. Girls' hearts are like spring, now sunny, now in shade.

216 ES   (FROM INSIDE THE CAVE LOOKING OUT) Cuiqiao runs into the cave. From under the *kang* mat she pulls out a pair of man's shoes,

made in the old-fashioned local style, with a needle and thread still sticking out. She picks up a bundle of straw and runs out …

217 SE … Cuiqiao runs out of the cave, puts down the straw by the door and sits down on it. The sun shines in her eyes, making her squint. She lifts her hand to oil the needle in her hair, then begins to sew with rapid stitches.

Gu Qing goes into the cave, puts on his army cap and walks out again.

Gu Qing: "If you like good luck sayings, why don't I write a pair of matching couplets for you?

Cuiqiao: "That would be nice … but I'm afraid we don't have any red paper at home. Besides, none of us can read, and if we can't read what you write, maybe our door isn't worthy of the honour." Suddenly she compresses her lips in a smile, and blurts out without thinking: "Menfolk sewing …" As she speaks she feels she has given herself away.—Still thinking of an official doing his own sewing, she blushes and lowers her head in order to hide a smile.

Gu Qing slowly raises his head.

25. The Family Plot (MORNING, EXT)

218 BE The father walks along the raised path between the fields towards the camera. Leading the ox forward, he flicks his whip. Hanhan follows behind, spreading dung.

The father urges on the ox: "Hoi … eh, how the fuck can we sow, how the fuck can we sow …"

219 BE	The hillcrest above the cave is the family plot. Gu Qing suddenly appears over the crest, walking from far off.
	Father (OS): "How the fuck can we sow, hoi hoi hoi hoi …"
220 MS	Gu Qing walks forward.
	Father (OS): "How the fuck can we sow, hoi hoi hoi hoi …"
221 ELS	It is a morning in early spring. A vapour like a light mist rises up from the vast brown earth …
	The father is ploughing, bare-footed and stripped down to a singlet. Hanhan follows after him, sowing seed. He is wearing a tattered jacket, open to show a red singlet underneath.
	Gu Qing suddenly appears left from the foot of the hill.
222 ES-MS	Gu Qing takes the whip from the father's hand and cracks it: "Eh,—move …"
	The ox obediently moves forward. Hanhan follows closely after Gu Qing. They cross into centre screen.
223 ES	Back view of Gu Qing and Hanhan moving away.
224 BE	The sound of Gu Qing urging on the ox, off screen.
	The father, crouched over, squats on his heels, looking sideways in the direction of Gu Qing.
225 ES	Back view of Gu Qing skilfully driving the ox and Hanhan spreading dung.
226 BE	The old man, squatting on the path between the fields, looks at Gu Qing moving into the distance. The expression on his face doesn't change.

227 ES	Back view of Gu Qing and Hanhan moving away.
228 ES	The old man squatting on the path.
229 ES-MS	Gu Qing and Hanhan move towards the camera.

          Gu Qing: "Round you go ..."

The father crosses in right, catching up with Gu Qing and Hanhan. He pulls off Hanhan's seed pouch and says: "Spread dung!"

Not saying a word, not lifting his head, the old man silently begins sowing.

Gu Qing turns his head and looks at the old man.

Without even raising his head, as if he has grown eyes in his forehead, the father says roughly: "Keep your eyes front!"

Gu Qing: "Der-tchk!"

Gu Qing smiles. He knows that peasants have their own ways of showing affection towards their friends.

230 BE   Back view of the three figures moving away over the soil.

Gu Qing:"Der-tchk! Move, tchk ..."

231 MS   (TPL) The three figures walk towards the camera.

As they talk it is apparent from the old man's words that he has finally accepted Gu Qing as one of them.

Gu Qing: "Tchk ... Any kids besides Cuiqiao and Hanhan, uncle?"

Father: "An elder daughter, married off."

Gu Qing: "Eh—, move ... You fix it up yourself?

Father: "Her ma went long ago, it was in my care."

Gu Qing: "She didn't mind?"

Father: "Yes."

Gu Qing: "How's that?"

Father: "Something to eat at their place." The old man hesitates, then adds: "She minded later on."

Gu Qing: "How's that?"

232 ECU (PAN) The warm earth, turned up under the plough.

A silence.

Father (OS): "Nothing to eat at their place!"

233 MS (TPL) Gu Qing:"That was the reason? Or because there wasn't any affection?"

The father looks at Gu Qing.

Gu Qing: "Mm, I mean love between man and wife."

Father: "There's a saying here: 'Meat and wine friends, rice and wheat spouses.' Where's love when there's no food?"

234 ECU The point of the plough, deeply scoring the soil …

Gu Qing (OS): "Move, move …, tchk … tchk …"

235 BE In the distance, Cuiqiao appears at the foot of the hill, carrying two black earthenware food jars. She walks forward.

Gu Qing (OS): "Tchk …, move …"

236 MS Cuiqiao full face. She is surprised at Gu Qing's skill on the job.

Gu Qing (OS): Move …, der …, tchk …"

237 MS (TPL) The three men walk towards the camera.

The father goes on: "… our daughter ran back home, said her husband beat her, … 'a beaten wife, a kneaded dough'—rich or poor, she wouldn't go back."

Gu Qing: "Afterwards?"

Father: "I told her, girl, though 'He who gets a

wife is glad, she who gets a man is sad', we poor folk have to keep our word, that's to say, stick to your man even if you have to beg for food. Besides, poverty doesn't strike root, you can't spend your whole life with your guts squeezed like a rope. Who knows when the likes of us might cast off our poor skins and maybe wake up rich?"

The old man chuckles. Lifting his head, he sees Cuiqiao coming with the food.

238 BE Cuiqiao coming with the food jars …

239 MS Into the camera, the father loudly whistles the ox to halt: "Heu—" and picks up his black padded jacket from its back.

Gu Qing, after a long silence, asks: " Tell me, why does your daughter have such a hard life?"

The father brushes the earth off his jacket, then says very seriously and positively to Gu Qing: "Fate."

Gu Qing: "And Cuiqiao, afterwards do you plan on …"

The father slings his jacket around his shoulders and gives him a keen sidelong glance. As he turns his head away, however, he can't supress a soft sigh.

240 MC Hanhan's apparently expressionless face, as before.

241 BE The father crosses out, not even turning his head.

Gu Qing: "Uncle, …"

It seems as if he wants to ask something, but then he discovers that Cuiqiao has already entered from the left and is walking over to him. He hastily greets Cuiqiao, concealing from her the topic of their conversation.

Cuiqiao looks alertly at Gu Qing, then looks over to where her father has gone. She asks suspiciously: "What have you been talking about?" —She certainly realizes that they have been talking about her.

242 MC   Hanhan's expressionless face. However, a careful look reveals that the glance he gives his sister shows a warm affection.

26. The Clifftop at the Edge of the Field (DAY, EXT)

243 BE   Hanhan, Cuiqiao and Gu Qing sit in a circle on the ground. Cuiqiao opens the earthenware jars and sets out on the ground the coarse, chipped earthenware bowls. There comes the sound of the father coughing.

The father crosses in left and sits down beside the others.

This is a meal between sky and earth, with the Yellow River flowing at the foot of the cliff behind them ...

244 MC   Cuiqiao fills half an extra-large bowl with millet gruel and hands it to her father.

He motions her to give it to Gu Qing.

Cuiqiao then fills up the bowl (PAN) and offers it to Gu Qing with both hands.

The father stands up. (ONE ACTION AFTER THE OTHER)

245 MC-BE   The father stands up. TILT UP to the sky. Against the sky in the background, his figure appears

at the bottom of the screen. With half-closed eyes he looks up. On his face appears an expression of piety and fear. He mutters: "Always clouds, but no rain … Looks like a drought for this year's harvest."

Holding a bowl of gruel in both hands, Cuiqiao appears at the bottom of the screen and hands the bowl to her father. She then disappears off screen.

With the piety of a peasant towards heaven, he picks out a drop of gruel with his chopsticks and casts it towards the sky. He mutters something, but only these words can be heard: "… five grains sprout, may the rains soon fall."

From off screen comes the sound of Gu Qing's well-meaning laugh.

(TILT DOWN) The father sits down again in his original position. He earnestly admonishes Gu Qing: "Young folks don't understand. You shouldn't grudge this bit of food."

He takes up a handful of yellow earth. "This old yellow earth, it lets you tread on it, plough it up—would you be willing?—Haven't you got any respect for it?"

246 MS   Gu Qing, holding his bowl in both hands, looks at the father. He seems to be very moved.

247 MS   Father: "This is millet from the year before last, eat up …"

Gu Qing murmurs assent, and slowly raises the bowl of pure millet gruel. It is something that farmers rarely get to taste.

248 MS   They begin to eat. When farmers eat their midday meal, chopsticks are superfluous. All that can

be heard is a cheerful slurping noise, which expresses a kind of happy contentment that ordinary people never experience.

249 MC   Gu Qing sucks in the millet gruel, his mouth wide open. (PARTIAL VIEW OF CUIQIAO'S BACK)

250 MC   Cuiqiao quietly eats her millet gruel, her head lowered. (VIEW OF THE FATHER'S HEAD)

251 BE   In the sunlight over the rolling hills, the distant ox, its head lowered, lightly flicks its tail ...

252 MC   The father sucks at his bowl, then pours out what is left for Hanhan, who has an astonishing appetite. He licks the bowl, gives a deep sniff and puts down the bowl contentedly. Over his face floats the peaceful pleasure of a farmer who has just eaten.

Hanhan, not saying a word, eats with his mouth wide open.

Cuiqiao puts down her bowl. She hands over the shoes she has just made to her father. "Try them on, pa, see if they fit!"

Gu Qing feels a bit tired. The early spring sun at noon makes him comfortably warm. With a smile he stretches out a hand and ruffles the tuft of hair on Hanhan's head.

Hanhan smiles at him for the first time. He has a very engaging smile.

253 SE   The father tries on the shoes. He looks at them first from one side and then from the other, moving his feet in them. He mutters: "Not as good as your ma used to make."

An idea occurs to him, and he asks Gu Qing cheerfully: "Mr Official, you said last night that this trip of yours is for collecting something?"

Gu Qing: "I want to collect the folksongs of our Shaanbei."

The father for the first time breaks into a laugh. "What folksongs—our poor local ballads?"

Gu Qing: "Can you sing, uncle?"

Father: "… Sing what? If you're not happy and not sad …"

254 MC (WITH A PARTIAL VIEW OF THE FATHER) Cuiqiao collects the bowls, her head lowered …

255 SE Gu Qing: "There are hundreds and thousands of our Shaanbei folksongs. Tell me, how can you know them all, and remember them all?"

The father thinks for a while before answering. "You remember them when times are hard."

Gu Qing nods, smiling wryly. He feels there is no chance of getting the old man to sing.

Cuiqiao: "What's it for, collecting our local ballads?"

256 MC (WITH A PARTIAL VIEW OF THE FATHER) Cuiqiao collects the bowls, her head lowered …

257 MS In the foreground is Cuiqiao, her back to the camera.

Gu Qing is sitting down, his legs crossed, deeply immersed in his thoughts.

Gu Qing: "When we've collected the folksongs and written new words to them, we turn them over to the Eighth Route Army troops, boys and girls of Cuiqiao's age …"

258 MC	Cuiqiao, collecting the bowls, keeps her head lowered.
	Gu Qing (OS): "… to sing, so everyone can understand why our suffering people are living in fear and wretchedness,"
259 CU	(A PARTIAL VIEW OF CUIQIAO AS FOREGROUND) The father half opens his mouth and blinks.
	Gu Qing (OS): "… why wives and daughters are beaten …"
260 MC	Hanhan's expressionless face.
	Gu Qing turns his face to one side and continues speaking: "… why labourers and farmers are carrying out a revolution. After hearing these songs, our Eighth Route Army troops ford the Yellow River and march east, to fight the enemy and struggle against the moneybags, fearing neither bloodshed nor loss of life …"
261 MS	Cuiqiao's lowered eyes.
	His back to the camera, Gu Qing says with a smile: "… Our Chairman Mao and Commander Zhu love listening to folksongs."
262 MC	The father stares dully at him, as if listening to some incomprehensible scripture. He looks at Cuiqiao, then looks back at Gu Qing.
	With his face turned to one side, Gu Qing continues: "Our Chairman Mao doesn't just get us to sing …"
263 MC	Cuiqiao's back in the foreground.
	Gu Qing: "… he also gets us to read and write. All the girls in Yenan go round with a stone tablet under their arms, they write … draw …"
264 MC	Cuiqiao slowly lifts her eyes.

Gu Qing (OS): "... our Chairman Mao wants to get all of our suffering people of China to eat millet without husks or weeds ..."

Cuiqiao's eyes gaze at Gu Qing. A long pause.

265 MC Cuiqiao in the foreground.

There is an expression of rebuke on the father's face.

266 MC Cuiqiao, in the foreground, seems to sense that something is wrong, and hurriedly lowers her eyelids ...

267 BE The four sit quietly together after their meal.

End of Reel IV (903.3 feet)

Reel V

268 SE Gu Qing, the father and Hanhan, seated.

Father: "Blasted girl! Leaving without a word!"

Gu Qing gazes after Cuiqiao off screen in the distance.

269 ES Cuiqiao walks away, carrying the black earthenware jars. She says nothing, and her gait is neither fast nor slow.

270 ELS Cuiqiao walks away. She makes a conspicuous red patch on the white path on the hillcrest.

271 CU-MS Turning her head to left screen, Cuiqiao sees Gu Qing watching her. She swiftly turns her head and walks on.

272 BE (TILT DOWN) The three figures at the edge of the cliff, the Yellow River behind them.

273 ELS Cuiqiao goes down the hill, leaving behind an empty hillcrest.

27. **The Family Plot** (DAY, EXT)

274 SE

The father takes the new shoes off, letting his big peasant's feet tread the spring earth.

Father: "Going barefoot's better than wearing shoes …"

He fondly pats the soles and sticks them in his belt, one on either side. Looking at Gu Qing, he turns red and then chuckles.

The father puts his hand to the plough but doesn't move. After some time passes, he asks with his head lowered: "You say that girls down south can read and write … is it true?"

28. **The Cliffside at the Edge of the Field** (DAY, EXT)

275 ELS

The evening sun is about to set behind the hillcrest. The sound of the father urging on the ox reverberates against the earth and sky, plaintive and lingering. The row of three small figures, ploughing, sowing and spreading dung, proceeds slowly along the hillcrest, just as our people have proceeded throughout their long and arduous history …

29. **The Bank of the Yellow River** (DUSK, EXT)

276 CU-MS

The shore of the Yellow River. Cuiqiao's back appears at the bottom of the screen, carrying a shoulder pole with a water bucket at each end.

277 CU

The Yellow River current …

278 CU

A blackened wooden bucket dips into the water

with a plop, and the water splashes in. TILT UP to Cuiqiao's calm face. Absorbed in rinsing out the bucket, there seems to be nothing on her mind, but a *xintianyou*, sung in a low, light voice, pours forth:

"Ducks float along the river // and geese swim ..."

279 CU-ECU   The muddy river water fills up the wooden bucket. A girl's hand picks it up, and a string of drops falls away. (LEFT FOLLOW) The bucket is placed on the shore, and the water inside settles, spreading ripples ...

"The Official doesn't know // that I, Cuiqiao, can sing." (sings)

280 ES   The Yellow River current.

"Poplars and willows // eighteen in a row ..." (sings)

281 MS-CU   Cuiqiao, carrying water, walks towards the camera along the well-trodden path.

"Cuiqiao longs to speak // but how she doesn't know." (sings)

282 ES   The muddy water of the Yellow River flows east.

"She doesn't know, o daughter o." (sings)

30. On the Hillside (DAY, EXT)

283 ES   (SLIGHTLY LOW-ANGLE) On the brown hillside, Gu Qing is driving a flock of sheep, walking from right to left across the hillside. Gu Qing and the silent Hanhan are now on more familiar terms.

Gu Qing's laugh can be heard in the distance.

284 MS   (PAN) Gu Qing comes up to Hanhan. He takes

from his hands the shovel-shaped shepherd's stick and digs up a few clods of earth, which he throws at an unruly ram. The ram bleats, and Gu Qing laughs.

Weaving his sheepskin jacket, Hanhan stands there in silence. Although he doesn't smile he looks happy.

Gu Qing plants the stick in the ground. With his right hand grasping the stick, he pats Hanhan on the shoulder with his other hand, saying: "Come here, Hanhan!"

Embarrassed, Hanhan turns to left screen …

285 ES   On the empty hillside. Cuiqiao appears, carrying water. Seeing Gu Qing and Hanhan, she stops.

286 MS   (PAN) With the hills in the background, Gu Qing walks smiling over to Hanhan's right, then sits down, not looking at Hanhan.

287 BE   Gu Qing sits on the ground. Hanhan, back to camera, stands at right screen. Behind them are the sheep.

288 MS   Gu Qing (OS): "… come on!"

Supressing a smile, Cuiqiao sits on her carrying pole, watching Gu Qing and Hanhan.

289 BE   Hanhan, back to camera, slowly turns his head to the left look at Gu Qing, sitting on the ground.

Gu Qing turns his head.

Their glances meet. Embarrassed, Hanhan turns his head away again.

290 BE   (REVERSE: HANHAN FACING THE CAMERA, GU QING BACK TO THE CAMERA) Hanhan blinks, and standing bolt upright begins to sing, showing not the slightest shyness:

"When the pomegranate flowers // the
    leaves start to grow,
My mother sold me off to him // without
    letting me know.

All I ever wanted // was an honest man to
    wed,
What I ended up with // was a little wet-
    a-bed.

You pee // I pee,
Damn you // together we pee.
Ai-hei, damn you, together we pee."
Gu Qing, sitting on the ground, chuckles.
Throwing out his chest, Hanhan sings with great
    earnestness:
"In spring next year // when the flowers
    turn red,
Frogs will start croaking // under the bed.

Down to the east // flows a river of pee,
To the Dragon King's palace // under the
    sea.

The Dragon King laughs // when he hears
    the pee:
'This little wet-a-bed's // in the same line
    as me,
Ai-hei, this little wet-a-bed's // in the
    same line as me.'"

291 BE   Gu Qing bursts out laughing.
The figure of Hanhan standing with his back to
    Gu Qing.

292 BE   Facing the camera, Hanhan doesn't laugh. He
feels that he has not sung well. Gu Qing, sitting

	beside him with his back to the camera, laughs in spite of himself.
293 BE	Facing the camera, Gu Qing laughs even harder.
294 BE	Cuiqiao, sitting far away on her carrying pole, begins to laugh.
295 MC	Laughing, Gu Qing gives Hanhan a hug, and the two walk away to the right.
296 MS	Cuiqiao's expression of concentration, in the distance.
297 BE	Gu Qing and Hanhan standing on the hillside.

297 BE — Gu Qing and Hanhan standing on the hillside.

Gu Qing: "Sing after me." (sings)

> "The hammer, the sickle // and the scythe …"

Hanhan doesn't utter a sound.

Gu Qing: (sings)

> "The hammer, the sickle // and the scythe …"

Hanhan still doesn't utter a sound.

Gu Qing: (sings)

> "For workers and peasants …"

Hanhan suddenly opens his mouth: (sings)

> "The hammer, the sickle // and the scythe, The hammer, the sickle …"

Delighted, Gu Qing pats Hanhan on the head: "Right, that's it!"

298 MS. — Not moving, Cuiqiao gazes at them. As she listens intently to Gu Qing's song, a deep emotion fills her eyes …

Hanhan (OS): (sings)

> "… and the scythe."

Gu Qing (OS) laughs.

299 BE — On the hillside, Gu Qing says something to Hanhan.

300 MS	Cuiqiao looks at Gu Qing and Hanhan.
301 BE	(SLIGHTLY LOW-ANGLE) On the hillside, Gu Qing and Hanhan sing as they drive the sheep down the hill … "The hammer, the sickle …"
302 BE	On the hillside, Gu Qing and Hanhan drive the flock down. They sing: "… and the scythe, For workers and peasants // shall build a new life. The piebald cock // flies over the wall, The Communist Party // shall save us all." They become gradually obscured behind the hill, but their singing continues to be heard: "The piebald cock // flies over the wall, The Communist Party // shall save us all." The empty hill top …
303 BE	(SLIGHTLY LOW-ANGLE) All that remains on the hillside is Cuiqiao in her red jacket. As if she had taken root there, she gazes for a long time at the vast brown earth …

31. On the Road Home (DUSK, INT)

304 MC	(TPL) Cuiqiao, carrying water, walks like a gust of wind along the path.
305 CU-ES	Cuiqiao, carrying water, appears behind the hillside opposite her home. She walks like a gust of wind along the path.
306 BE	Cuiqiao, carrying water, walks up from the bottom of the gully.

32. Inside Cuiqiao's Cave Home (DUSK, INT)

307 ECU	The cave door is pushed open with a squeak. Cuiqiao's ecstatic face abruptly turns fiery red.
308 SE	(FROM OUTSIDE THE CAVE LOOKING IN) A matchmaker, sitting on the edge of the *kang* and holding a bowl in her hand, looks at Cuiqiao in the doorway. Wedding clothes and various colourful items are scattered over the *kang*.
	The father is sitting in front of the stove, in silence.
309 ES	(FROM INSIDE THE CAVE LOOKING OUT) The three people in the cave are silent. After a moment, the matchmaker gets off the *kang*, and silently squeezing past Cuiqiao on tiptoe, goes out the door.
310 ECU	Cuiqiao's face. Her still eyes register indescribable shock and suffering.
	Silence.
	Father (OS): "… the husband's family have sent over a message, they've also sent over the wedding clothes … They'll fetch you at the beginning of Fourth Month … Now your ma can close her eyes. You've felt the back of my hand already over this business … Every girl takes this path …"
	On Cuiqiao's wooden face there is, however, an expression of despair.
	Father (OS): "… I reckon your fate might turn out better than your sister's … Your future husband's a good fellow; even if he's a bit

older, it's better that way, he's honest and reliable."

Cuiqiao's still eyes …

Father (OS): "… Besides, you were betrothed as a child, half the money went for your ma's funeral, the other half will make up the amount for your brother to get betrothed … it just works out …"

Cuiqiao slowly lowers her eyelids, hiding her tears, and nods her head.

311 ES   Cuiqiao is left alone in the cave. She sits silently on the edge of the *kang*. After a short while, she picks up the new, bright-red wedding jacket.

312 MS   Cuiqiao holds the wedding jacket up to her chest. She holds out the sleeve and slowly compares it to the one she is wearing. She smiles, a sad, bitter smile.

313 ES   Cuiqiao throws down the jacket and sits still, thinking. Suddenly she crawls to a corner of the *kang*, takes out a cloth bundle and wraps it up.

She holds the small bundle, her face a blank …

End of Reel V (912 feet)

Reel VI

33. The Hillside opposite Cuiqiao's Home
(DUSK, EXT)

314 LS   On the hillside the father, leading a black donkey on which the matchmaker is seated, walks slowly away …

34. The Yard outside Cuiqiao's Home
(DUSK, EXT)

315 ES — Leaning against the door, Cuiqiao gazes after her father ...

35. The Hillside opposite Cuiqiao's Home
(DUSK, EXT)

316 LS — On the hillside, the father, leading the black donkey on which the matchmaker is seated, walks slowly away.

36. The Yard outside Cuiqiao's Home
(DUSK, EXT)

317 ES — Cuiqiao stands blankly against the door. In days to come, her father will lean against the door watching someone carry away his daughter ...

37. Inside Cuiqiao's Cave Home (DUSK, INT)

318 ECU — The muddy Yellow River flows once more into the water vat ...

319 ES — (FROM INSIDE THE CAVE LOOKING OUT) Cuiqiao puts down the bucket, turns around and goes over to the *kang*. From under the mat she takes out a pair of shoe soles that she hasn't finished embroidering.

The pattern embroidered on the soles is "Cinnabar phoenix aface the sun".

38. The Yard outside Cuiqiao's Home
(DUSK, EXT)

320 SE (THE YARD FROM INSIDE THE CAVE) Seated on the small straw stool in front of the cave, Cuiqiao embroiders the shoe soles. Her face is calm, her head bent.

Gu Qing comes up the path.

Cuiqiao, her head bent: "You're back?"

Gu Qing: "Yes—what's up, Cuiqiao?"

Cuiqiao: "Nothing, I'm working."

Gu Qing: "Oh …"

As he speaks he goes inside.

321 BE Cuiqiao is bent over her embroidery. "The food is in the pot. Go ahead and eat."

Gu Qing (OS): "Oh."

Cuiqiao oils the needle in her hair. "My brother is silly, isn't he?"

Gu Qing (OS): "Not at all. Hanhan doesn't say much, but he's a bright lad."

Cuiqiao gives a faint smile.

The sound of Gu Qing packing.

Cuiqiao: "Do you have girl soldiers in your army?"

Gu Qing (OS): "Lots of them."

Cuiqiao: "You don't want people who can't sing."

Gu Qing (OS): "Who says that?"

Cuiqiao: "But people who can sing?"

Gu Qing (OS): "There's a place for them in our army."

Cuiqiao moistens the needle, and lowers her head again. "Is it far to Yenan, by the main road south?"

Gu Qing (OS): "Mm, about 200 miles."

Cuiqiao: "Oh—that far!"

Gu Qing (OS): "Why do you ask?"

Cuiqiao: "Just asking, it's nothing."

The sound of packing.

Cuiqiao: "What are you doing in there? There's water in the vat, pour out a basinful and have a wash."

Gu Qing (OS): "No, I'll go down to the Yellow River tomorrow and have a proper wash."

Cuiqiao: "Why go to the river, there's water here."

Gu Qing (OS): "I'm leaving tomorrow."

Cuiqiao, panic-stricken, stops sewing.

Cuiqiao: "Where are you going?"

Gu Qing (OS): "I've been away for a few months, I have to go back."

Cuiqiao: "You won't collect folksongs? You won't help pa with the ploughing? You won't teach my brother some songs?"

Inside, Gu Qing is silent. After a while he answers. "Cuiqiao, I've put the money for my food for these days on the *kang*, see if it's enough. If there's enough, go to the market and buy a few yards of fancy cloth to make yourself a shirt."

Cuiqiao's eyes redden and fill with tears. To stop herself from crying, she takes a deep breath, then says: "… I have some."

Cuiqiao twists round towards the cave, then stops. It seems as if she has something more to say to Gu Qing inside.

39. A Distant View of the Hillcrest (NIGHT, EXT)

322 BE   The hillcrest is bleak and empty, with no sign of human presence except a white path twisting upwards along the brown earth and disappearing over the hill. A lonely wild pear tree stands at the crest.

40. Inside Cuiqiao's Cave Home (NIGHT, INT)

323 CU   With the oil lamp in the foreground, Gu Qing's face in the faint light, his eyes staring straight ahead.

324 ES   Cuiqiao, in front of the stove, is lighting the fire. Hanhan is sitting at the edge of the *kang*, while Gu Qing and the father are sitting opposite each other, in silence.
The father pushes over the red dates on the *kang* table and beckons to Gu Qing: "Have some."
In answer Gu Qing takes some dates and stuffs them into Hanhan's hand.
Gu Qing: "Uncle, I've put you to some trouble over the last few days. Thanks!"

325 MC   With the oil lamp in the foreground, the father lowers his eyes and laughs softly.
Gu Qing (OS): "When I have time later I'll drop by and see you."
Father: "You mean well enough—but you won't show up, you won't show up."

326 MC   In front of the stove, Cuiqiao's troubled face in the fire light.

327 MC   With the oil lamp in the foreground, the father:

"You haven't collected any of our local ballads while you've been here. You'll lose your job when you go back."

Gu Qing (OS): "I've gained experience here."

The father remains impassive, as if he hasn't heard. After a while he chuckles.

328 MC   Gu Qing smiles—he is used to the old man's ways.

329 CU   With the circle of light from the lamp in the foreground, the father, his head lowered and his hands tucked in his sleeves, suddenly breaks into song:

"The first hour // of First Month strikes ..."

330 CU   With the circle of light from the lamp in the foreground, Gu Qing is startled. He hasn't expected that the father would end up singing for him. (HALF SILHOUETTE)

331 ECU   With the circle of light from the lamp in the foreground, the father does not look at Gu Qing. His voice is ancient, bleak and full of feeling: (HALF SILHOUETTE)

"Big bright eyes // two shining lights.

Curving eyebrows // two arched bows ...

332 MC   Cuiqiao, tending the stove, listens intently to the song ... (HALF SILHOUETTE)

333 SE   Cuiqiao gets up from where she has been sitting in front of the stove. From the top of the stove she picks up a patched sack of grain, then facing the camera, walks over to the cave door and goes out left.

The father, sitting on the *kang*, sings:

"All adore her // wherever she goes."

334 ECU	With the circle of light in the foreground, the father's face as he sings: (HALF SILHOU-ETTE) "Betrothed at thirteen // at fourteen a wife, At fifteen a widow // for the rest of her life."

41. The Yard outside Cuiqiao's Home
(NIGHT, EXT)

335 BE	Cuiqiao goes out through the door, holding the sack of grain in her hand. She looks around the small yard, five foot by five foot, in the frosty night. It is as if this is a strange place, or if not, then a place she was loathe to leave … The father's voice is heard off screen, singing: "Three loud cries // on all ears fell …"
336 CU	A hand holding a small broom slowly sweeps the mill base … The father's voice, singing, off screen: "Three low cries // she jumps into the well."
337 CU	Cuiqiao's face in the darkness. The father's voice, singing off screen.
338 ECU	Two hands carefully untie the rope around the neck of the sack, and a stream of millet pours out on to the mill base. The father's voice, singing off screen: "Ai—"
339 CU	The roller, which has begun to move. The father's voice, singing (OS): "Ai—"
340 ES	From the hillside opposite the small yard PAN SLOWLY to inside the yard. Cuiqiao is

	pushing the roller, silently, sturdily. A dim light from the window shines on Cuiqiao's figure in centre screen.
341 MC	Cuiqiao stops, and then starts pushing again, silently, sturdily ... The sound of the roller crushing the grain ...
	Cuiqiao's figure disappears and reappears on the screen.
342 BE	From inside the cave, the dim lamp shines on a small figure leaning against the door. It is Hanhan, watching his sister ...

42. Hanhan Sees Gu Qing off (MORNING, EXT)

343 BE	Early morning. Gu Qing is on his way, followed by Hanhan.
	They go up the slope opposite the cave, taking the white path, and are hidden behind the slope.
	Morning. Wind soughs faintly through the valleys ...
344 ES	Behind the slope, Gu Qing and Hanhan appear at the bottom of the screen, Gu Qing in front, Hanhan behind.
	Hanhan walks fast and catches up with Gu Qing on the right. They enter a gully.
	The wind soughs ...
345 ES	A ridge with a smooth gradient. The silhouettes of Gu Qing and Hanhan appear in right screen, walking.
	Gu Qing stops and turns his head. "Go home now, Hanhan."

Gu Qing stands still. As he starts walking again, Hanhan still follows him.

Morning. Wind soughs through the valleys …

346 LS   The figures of Gu Qing and Hanhan follow a winding path up a hillcrest. Hanhan is in front, Gu Qing behind.

The wind soughs …

347 MS   With the sky in the background, Gu Qing and Hanhan stand on the hillside.

Gu Qing turns round and puts his arm around Hanhan's shoulder. "I'm not leaving. Let's turn back."

Hanhan doesn't speak. Gu Qing doesn't speak either, watching Hanhan.

Hanhan stretches out a hand, pulls over Gu Qing's small satchel and undoes the straps. He reaches in his own jacket, feels around and then brings out two pieces of yellow millet cake. He puts them in Gu Qing's satchel and does up the straps. After a pause, he tucks his hands into the sleeves of his sheepskin jacket, and stands there motionless.

Gu Qing's hands slowly stroke Hanhan's head for some time.

348 ES   A hillcrest. Both Gu Qing and Hanhan stand there. Hanhan stands to the left, Gu Qing to the right.

A slight pause. Gu Qing follows the small path downhill. Hanhan stands motionless.

The wind soughs …

349 CU   Neither smiling nor weeping, Hanhan just stands there, as at the first time he saw Gu Qing. His glance travels to right screen.

	The wind soughs …
350 MC-ES	Gu Qing appears on screen, back to the camera. He turns towards left screen, lifts his hand to wave to Hanhan, then turns round and goes downhill …
	The wind soughs …
351 CU	Neither smiling nor weeping, Hanhan just stands there, as at the first time he saw Gu Qing. His glance travels to right screen.
	The wind soughs …
352 MC	Against the background of the sky, Gu Qing appears on screen, back to camera. He silently turns his head again, looking at Hanhan off screen.
	The wind soughs …
353 LS	A hillcrest. Hanhan becomes a black spot in centre screen.
	The wind soughs …
354 ES	(PAN FROM RIGHT TO LEFT) Gu Qing walks silently towards the camera, with the hills in the background.
355 MS-CU	(TPL) Gu Qing walks towards the camera, with the gullies and ravines in the background.
356 MS-CU	(TPL) Gu Qing walks towards the camera along a hillside, with the sky in the background.
357 MS-CU	(TPL) Gu Qing walks towards the camera, with the horizon in the background.
358	Back view of Gu Qing going downhill along the long path. At the foot of the hill Gu Qing stops, then slowly takes a few steps forward again …

End of Reel VI (934.5 feet)

Reel VII

43. Cuiqiao Sees Gu Qing off (MORNING, EXT)

359 MS	Gu Qing walks a few steps and then stops. Facing slightly towards left screen, he seems to be surprised but at the same time to have expected what would happen.
360 ES	Cuiqiao, sitting on the incline of a cliff, wearing a red jacket.
361 MC	Gu Qing's face.
362 BE	Cuiqiao, sitting on the incline of a cliff, wearing a red jacket.
363 MC	Gu Qing's face.
364 BE-MS	Cuiqiao lifts her head, looks at Gu Qing and lowers her head again. She sits motionless on the incline. After a pause, she stands up slowly and walks over with heavy steps ... Far away the wind soughs faintly through the valleys. Cuiqiao lowers her head ...
365 ES	Both stand still: Cuiqiao to the left, Gu Qing to the right.
366 MC	Gu Qing's face.
367 MS	Cuiqiao's face.
368 MC	Gu Qing's face.
369 CU	Cuiqiao slowly lifts her head, her eyes weighing up her decision ... Cuiqiao: "Take ... me with you."
370 MC	Gu Qing's silent face.
371 MS	Both in midground, Cuiqiao to the left and Gu Qing to the right. Cuiqiao's hands are empty: she has not brought anything with her.

Cuiqiao: "... I made up a bundle, but I didn't bring it. I can go like this."

Gu Qing: "Cuiqiao, has something happened?"

Cutting Gu Qing short, Cuiqiao says: "I can do everything: wash clothes, carry water, make food, even ... cut my hair short."

Gu Qing lifts his head and looks at Cuiqiao.

Cuiqiao: "What's wrong?"

Gu Qing: "Cuiqiao, we officials are bound by official regulations, it would have to be approved by the leadership."

Cuiqiao: "Can't the regulations be changed?"

Gu Qing: "We officials need these regulations to conquer the land."

With a look of disappointment in her eyes, Cuiqiao slowly lifts her head.

Cuiqiao: "Oh ..."

372 MS   (TPL) Gu Qing and Cuiqiao walk slowly towards the camera, with the sky in the background.

Gu Qing: "... When I get back, I'll speak to the leadership. I'll tell them that there's a young lass by the Yellow River called Cuiqiao who wants to join up—. Once the leadership has approved I'll definitely come back for you."

Cuiqiao: "Could you be back before Fourth Month?"

Gu Qing and Cuiqiao stop walking.

Cuiqiao lowers her head. Gu Qing: "Cuiqiao, I'll definitely be back."

Cuiqiao finally nods her head and gives a bitter smile.

"I believe you ..."

Gu Qing seems to think that he understands the whole matter.

373 MC   Gu Qing's face.

374 MC   (TPL) They look at each other in silence. After a pause, Gu Qing walks towards the camera ...

Cuiqiao: "Brother Gu!"

Gu Qing stops. This is the first time Cuiqiao has called him "brother Gu." He doesn't turn his his head, but stands firmly where he is.

Cuiqiao is about to speak, but in the end suppresses what she would like to say. A slight smile flits across her face, as if she has forgotten her own grief.

Cuiqiao: "Did my brother give you the yellow millet cakes? ... Try them on your way, see if they taste good. Look out for a fellow-traveller, you won't feel tired if you're chatting with someone. If you get thirsty, drink water that has run clear. When it's getting on for night, stop and rest at a poor folk's place ..."

Gu Qing stands there.

375 LS   (HIGH ANGLE) Gu Qing at right front on the incline, Cuiqiao at left back. They make their silent farewells.

Gu Qing walks to left screen.

376 MC   Cuiqiao standing on the slope ...

377 LS   (HIGH ANGLE) Gu Qing at right front on the incline, Cuiqiao at left back. They make their silent farewells.

Gu Qing walks to left screen.

378 ES   Gu Qing turns to the left on the slope ...

Cuiqiao (OS): "Take out your notebook, brother Gu!"

379 BE   Cuiqiao walks along the slope and sings, crossing in left screen. This is the first time she has sung at full strength. Her voice is very sweet and clear, and burning with passion.

Cuiqiao: (sings) "Ai ..."

380 ES   Gu Qing, who has been silently looking back left, turns round slowly and walks away ...

Cuiqiao's song (OS):

> "The piebald cock // stands by the tree,
> From the Communist Party // comes a man who's free.
>
> Choosing one horse from many // one beats the rest ..."

381 BE   The empty valley.

Cuiqiao's song (OS):

> "Comparing you with the others // our Official's the best,
> Yi-ai-yo!"

382 ES   At the bottom of the gully, a back view of Gu Qing walking away ...

Cuiqiao's song (OS):

> "Should the Eighth Route Army // only bid me prepare,
> I'll discard my red shoes // and straw sandals wear.
>
> Two ounces of cotton // are spun into a skein ..."

383 ES   Another ridge. Cuiqiao's red clothes flash. She goes down the ridge from the right.

Cuiqiao's song (OS):

> "I'm afraid that from now on // I'll never see you again,

	Never see you again ...″
384 ES	A back view of Gu Qing, walking along the gully ...

Cuiqiao's song (OS):

> "The wind has dropped // but willow tips sway,
> For your return // I long night and day."

| 385 LS | Gu Qing walks up a hillside ... |

Cuiqiao's song (OS):

> "As soon as I hear // our Official return,
> Two holes in the window // shall my eager eyes burn."

As Gu Qing reaches the hilltop, the sound of the song is abruptly halted. The only sound to be heard is the wind soughing faintly through the hills.

386 MC	With the sky in the background, Gu Qing turns to the left and looks back ...
387 LS	On the ridge, Cuiqiao's figure has become a red dot.
388 BE	Gu Qing, who has been standing on the ridge, slowly goes down the hill.
	All that is left is the empty ridge.
389 BE	Cuiqiao, standing on the ridge, sings:

> "Larks crossing the river // won't fall to the bottom,
> For the rest of my life // you'll not be forgotten."

| 390 BE | The empty hillside. |

Cuiqiao's song (OS):

> "Onions can't root // in bare stony ground ...″

| 391 LS | (SLOW PAN FROM RIGHT TO LEFT) Gullies |

and ravines …

Cuiqiao's song (OS):

> "When can we poor folk // turn our fate round,
>
> Turn our fate round?!"

The lingering notes reverberate for a long time.

392 CU   Cuiqiao's face, showing neither grief nor tears, only a calm intentness.

393 MC-ECU   Cuiqiao walks towards the camera.

The song continues, light and low, in Cuiqiao's heart.

394 ES   On the ridge, a back view of Cuiqiao returning home slowly. She gradually becomes a red patch.

Cuiqiao's song:

> "Behind the cloud // the sun dips low.
>
> My lips can't speak // my heart's sorrow.
>
> Green grass and cow dung // can't put out a fire,
>
> Folk songs can't save me // poor Cuiqiao.
>
> Poor Cuiqiao, o daughter o."

After crossing over the ridge, Cuiqiao gradually disappears at the end of another ridge. It seems that her fate has been determined …

44. The Ridge (DAY, EXT)

395 ELS   (FOLLOW FROM LEFT TO RIGHT) A wedding procession comes down from the ridge.

396 BE   The procession, which includes several musicians, the receiving and dispatching female attendants astride donkeys, and a red bridal palanquin, comes down from the ridge along

the winding path. There are several dozen people altogether.

397 BE (FOLLOW FROM LEFT TO RIGHT) The procession forms a group along the ridge.

45. The Riverbed (DAY, EXT)

398 CU-ECU The suona, blaring vigorously into the camera, their red silk streamers fluttering ...

399 CU The gongs in the bridal procession, struck with their sticks ...

400 CU The donkeys in the bridal procession, bearing red rosettes ...

401 CU One side of the bridal palanquin in the bridal procession, hung with red silk ...

402 CU The top of the palanquin in the bridal procession ...

403 ECU The red shoes worn by the receiving attendants, embroidered with a pattern of pomegranate flowers, swaying from side to side with the movements of the donkeys ...

404 MS-CU Among the suona players, one old man comes towards the camera, blowing with particular energy ...

405 CU-ECU Coming towards the camera, the palanquin in the wedding procession gradually fills the entire screen.

46. The Yard outside Cuiqiao's Home (DUSK, EXT)

406 BE The father stands in the small yard, watching the approaching wedding procession ...

407 MC The small yard is full of people come to conduct

<table>
<tr><td></td><td>the wedding and to enjoy the excitement. The palanquin is set down, occupying almost the whole screen. The attendants lift up the red curtains ...</td></tr>
<tr><td>408 ECU</td><td>The blank face of Hanhan, who is wearing new clothes, and the side of the palanquin together occupy the whole screen.</td></tr>
</table>

The noise seems to have faded away except for the sound of one solitary suona. The music rises and falls, sounding both sad and joyful. The sadness and joy are mixed together, as if telling an ancient and yet very common tale.

409 ECU · · · · · · A pair of "Happiness" characters in red, on the shabby old window paper ...

410 ECU · · · · · · The mill base, littered with paper from the fire-crackers ...

47. Inside Cuiqiao's Cave Home (DUSK, INT)

411 CU · · · · · · On the *kang*, neatly-folded red clothes and quilts ...

48. The Yard outside Cuiqiao's Home (DUSK, EXT)

412 CU · · · · · · New red strips of paper on the door.

413 ECU · · · · · · By the door, the old, yellowing straw stool that Cuiqiao used to sit on ...

The sound of the suona rises and falls, lingers in the visible world, then gradually gets weaker and further away ...

49. The Hillside opposite Cuiqiao's Home
(DUSK, EXT)

414 BE The wedding procession gradually moves into the distance, along the white path that Cuiqiao used to take every day ...

50. The Yard outside Cuiqiao's Home
(DUSK, EXT)

415 ES The father leans against the door, looking after the procession in the distance. The music has become as thin as gossamer, but he still stands there blankly, looking very old. His eyes seem as if they can still penetrate everything before them. After a while, he bends over and picks up the old, yellowing straw stool that Cuiqiao used to sit on, putting it under his arm like some precious object, and goes into the cave.

51. A Distant View of the Hillcrest (DUSK, EXT)

416 BE On the hillcrest, the wild pear tree, bare of all its leaves, stands in silence.

End of Reel VII (926.6 feet)

Reel VIII

52. Cuiqiao's Wedding Chamber (NIGHT, INT)

417 ES The wedding quilts and pillows are laid out on the *kang*.

> Cuiqiao, a red headcloth over her head, sits motionless facing the wall.
>
> Off screen comes the noise of the door opening, then the door being shut, then footsteps approaching ...

418 CU-MC   The bright red headcloth.

> A large male hand appears on the screen, touching the red headcloth.
>
> Under the red headcloth is revealed Cuiqiao's frightened face. Filled with an inexpressible fear, she shrinks back, without a sound, further back ...

53. The Waist-drum Dance (DAY, EXT)

419 ECU   The sky and cymbals.

420 CU   A farmer leaps up and down, clashing a pair of cymbals.

421 MS   (INSERT TITLE) **YENAN**

> With a waist-drum troupe behind them, a band of farmers leap up and down, clashing their cymbals.
>
> The grand, awe-inspiring sound of the drums is added.

422 CU   With the waist-drum troupe behind them, peasants play the suona with swollen lips ...

423 BE   A full view of a lead drummer, wearing a sleeveless sheepskin jacket. Behind him are countless farmers beating drums. They leap up and down, their movements bold and vigorous ...

424 BE   Another full view of the lead drummer. Behind him as before are countless farmers, leaping up

	and down, their movements bold and vigorous …
425 CU	Peasants playing the suona with swollen lips …
426 CU	Three red banners appear from the bottom of the screen, with the blue sky in the background: "Farewell to our sons, in the army to beat the Japs!" "Recruit the masses, join the anti-Japanese forces!" "Down with the Japanese devils!"
427 CU	A file of mules. TILT UP to a peasant's chest festooned with a red rosette. TILT UP to his face.
428 CU	A file of mules. TILT UP to a peasant's chest festooned with a red rosette. TILT UP to his face.
429 CU	A file of mules. TILT UP to a peasant's chest festooned with a red rosette. TILT UP to his face.
430 MS	As the waist-drum troupe moves from left to right, Gu Qing crosses in right screen. This is a Liberated Area. Gu Qing stands in the middle of the excited crowd.
431 BE	(SLIGHTLY LOW-ANGLE) The drummers fill the screen.… These are the peasants who only look at you blankly, their hands tucked in their sleeves. The drums and the shouting are tremendous, solid, intoxicating, like a sudden clap of thunder that has been nurtured underground …
432 ES	(SLIGHTLY LOW-ANGLE) Beating their waist-drums wildly, the peasants go down the hillside. Leaping and twisting, they fill the screen.
433 MC	(TPL) (VERTICAL SHOT) The drummers in vertical file disappear left screen.

434 ES	(SLIGHTLY LOW-ANGLE) Beating their waist-drums, the peasants go down the hillside. Leaping and twisting, they fill the whole screen.
435 MC	(TPL) (VERTICAL SHOT) The drummers in vertical file cross out right screen.
436 MC	(TPL) (VERTICAL SHOT) The drummers in vertical file cross out left screen.
437 MC	(TPL) (VERTICAL SHOT) The drummers in vertical file cross out right screen.
438 ECU	(PAN FROM RIGHT TO LEFT) The whole screen is a composition of black, red and yellow. All that can be seen are countless waist-drums, soaring upwards, hurtling down, whirling and turning. The screen is full of the leaping and twisting mid-sections of peasants wildly beating their waist-drums.
439 ECU	(PAN FROM LEFT TO RIGHT) The peasants beat their waist-drums wildly, their joyful faces filling the whole screen …
440 MS	(PAN) The camera pans across the whole screen, amid the waist-drum troupe. On all sides there are leaping figures and excited, honest faces …
441 ES	From the sky, PAN to the moon.
	The sound of the waist-drums reaches to the clouds …
442 BE	Below a great mountain range is a flat ridge wide enough for a horse to ride along. The sound of drumming comes from behind the ridge. The lead drummer slowly appears on screen, then two flashing cymbals. Behind them come the parasols, and then the drummers appear on screen, first in groups of three then five, then

ten, pouring on in a constant succession of waves …

The earth-shaking sound of the drums.

443 CU   In the silence, after the dust has subsided, Gu Qing's solemn face.

54. Inside Cuiqiao's Cave Home (DUSK, INT)

444 ES   (FROM INSIDE THE CAVE LOOKING OUT) The lamp has not yet been lit. Inside the cave, the father is sitting on the *kang*, silent, not moving.

Hanhan opens the door and come in. He puts down his shepherd's stick, takes off his shoes, picks up the buckets and goes outside. This heavy task now falls on his frail shoulders.

55. On the Ridge (DUSK, EXT)

445 BE   An undulating ridge in the twilight.

The small figure of a woman walks quickly along the ridge.

56. The Rocky Shore (DUSK, EXT)

446 BE   On the river shore, where the pounding of the current has formed a pattern of overlapping ripples, is a line of footprints left behind by hurried steps. Just here the shore is covered with rocks. These countless stubborn rocks are brought by the Yellow River from the drought-stricken land. Strewn at random over the shore, they maintain a stubborn silence.

At the edge of the shore, at the end of the line of footprints, a small figure is running.

57. The Bank of the Yellow River (DUSK, EXT)

447 MS	By the fading light in the west wind, Hanhan walks towards the river bank, carrying the buckets.
448 CU	The Yellow River current.
449 MC	Hanhan's hands, holding the bucket, stretch towards the Yellow River, and the current slaps against the side of the blackened bucket. A girl's hand appears right screen and deftly picks up the bucket filled with river water. A string of drops falls away. (PAN) The bucket is set on the bank. The water in the bucket doesn't settle but rocks from side to side ...
	It is Cuiqiao. She picks up the other bucket and crosses out left screen.
450 MS	At the bottom of the screen, set off against the Yellow River current, Hanhan slowly straightens up and looks blankly at left screen.
451 CU	The Yellow River current.
452 MC	Hanhan stands there blankly, set off as before against the Yellow River current.
453 MC	The full bucket is placed on the bank. TILT UP to Cuiqiao's face as she straightens up. She is now dressed as a married woman. Already all trace of her former gentleness has disappeared. Her expression· is confused, dull,

blank, as if she could easily be startled. Her
married life can be known by the grief and fear
contained deep in her eyes.

Cuiqiao gazes blankly at the river water.

454 MC   Hanhan's frightened face, set off as before against
          the Yellow River currrent.

455 MC   Cuiqiao's face, set off against the Yellow River
          current, gazes blankly at the river water, then
          gradually turns towards Hanhan.

456 ES   Brother and sister stand there looking at each
          other.

          Cuiqiao hastily picks up the buckets. Hanhan
          goes to the bank and picks up her bundle. He
          follows behind her …

457 MS   (TPL) With the Yellow River current as back-
          ground, the two walk towards the camera,
          Cuiqiao carrying the water, Hanhan following
          behind …

458 MS   (TRUCK) Cuiqiao, carrying the water, walks
          swiftly. Hanhan, following behind, breaks into
          a trot …

459 MC   (TRUCK) Cuiqiao walks swiftly …

460 MC   (TRUCK) Against the darkening sky, Cuiqiao
          walks swiftly. Hanhan, following behind,
          breaks into a trot …

461 MC   (A PARTIAL VIEW OF CUIQIAO AS FORE-
          GROUND) Hanhan approaches the camera,
          swiftly, vertically.

462 MC   Cuiqiao's and Hanhan's swift feet, approaching
          the camera …

463 CU   From the suddenly lowered bucket, PAN to the
          lamplight from Cuiqiao's home.

464 MS   (TPL) The brother and sister, seen from behind,

with the lamplight from the cave as background. Their silhouettes fill the screen.

Hanhan: "Sister, are you going to look for brother Gu?"

Cuiqiao murmurs: "No! I'm not looking for brother Gu, I'm going to cross the river. The Eighth Route Army lies east of the river ..."

Cuiqiao: "... When I'm gone, you must do your best to look after pa. He's getting old. When you get hungry, and make yourself something to eat, and don't forget to keep adding firewood. In the summer, wear the belly-apron I made you, it's under the *kang* mat ..."

465 MC   (TPL) The lamplight from the cave ...

Cuiqiao (OS): "When it comes time for you to get married, you should decide for yourself ..."

466 MS   (TPL) With the light from the cave in the background, both have their backs to the camera. Cuiqiao takes the bundle from Hanhan and takes out a neatly-cut braid. She hands it over to Hanhan.

Cuiqiao: "This ma and pa gave me, I'm giving it back to them. Tell pa, Cuiqiao has gone now, it isn't anything to do with him. If he still thinks of me, he can look at this and then see me. This water is for pa ... When I come back ..., I'll look after him again ..."

467 ECU   (TPL) Hanhan's hands hold up a long braid, neatly-cut and still tied in a red ribbon.

468 MS   (TPL) With the light from the cave in the background as before, both have their backs to the camera. Hanhan's hands holding Cuiqiao's braid ...

Looking at Hanhan standing there blankly, Cuiqiao then says: "Go home now, pa's waiting for the water ... Go home! Go home!"

Taking the bundle from Cuiqiao's hand, Hanhan turns and crosses out left screen.

Looking at the light coming from the cave, Cuiqiao leaves slowly, crossing out left. The lamplight ...

58. The Shore (NIGHT, EXT)

469 BE The moon and the Yellow River current.

59. The Ford at the Yellow River (NIGHT, EXT)

470 ES The fast running Yellow River appears on screen. (PAN FROM RIGHT TO LEFT) A small flat-bottomed boat is tied to the bank, rocked to and fro by the river water.

471 MS Back to camera, Cuiqiao walks slowly at the bottom of the screen towards the river ...

Hanhan follows behind, the bundle in his hand.

472 MS Seen front-on, Hanhan faces the Yellow River, the bundle in his hand.

The sound of the waves reverberates.

Hanhan is shaken. He looks around.

473 ES With Hanhan's side back as foreground, Cuiqiao kneels to untie the rope. The knot is tight, and she has to struggle with it. An irritated expression appears on her face.

Hanhan: "Sister, you can't cross over."

The sound of the waves.

Cuiqiao struggles with the knot.

Hanhan: "Sister, the south road to Yenan would
be easier ..."

The sound of the waves.

Cuiqiao, not saying a word, struggles with the
knot.

Hanhan: "Sister, wait for daybreak, ask the ferry-
man to take you across ..."

The sound of the waves.

Cuiqiao, with an extra burst of effort, manages to
untie the knot. She stands up slowly.

End of Reel VIII (930 feet)

Reel IX

474 BE	Cuiqiao stands by the river bank.
	With a side view of Hanhan, Cuiqiao: "Hanhan, I'm suffering, I can't wait any longer ..."
475 BE	Cuiqiao goes up to Hanhan and takes the bundle from his hand. She takes out something from it.
	Cuiqiao: "When brother Gu comes back ..."
476 CU	Cuiqiao (OS): "... give him this."
	Hanhan takes it in his hand. It is a pair of soles, embroidered on the top with the pattern "Cinnabar phoenix aface the sun".
	Hanhan stretches out his other hand—it is a sewing kit, embroidered on top with a red star.
	Cuiqiao (OS): "Yes, I've seen it. Best you keep it."
	TILT UP to Cuiqiao's face, sorrowful, resolute ...
477 BE	The brother and sister with the Yellow River in

	the background. Cuiqiao strokes Hanhan's head, then walks away …
478 MC	The sound of Cuiqiao jumping into the boat.
	Hanhan: "Sister, set the scull fast."
	Cuiqiao (OS): "Yes."
	Hanhan: "Sister, try to manage."
	Cuiqiao (OS): "Mm."
479 MC	Cuiqiao stands on the boat, sets fast the scull, raises her head and looks at Hanhan …"
480 CU	Cuiqiao's smiling face.
481 MC	Hanhan's face.
482 BE	Cuiqiao, standing on the boat, shouts: "Tell brother Gu, Cuiqiao is going to become an official."
483 MC	The sound of the waves.
	Hanhan's face.
	Cuiqiao (OS): "Han—han—, go back—!"
484 BE	On the river, the figure of Cuiqiao rowing the boat gradually becomes distant …
	From the distance comes the sound of Cuiqiao singing:

> "The hammer, the sickle // and the scythe,
> For workers and peasants // shall build a new life.
>
> The piebald cock // flies over the wall …"

60. The Shore (NIGHT, EXT)

485 BE	From the Yellow River TILT UP to the moon.
	Cuiqiao's song (OS) is suddenly broken off:

> "The Communist …"

61. **The Ford at the Yellow River** (NIGHT, EXT)

486 CU   Hanhan, holding in his hands the braid and the soles, cries out: "Sister ..."

62. **A Sequence of DISSOLVE SHOTS**

487 ES   The Yellow River current at night.

Hanhan (OS): "... Sister—"

488 CU   (DISSOLVE) The Yellow River current by day.

489 CU   (DSSOLVE) (HORIZONTAL PAN FROM LEFT TO RIGHT) The Yellow River current at dusk ...

490 CU   (DISSOLVE) (HORIZONTAL PAN FROM RIGHT TO LEFT) The Yellow River current at night ...

491 CU   (DISSOLVE) (SLOW MOTION) The Yellow River current at dawn ...

492 ES   (DISSOLVE) Dawn. A large rock on the river shore.

63. **The Hillside** (DAY, EXT)

493 BE-MS   Ravines. SLOW PAN to Gu Qing walking along the horizon of the hillside. He is wearing a grey cotton army uniform. The sweat on his face shines as he walks with hasty steps towards the camera.

He stops, trying to hear something ... then walks forward again.

64. The Yard outside Cuiqiao's Home
(DAY, EXT)

494 ES   From the hillside opposite Cuiqiao's home PAN to the small yard in front of the cave.
Gu Qing (OS): "Uncle, Hanhan, Hanhan …"

65. Inside Cuiqiao's Cave Home (DAY, INT)

495 ES   (FROM INSIDE THE CAVE LOOKING OUT) Gu Qing (OS): "Cuiqiao …"
The cave door is pushed open. Gu Qing comes inside and looks around.

66. The Yard outside Cuiqiao's Home
(DAY, EXT)

496 MC   The closed door is opened by Gu Qing, who comes outside. He pushes the door shut again. Behind him, the strips of red paper on both sides of the door, printed with black circles, are in tatters.
Gu Qing crosses out left, beyond the yard …

67. A Blank (DAY, EXT)

497 ES   In the middle of a pale screen the shape of the sun can be seen indistinctly.

68. The Rain Prayer (DAY, EXT)

498 BE   With the sky in the background, the father stripped to the waist, is kneeling on the ground. Behind him are countless peasants, also stripped to the waist, prostrate on the

ground, making a square formation for the rain prayer.

The calm in his aged face and lowered eyes seems to convey deep grief.

Silence ...

Father: "Venerable Dragon King, the crops in the northern fields have dried up and died, and the crops in the back fields have dried up and died ... We beg you for rain ... Venerable Dragon King, have you brought up the sea ... not yet ..."

The peasants prostrate on the ground straighten their backs, appearing on screen.

499 BE   With the sky in the background, another section of the peasants prostrate on the ground straighten their backs and appear on screen.

500 BE   With the sky in the background, yet another section of the peasants prostrate on the ground straighten their backs and appear on screen.

(SLOW TILT UP) The sky and the sun. In the harsh glare of the sun, the rain prayer chanted by the father reverberates against the sky:

> "Dragon King of the Sea // let the good rains fall,
>
> Send cool wind and gentle rain // to save us all ..."

501 ECU   The spirit tablet of the Dragon King of the East Sea is outlined against the sky ...

The peasants (OS): "Ai, save us all!"

502 CU   The father's face. Muddy tears gush up in his eyes as the rain prayer pours forth from his chest, vigorous, deeply felt and full of longing.

Father: (sings)

"Dragon King of the Sea // let the good rains fall,

Send cool wind and gentle rain // to save us all!"

503 MS   Hanhan is also present, in the middle of the peasants.

They cry out: "Ai, save us all!"

504 CU   The father's face. Muddy tears gush up in his eyes as the rain prayer pours forth from his chest, vigorous, deeply felt and full of longing.

Father: (sings)

"Dragon King of the Sea // let the good rains fall,

Send cool wind and gentle rain // to save us all!"

505 MS   The farmers' faces, filled with longing, pack the screen.

They cry out: "Ai, save us all!"

506 MS   The peasants in their prayer for rain gaze at the sky. The spirit tablet of the Dragon King of the Sea stands out prominently among them.

507 ECU   A jar of holy water lies motionless in the pond.

508 ECU   Their backs to the camera, the peasants kowtow devoutly.

509 ES   Their backs to the camera, filling the screen, they kowtow.

510 ES   (HIGH ANGLE) A full shot of the kneeling peasants gazing at the sky, their heads at the bottom of the screen, which is four-fifths sky. They wait …

511 ECU   The jar of holy water lies motionless in the pond.

512 MS   The father, kneeling in front of the farmers, wipes away his tears with his hand …

513 CU	(FRONT ON) The screen is filled with men kowtowing as they pray for rain ...
514 CU	(FRONT ON) The men kowtowing as they pray for rain.
515 ECU	(FRONT ON) One old man wipes away his tears.
516 MS	(FRONT ON) Men kowtowing as they pray for rain.
517 CU	(FRONT ON) Men kowtowing as they pray for rain.
518 ECU	(BACK VIEW) The farmers kowtowing ...
519 ECU	The jar of holy water in the pond gradually sinks into the water.
520 BE	With the sky as four-fifths of the screen, the farmers are dumbstruck as they hear the sound of the jar of holy water sinking. They remain still, their eyes lifted upwards ...
521 ES	As before, the rows of men praying for rain remain still, their eyes lifted upwards ...
522 ECU	The spirit tablet of the Dragon King of the Sea.
523 ES	The still, dumbstruck men suddenly burst into life. They raise high the Dragon King's spirit tablet, and their shouts fill the screen ...
524 ECU	The father's face, streaming with tears. In the foreground and background, the men spring to their feet and start running, shouting with joy ...
525 MC	Hanhan, in the middle of the moving crowd, does not know what to do. Turning around, he suddenly catches sight of Gu Qing ...
526 BE	Gu Qing's figure approaches from far away.
527 ES-CU	Hanhan runs towards the camera against the massive human current. He waves his hand and shouts: "Brother Gu! ..."

	The sound is quickly drowned in the joyful shouts of the crowd.
528 ES-MC	Hanhan, submerged in the human current, still tries desperately to run forward, waving his hand at Gu Qing ...
529 ES	Hanhan still runs against the human current.
530 BE	Gu Qing's figure approaches from far away. The farmers shouting (OS): "Ai, save us all! ..."
531 ES	Hanhan runs desperately against the human current.
532 ES	Hanhan runs desperately against the human current.
533 ES	Hanhan still runs desperately against the human current.
534 BE	Gu Qing's figure approaches from far away. The farmers shouting (OS): "Ai, save us all! Ai, save us all ..."
535 ES-ECU	(SLOW MOTION) Hanhan runs toward the camera against the massive human current, alternately drowning and reappearing ... The cry "Ai, save us all!" congeals into a huge wave of sound, reverberating across the whole screen. Hanhan's hand falls on to the screen ...

69. The Yellow Earth

536 BE	(TILT FROM ABOVE) From the sky above (DOWN) to the thick yellow earth. In the silence, as if rising from the earth to soar up to the sky, comes Cuiqiao's song from far away:

"The piebald cock // flies over the wall,
The Communist Party // shall save us all."

The song gradually fades away into the distance. The yellow earth is silent and still …

537 (END TITLES)

Guangxi Film Studio

Youth Production Unit

538 Director: Chen Kaige 陳凱歌

Cinematographer: Zhang Yimou 張藝謀

Art Director: He Qun 何羣

539 Music: Zhao Jiping 趙季平

Sound: Lin Lin 林臨

Set Adviser: Zhong Ling 鍾靈

540 Assistant Director: Tan Yijian 覃一堅

Script Editor: Wan Liu 萬流

Film Editor: Pei Xiaonan 裴小南

541 Lighting: Zhang Shubin 張樹斌

Costume: Tian Geng 田耕 and Chen Bona 陳伯娜

542 Makeup: He Hong 何紅

Props: Zhang Jianyang 張建揚 and Jiao Zhigang 焦志剛

543 Set Manager: Xue Fei 薛飛

Sound Effects: Liu Quanye 劉筌業

Production Manager: Guo Keqi 郭可琦

544 CAST

Cuiqiao	Xue Bai 薛白
Gu Qing	Wang Xueqi 王學圻
Father	Tan Tuo 譚托
Hanhan	Liu Qiang 劉强

545 PERFORMERS

The Orchestra and Traditional Music Ensemble of the Xi'an Academy of Music

546   Conductors: Liu Dadong 劉大東 and Lu Rirong
           魯日融

           Soloist: Feng Jianxue 馮健雪

547   The Peasant Waist-Drum Troupe of Ansai County

End of Reel IX (908 feet)
Total length: 2385 metres